# Peril on the Indian Pacific

**C.A.** Larmer is a journalist, editor, teacher and author of multiple crime series, stand-alone novels and a non-fiction book about pioneering surveyors in Papua New Guinea. Christina grew up in PNG, was educated in Australia, and spent many years working in Sydney, London, Los Angeles and New York. She now lives with her musician husband, boomerang sons and their very cheeky Bluey on the east coast of Australia.

Sign up for news, views and giveaways:
**calarmer.com**

## ALSO BY C.A. LARMER

The Murder Mystery Book Club series:
*The Murder Mystery Book Club* (Book 1)
*Danger On the SS Orient* (Book 2)
*Death Under the Stars* (Book 3)
*When There Were 9* (Book 4)
*The Widow on the Honeymoon Cruise* (Book 5)
*Gone Guest* (Book 6)

The Ghostwriter Mystery series:
*Killer Twist* (Book 1)
*A Plot to Die For* (Book 2)
*Last Writes* (Book 3)
*Dying Words* (Book 4)
*Words Can Kill* (Book 5)
*A Note Before Dying* (Book 6)
*Without a Word* (Book 7)

The Posthumous Mystery series:
*Do Not Go Gentle*
*Do Not Go Alone*

The Sleuths of Last Resort:
*Blind Men Don't Dial Zero*
*Smart Girls Don't Trust Strangers*
*Good Girls Don't Drink Vodka*

**PLUS**
*After the Ferry: A Gripping
Psychological Novel*

*An Island Lost*

# C.A. LARMER

# Peril on the Indian Pacific

## The Murder Mystery Book Club
### (Book 7)

LARMER MEDIA

Published by Larmer Media
Northern NSW, Australia
calarmer.com
ISBN: 978-0-6459449-3-8

Cover design by Nimo Pyle
Cover photography by Christian Pyle
Edited by D.A. Sarac, The Editing Pen
& Elaine Rivers, with thanks

To Simone,
for spurring me on

# PASSENGERS ON
# THE INDIAN PACIFIC

### *The Murder Mystery Book Club:*
Alicia Finlay (club founder/journalist)
Lynette Finlay (her sister/restaurant manager/chef)
Claire Hargreaves (vintage-store owner)
Missy Corner (librarian)
Perry Gordon (palaeontologist)
Veronica "Ronnie" Westera (wealthy philanthropist)

### *The Dartmoor Family:*
Clayton "Clay" Dartmoor (wealthy "Wheat Baron",
widower to Daisy)
Flynn Dartmoor (their eldest son)
Fiona "Fi" Dartmoor (their daughter)
Patrick "Paddy" Dartmoor (their youngest son)
Posey Dartmoor (Patrick's wife)
Phillip "Phil" Dartmoor (Clay's younger brother)

### *Other Notable Passengers:*
Jock and Iris Gleeson (elderly wheat farmers,
Dartmoor neighbours)
Alan J. Taggart "Tag" (amateur palaeontologist)
David Jules (old school friend of a Dartmoor cousin)
Sara, Paul and Brenda (new Perth friends)

***Notable Crew:***
Jacinta "Jac" McClaren (Hospitality Attendant,
Gold Class)
Walker (Hospitality Attendant, Platinum Class)
Arlo (trainee Attendant, Platinum Class)
Marvin (Guest Experience Manager)
Agnetha (bartender)
Hana Sato (Journey Manager)


## READING MATERIAL

*The 4.50 from Paddington* (Agatha Christie)
*The Mystery of the Blue Train* (Christie)
*Murder on the Orient Express* (Christie)
*The Girl on the Train* (Paula Hawkins)
*The Sleeping Car Murders* (Sébastien Japrisot)
*The Girdle of Hyppolita* (Christie)
*The Girl in the Train* (Christie)
*The Plymouth Express* (Christie)

# PROLOGUE

As she watched the figure fall from the train, Alicia Finlay did four things. She sat up with a start, smashing her head hard on the roof above, she scrambled for the window, tripping herself up on the tangled sheet, then she fell onto the cabin floor, narrowly missing the ladder as she burst into peals of laughter.

The first three responses were completely understandable—Alicia was ensconced in a fast-moving sleeper carriage after all, hurtling across a train track at a hundred kilometres an hour, and the last thing she expected to see as she stared blearily out from her cosy bunk bed was a plummeting human being.

The laughter, however, was unforgiveable.

It was just that the Murder Mystery Book Club founder could not believe her eyes. Another one? *Seriously?* Her detective fiancé would kill her! And he wasn't the only one. As Alicia gulped back her laughter and returned to her bed, her roommate was sounding murderous.

There was a stream of mumbled expletives, then a grumpy, "What are you *doing* down there? It's like... four in the morning."

Alicia swept her eyes towards the top bunk. "Sorry, Lynny, but I think I just saw someone fall off the train!"

"Huh?"

"I saw a flash of something, like a green-and-white shirt. I think maybe someone fell!"

A pause. A grunt. Then Lynette Finlay said, "You're still drunk. Go to sleep."

That brought an indignant scoff from Alicia, although her sister made a valid point. Alicia's head had been spinning since she hit the pillow five hours earlier, largely thanks to

1

the fact that it was the first night of her hen's party aboard the Indian Pacific and someone (well, the hens) had plied her with far too much champagne. It was the reason she'd woken at such an ugly hour, tongue wedged to palette, frantically searching for her water bottle.

"No, no! Honest to God, I saw something," Alicia persisted. "I think it might've been that farmer guy, you know? The one we saw at the bar, in the green checked shirt. I'm sure of it."

Eventually a mumbled, "How sure?"

Alicia wavered. "Kind of, sort of sure. I mean… it was definitely his shirt."

There was another stream of cursing, clearer this time, then a very stern, "You were dreaming. Go back to sleep."

"But you know what our record's like. It could've been him."

"Or it could be your mad mind. Sleep, Alicia. Now."

"Lynny!"

A longer pause this time. Maybe even a snore.

"Lynnnnny?"

"*What!*"

"We have to pull the emergency cord or something."

Suddenly a swish of long blond hair fell towards Alicia, followed fast by a set of puffy emerald-green eyes. "Don't you bloody dare."

"But—"

"You are not stopping a seventeen-hundred-tonne train on a drunken whim, Alicia. For heaven's sake, don't you think the family would've done that if it had actually happened?"

"That family? No *way*. They hated him."

The puffy eyes narrowed. "What're you talking about? You saw them for five seconds."

"Could just tell. And now he's been pushed off the train."

"Pushed? I thought you said he fell."

Alicia's eyes turned towards the window again. "He could've been pushed."

While she hadn't actually *seen* the push (let alone the body if she were being honest), she had a bad feeling about that family…

Her eyes swept back to her sister. "What if he was *murdered*?"

The ponytail disappeared. There was a long release of air, then a weary, "I swear to God, sis, if you do not go back to sleep right now, I am going to push you from the train myself. Nobody's been murdered on this train or any train. Just go… the hell… *to sleep*."

And with that Lynette returned to snoring while Alicia glared up at the bunk above her head and scoffed, "Yeah right." Scoffed again. "Tell that to Mrs McGillicuddy."

Nobody believed that old lady either when she witnessed a murder through a train window. Nobody, of course, except her good friend Miss Marple.

Alicia's eyes turned to the tiny shelf beside her bed where, beneath the much-needed water, she could just make out a silhouette of the book she'd been reading—Agatha Christie's *4.50 from Paddington*. She was only a few pages in and already loving it, if only because it featured Christie's least-lauded yet equally brilliant amateur sleuth. In this story, Mrs McGillicuddy witnesses a woman being strangled on a passing train, and when nobody takes her seriously (the patronising prats, thought Alicia, glaring above her head again), she turns to Miss Marple.

"*Most* distressing for you," Jane says to her friend, "and surely *most* unusual. I think you had better tell me about it *at once*."

It's a pity St Mary Mead's most solicitous citizen isn't in the bunk above, Alicia thought grumpily as she took a swig from the bottle then returned her gaze to the screeching darkness and her mind to the riveting train mystery she'd been reading.

And it wasn't Christie's only one…

# CHAPTER 1
## Seventeen Hours Earlier...

**P**erry Gordon glanced from his battered copy of *The Mystery of the Blue Train* and then up to the train he was about to board and gasped. Blimey! Apart from its pretty canary trimming, the blue front locomotive of the Indian Pacific was eerily similar to the blue train on the cover of his 1962 Agatha Christie imprint, the likeness quite surprising.

Of course, Christie's cover also featured a glamorous auburn-haired corpse sprawled on the platform, and as far as he could see, at that point everybody on *this* platform was still in the vertical position. But if there's one thing Perry had learned from hanging out with his beloved Murder Mystery Book Club, you could never take that for granted.

Murder and mayhem were often just a shoulder chip away.

The very thought should have sent shivers through Perry's velvet-jacketed shoulders, but instead, he felt a frisson of excitement as he waited at the check-in counter on Platform 2 and wondered what adventures awaited his fellow sleuths on their journey.

Then he immediately tsked. *Oh Perry,* he hushed himself. *Behave!*

They were there for fun and romance—it was Alicia's hen's party after all—and the less murder and mayhem the better. Perry was travelling as an honorary hen (there was no way he was missing out just because he happened to be a rooster), and there was no way anything ominous was going to happen on this journey.

He simply would not allow it.

Besides, now that he thought about it, the two trains weren't *that* similar. Agatha's Blue Train was really the

Calais-Méditerranée Express, a French train that carried the rich and famous between Calais and the French Riviera circa 1920, while this one was supermodern, more Australian than Bluey, and heading for the great outback.

What's more, he realised, as he handed over his luggage to the woman at the desk, only the front carriages of the Indian Pacific were blue. The rest were all a dazzling silver. At least, he assumed they were. The poor creature had been lopped into three inglorious pieces so that her almost-one-kilometre torso could fit snugly into Sydney's Central Station.

But even in her dismembered state, she really was a beauty. Forget the Blue Train. Add some wispy smoke and Claire Hargreaves-style frocks and you'd imagine you were back on the more infamous Orient Express.

Oh no, he'd done it again! *There was a sprawling corpse on that train too...*

"Everything okay, sir?" came the chirpy voice of the counter clerk, cutting through his reverie. She was adorned in a rather dapper uniform in shades of red, navy blue and taupe, with classic Aussie touches, including an R. M. Williams leather belt and a wide-brimmed Akubra hat (think Crocodile Dundee, minus the snakeskin and croc teeth).

Perry blinked, smiled, then shoved the book back into his hand luggage and assured her everything was "simply fabulous!" He thanked her for the lanyard she was offering, arranged it carefully around his neck, then followed her directions back across the Grand Concourse to the Eternity Café where, she assured him, his fellow passengers were gathering for pre-departure canapés and beverages, including, apparently, his book club.

If only he could find them.

The place was pumping. More like a night club than a departure lounge, the elegant art deco café was packed with revellers of all persuasions, the mood verging on hysterical as they clinked champagne glasses, hoovered up cakes and sandwiches, and shrieked with excitement. And really who could blame them?

*Was* there anything more thrilling than farewell drinks before a long-distance voyage?

"This is a bore," came a voice nearby, and Perry glanced around to see a short, buxom woman with long black tresses cut into chunky layers, rolling her eyes at a man with a golden-red beard and matching curls poking out from beneath a rabbit fur-felt bushman's hat. It, too, was an Akubra, crisp and fawn in colour with a plaited leather band. The man's skin was badly sunburnt, peeling in places, his lips dry and chapped.

"Chill, babes," he muttered beside her. "It'll all be over before you know it. Let's just get a drink and get through this." Then he grabbed her manicured hand and plunged through the crowd towards the bar. Perry didn't like their attitude—how could you wish *this* train trip over?—but he did like their direction and followed in their wake.

While they waited for the waitress to fill champagne flutes, he heard the two grumble some more—mostly about a "chicken-shit older brother" and a "useless lump of an uncle".

"D'ya think he'll have the balls to do it?" the woman asked.

"Said he would," the man replied.

"Oh, then he's *sure* to," she snapped back, her sarcasm as dry as the complimentary olive she'd just popped into her mouth, before they both grabbed drinks, wedged stiff smiles to their lips, and made their way back across the room to a group seated to one side. Probably the pilloried relatives, Perry decided, judging by the matching hats, snarls and sunburn.

And that's when Perry finally spotted his favourite people at a corner table just nearby. The Murder Mystery Book Club were the antithesis of snarly—laughing, clapping and clearly sharing a joke.

He sighed happily, stroking his chiselled goatee as he waited for his glass to be filled, and kept watching. Club founder, Alicia Finlay, was chuckling and shaking her shaggy blond locks at something her younger sister, Lynette, was saying, Lyn's longer, more luscious hair bundled into a high ponytail, her bare, tanned arms gesticulating wildly. Across from them, Claire Hargreaves smiled demurely like an Asian Grace Kelly in her vintage silk shirtwaist dress, while young Missy Corner giggled uncontrollably into her ample cleavage, her zebra-print glasses almost falling off. Missy's corkscrew curls were now dyed a vivid mercury blue—probably to match the train, knowing Missy, he decided—while ashen-haired Ronnie Westera sat beside her, tsking like a dowager duchess in her trademark drab cardigan and pearls.

"What took you so long?" Ronnie called out, tapping her diamond-encrusted Cartier watch when Perry finally approached.

"We're already on our second champers!" added Lynette.

"Never you mind, lassies," he told them, holding up two flutes. "I'll be caught up long before you hear that train whistle."

An hour later and there was not so much as a coo-ee as the train began to crunch to life.

The café had now emptied, and the passengers were all aboard, the Indian Pacific back in one reassuring piece and steadily chugging its way out of central Sydney.

It would be a 4,352-kilometre journey across Australia's ample girth, from the east coast to the west—through the shadowy Blue Mountains and the dusty mining town of Broken Hill, to the South Australian city of Adelaide and then back up and across the vast red desert of the Nullarbor Plain all the way to Perth.

But for now, the book club's world had become comfortingly small, each of them ensconced in a cosy Gold-class twin compartment, although not all of them sharing like the Finlay sisters.

Being the only rooster in the group, Perry had booked a berth to himself, as had the oldest book club member Ronnie. She was also the richest and could easily afford the posher, first-class Platinum carriage with its more comfortable double bed, but there was no way she was separating herself from the action, she had told them. How dreary that would be!

Now that she was married to a wealthy businessman, Claire, too, could have upgraded, but she went one better and not only booked a twin cabin, she insisted that Missy bunk in with her for nix (without this offer, the lowly paid librarian was going nowhere).

The only club member missing was Queenie Dobson, and that had nought to do with finances. The executive assistant was currently on an all-expenses paid trip to Europe, courtesy of her boss (who also happened to be Claire's husband). He dubbed it "an exploratory work trip"—there to research five-star hotels apparently—but Claire told the group it was more of a reward for all Queenie's hard work.

It was just a pity about the timing, thought Ronnie, as she carefully unpacked her vintage Victorian carpet bag and placed her things in their cleverly designed spaces. The room was classically decorated in a muted shade of green with veneer wood panelling and shiny brass trimming, every inch utilised for comfort and storage. She had been informed there was not much room, and it was certainly tight, but Ronnie had never had a problem with size. She might reside in a McMansion, living the life of a wealthy widow, but all she really needed was a cosy nook, her knitting, and a good book. And right now she had all three, including the aforementioned *Murder on the Orient Express*.

Because, yes, Ronnie was the lucky duck who got to read this particular classic over the next four days. It was all Missy's brilliant idea. The young librarian had suggested they each choose an iconic train mystery to read while on an iconic train and then gather during the journey to compare them—when they weren't toasting Alicia, that is.

While the club had already discussed this book, Ronnie had not been part of the group then, and it didn't take much to convince them it was worth reviewing. After all, it was the most iconic train mystery of them all!

Fortunately, it had been decades since Ronnie had read it,

the details now fuzzy, and she sighed contentedly as she locked her expensive watch away in the cupboard safe (it had been a final gift from her beloved Bert; never went anywhere without it), then secured the door, clicked in the table by the window, and placed the book beside her knitting and silver spectacles. Then she dropped onto the three-seater couch and stared out of the thick, panoramic glass, wondering whether she'd even get a chance to read, let alone enjoy the passing view.

Knowing the book club, as she now did, she certainly wouldn't bet her McMansion on it...

~

If Claire were a betting woman, she'd put money on the killer in her book being someone outside of the hapless victim's sleeping car, not her fellow passengers. They were all far too obvious! Claire was twenty-two pages into the classic French mystery *The Sleeping Car Murders* (aka *The 10.30 from Marseille*), written by acclaimed French author Sébastien Japrisot. It was the vintage fashion-store owner's choice for a train mystery, and she was thoroughly enjoying it. A recent gift from her Paris-based, Hong Kong Chinese mother, the book had dry, subversive humour, a galloping pace, and a name other than Christie on the cover (what happened to the book club's determination to read fresh authors? Hmm?).

First published as *Compartiment Tueurs* in 1962, it was both hard-boiled crime and classic Christie-style whodunnit, although Claire was shocked the murdered woman had been sharing a sleeping car with strangers, most of them *men*. Miss Marple would never do something so scandalous, and nor would Claire! And, luckily, she didn't have to. Her roomie was a friendly female, who was tapping at her door that very moment.

Claire jumped up to find Missy standing out in the narrow corridor, holding up six coat hangers like they were trophies.

"No need to knock," said Claire. "These doors only lock from the inside, and I hadn't secured it."

"Oh soz!" said Missy, "but *look*." She waved the coat hangers about. "I nabbed these from the conductor. She is *sooo* sweet and so accommodating. Says we can come back for more if we need them. And there's tea down there, too, and hot chocolate and free bickies and stuff. A whole tearoom just for this carriage. And we can help ourselves any time we like."

Claire smiled warmly, but it wasn't teabags or coat hangers they were lacking, it was space, and it was their own silly fault. Both women were fans of fifties-style frocks—big skirts, tulle petticoats, fiddly shoes. And it didn't help that Claire had also brought four handbags, a makeup case and a hatbox crammed with a 1930's felt cloche, oversized straw hat and snug velvet turban.

And that's when Claire noticed a hat of a different kind. Two hats, in fact, both large tan Akubras bobbing down the corridor towards her. One was being worn by a short, stocky woman in classic country-style trousers and riding boots, her face hidden, cast downwards as though deep in thought. Behind her was a taller man in similar garb, eyes also on his boots, his closely shaved jaw tight as he walked.

Neither appeared to notice Claire until the very last moment, when they both looked up and into her feline eyes at the exact same time, and for the life of her, Claire felt like she could see straight into their souls.

And what she saw was shocking.

Their glance didn't last long, just a fraction of a second, but it was enough to send a shiver down Claire's spine, and she quickly closed the door and returned to her seat.

"Everything okay, possum?" Missy asked, sensing her mood change.

Claire nodded reassuringly, but she couldn't help shivering again, the strangers' expressions now imprinted on her brain. Because, at the risk of sounding like overly imaginative Alicia, Claire could have sworn both their minds were on murder.

And she wondered who they were thinking of and if they were also sharing a sleeping car…

As Claire settled into a strange, maudlin silence, Missy tucked a blue curl behind her ear and tried not to dance about the cabin like a loon. But *oh my God*. Here they were, on the majestic Indian Pacific! And she didn't care how squashed her dresses got or how much pride she had to swallow to accept Claire's generous offer to share the twin berth. She was *beyond* excited. Had been prepping for this for months (hence the hair—it had taken many trials and quite a few tears to get just the right shade).

Missy's excitement wasn't even dampened by the fact that she couldn't bring along her new boyfriend. Yes, *boyfriend*. Oh, how thrilling that sounded. Missy had waited a long time for true love to come knocking, and she had Ronnie to thank for the call. She had met Ronnie's lovely nephew, Seamus Jones, at Ronnie's seventy-fifth birthday party, the one positive thing to emerge from that ghoulish night, and Missy grinned again at the last thing Seamus said to her as he dropped her at Central Station: "Have fun, say hey to Aunty Ronnie, and don't get into any trouble this time!"

Ha! She thought. *As if.*

Then her mind darted to the train mysteries she was reading. Yes, *mysteries*. Plural! While the others had all chosen one full-length novel, the youngest book club member had opted for three Christie short stories, which, until now, no one in the club had heard of. That was the fun thing about being a librarian. Missy had access to the entire Christie catalogue. She had just started the oddly named *The Girdle of Hyppolita* ("A schoolgirl disappears on a train to Paris!"), and would then move on to *The Girl in the Train* ("A beautiful girl begs a bored playboy to hide her on a London train!") and finally, *The Plymouth Express* (which sounded suspiciously like *The Mystery of the Blue Train*; she would have to tell Perry).

But enough of all that. Mystery was supposed to play second fiddle on this journey. They were here to celebrate Alicia and her upcoming marriage to Detective Inspector Liam Jackson. Missy swooned just thinking about it. Couldn't wait for the wedding and the chance to finally bring along a proper plus-one! Her sister Henny would be so relieved.

She did a little jig, then turned to Claire. "Shall we finish unpacking and pop around to the Finlay cabin, see what the girls are up to?"

But Claire didn't respond, was still lost in her own thoughts—her brow tightly knotted, her eyes staring hard at the book in her lap. Missy smiled to herself. Ah, she thought. There really was nothing like a good murder mystery to take your mind off things!

~

Two doors down, Lynette also had a book in her lap, but it was the view flashing past the window that had the tanned blonde mesmerised. They were now travelling through the suburban outskirts of Sydney, and her big green eyes kept darting across the tracks, seeking out discarded clothing, not unlike the pile spotted by the poor, drunken Rachel in her book *The Girl on the Train*.

Also trying to break the mould, the younger Finlay had picked a more modern train mystery to devour. She was only a few pages into Paula Hawkins' 2015 blockbuster but could not get the opening sentence out of her head:

*"There is a pile of clothing on the side of the train tracks. Light-blue cloth—a shirt, perhaps—jumbled up with something dirty white."*

Urgh. She wrapped her arms around her long legs. It was such a simple image and yet somehow so *ugly*. And she wondered how a woman's shirt ended up on the tracks, let alone what sounded suspiciously like her underwear.

"Why would there be clothes strewn beside a train track?" she asked Alicia, who was busily unpacking her beaten-up leather duffle bag.

Alicia glanced across, confused, then down at the book in Lynette's hands. She smiled. "Creepy, isn't it? Makes you wonder if there's a body mixed up in all that gear, doesn't it?"

Lynette laughed. "No, it makes *you* wonder that, Ms Glass is Half-Empty. I was thinking someone had gotten seriously hammered and stripped off."

Alicia tsked. "Good to see where your mind's at. Speaking of gear... ever going to put yours away?" She nodded at Lynette's metallic-green Samsonite carry-on, then gave it a kick for good measure.

"Can't. You've hogged all the space."

"Have *not.*" Alicia pulled the cupboard door open to reveal some empty hangers. "At least hang up your good stuff so you won't be all crumpled for my first hen's drinks."

"Oh, it's all about *you,* isn't it?" Lynette said, winking.

Alicia laughed. "Hey, I'm only playing Bridezilla once. Humour me." But when she smiled down at her sister, she noticed Lynette's eyes had suddenly puddled up. She dropped beside her and grabbed her hands. "What's going on? Are you okay?"

Lynette shook her off. "Of course, you flop! Just *so* looking forward to this." Then she pushed her away, jumped up and reached for a coat hanger.

~

Clutching the coat hangers to her red-white-and-navy pinstriped blouse, the train conductor tried hard to calm her breathing. But it wasn't easy. Jacinta McClaren's heart was galloping at a terrifying pace, just like the chestnut mare she once rode with abandon, back on the farm, back when she was young and brave... and vulnerable.

Unloading the hangers, she snatched up the carriage manifest, shaky finger running down the page, stopping at cabin two, then cabin three... then, gulp, cabin number four. Her heart went into free fall, the past rushing up to fill the gap.

She remembered affection, then love, then ugliness and violence.

*Come on, Jacinta, what's the big deal?* she said to herself, trying to shake it off. *You knew that family was booked on this train; you had plenty of warning!*

And yet just seeing them, in the flesh, all these years later, had sent her into a spiral. She thought she'd moved past it. Gotten over it. Had forgotten the whole thing. But who was she kidding?

You didn't forget your demons.

Didn't forgive them either, especially when they swept straight past you with their country bumpkin get-up and haughty expressions, like they didn't even remember you. The nerve! Well, Jacinta remembered everything, and it was not a pretty memory.

But she couldn't focus on that now. She had so much work to do! The search for spare hangers had set her schedule right back. More than a conductor, Jacinta was the hospitality attendant in charge of this Gold carriage, and her priority right now was to pop on her brightest smile and drop into all nine cabins to wish her guests a hearty welcome, give them a tour of the amenities, and provide the all-important information on things like mealtimes and off-train excursions.

Problem was, that meant stepping into the haughty passenger's cabin too, and her heart hammered again just thinking about that.

"All good?" came a voice from the tearoom behind her, and Jacinta turned to see the attendant from the next carriage pilfering her stock of long-life milk.

"Of course it is, Arlo," she said breezily.

He held up the stash. "Soz, Walker asked me to grab these."

Her eyes narrowed. "How's your training going?"

He shrugged. "Preferred it down here. Less stress, you know?"

Ordinarily she would agree. But not now. She glanced out to the corridor, then back at the young trainee. "Hey Arlo," she said. "If you're going to steal my supplies, I'm gonna need something in return."

Then her stress levels fell away as she offloaded cabin number four.

# CHAPTER 2
## Toasting the Bride-to-Be

The atmosphere in the Outback Explorer Lounge was entirely too sedate for a hen's party, and Lynette and Perry quickly conspired to jazz things up. They had earlier demanded that everyone meet there for a predinner drink and hadn't expected it to be quite so... quiet.

"We need two tables together and buckets of champagne, pronto!" Lynette announced as she glanced about.

The room was ambiently lit and awash in rich burgundies, apricots and amber, communal lounges set along one side of the carriage, snug leather armchairs along the other. There was a hint of lemon and citronella in the air, and the vibe was both art deco and regal and *way too* tranquil! While the lounge was only half-full, the guests had spread out in clusters of two, keeping their distance as they peered through the wide double-glazed windows, watching the view stream by on both sides, others swiping through their devices like Facebook was more interesting, several staring up at the book club with a look of expectation.

Perry spied a bar at the opposite end of the carriage, and as they dragged seats together, he said, "I'll grab the first bottle of bubbly if you like."

"Are we allowed to drink anything other than champagne?" asked Ronnie, whose favourite tipple was scotch and soda.

"Not on the first night," said Perry. "We're in celebration mode. Get with the program, woman."

Ronnie tutted as Alicia said, "Well, go easy on me please. I'm a lightweight. Ask Lynny. I fall about after two drinks."

"Then we're in the perfect venue," said Missy, giggling as

she watched a tall, well-built man in a tan Akubra struggle past them, clutching onto the tops of the chairs as he headed towards the bar. "If you fall over, honeykins, you can just blame it on the bumpy train."

Lynette had clocked the man too—or smelt him really. His aftershave was subtle and expensive. So were the wheat-coloured moleskin trousers he was wearing.

"Actually, why don't I get the first round," she told Perry, who had also clocked the sweet-smelling forty-something. "I want to check out the wine list anyway."

"Sure you do," said Perry, watching as she scuttled after him. From the back, at least, he looked like a taller, straighter version of the grumpy, bearded hipster Perry had overheard in the café before they'd set off.

Sniggering, he took the seat next to Alicia and said of Lynette, "Usual tricks?"

Alicia sighed. "She told me she was sick of being single and was going to stop flirting with older, richer, commitment-phobes. That guy is like a walking template."

"You can tell all that from here?" asked Missy, eyes also turned to the bar. "All I can see is a handsome fella with a thirst."

"Ah, but it's the handsome thirsty ones you have to watch out for," said Perry, also sighing.

The handsome fella had not noticed Lynette approach, was too busy giving the bartender instructions, which included a round of cold beers and a glass of rosé with some ice on the side now, then two bottles of their finest champagne to be kept on ice for after dinner around nineish.

"What is your finest champagne?" he asked, thick eyebrows high above glacial-blue eyes.

The bartender, a pretty young blonde with a name badge that read AGNETHA, produced a small menu and handed it over. "In this bar, sir, we have two Australian sparkling wines, one from the Adelaide Hills, one from the Barossa Valley, both very good, but we can organise bottles of French champagne if you've booked the Platinum carriage."

"Yeah, well, my father has, so make that happen please. Any French will do."

She nodded. "And what beers would you like now?"

He glanced back at the list, just as he spotted Lynette patiently waiting beside him. "Oh, I am sorry," he said. "Please go ahead."

"No worries," Lynette replied. "I'm happy to wait."

He smiled, then tapped the bar menu and told Agnetha, "We'll have five of the James Squire Lashes Pale please. And a glass of the Sangiovese Rosé. Don't forget the ice."

Agnetha got to work while he turned and faced Lynette. "Shouldn't be too long." His smile widened as he soaked up the sight of her—long, smooth legs, flowing fair hair, a strappy cotton dress on. "So..." Pulling off his hat, he brushed some fingers through his neatly trimmed golden-red curls and turned his narrow blue eyes towards the lounge. "You're travelling with your husband... boyfriend?"

Lynette was smiling now. She knew a fishing expedition when she saw one and wished she could smugly tell him that yes, as it happens, she was happily on holiday with her rich, handsome beau. Except who was she kidding? She was now the book club's resident Miss Marple, practically the only one still on the shelf (Perry didn't count; he would always be their Poirot no matter what his relationship status).

"I'm actually on a hen's weekend with my sister and our Murder Mystery Book Club," she told him. Might as well fess up to that too. They were stuck together for four days, so he'd find out soon enough. She held up her naked ring finger and added, "And no, I'm not the chook getting married."

He laughed as she suspected he would, then said, "Sorry, I can't talk. I'm here with my siblings, my uncle, and my *dad*, so I think that makes me the biggest loser."

And now Lynette was laughing.

He held out a hand. It was large and thick-skinned, freckled, sunburned and callused. The hand of an outdoor worker and a hard worker at that. "Flynn Dartmoor. Of Dartmoor Downs, Western Australia."

She offered hers in return. Long, thin fingers, soft, supple skin. Not so much as a burn mark now that she was managing a restaurant instead of cheffing. "Lynette Finlay. Of plain old Woolloomooloo, Sydney."

He laughed again and said, "Let me guess. Your book club's reading *Murder on the Orient Express*."

"One of us is, not me. I'm reading *Girl on the Train* actually. But I'm guessing you're not much of a mystery man, Flynn."

"Well, I wouldn't say *that*..." He smiled. Alluringly. Then his head nodded back towards the lounge. "My sister's the crime fanatic in our family."

Lynette followed his nod to see a slightly stocky woman with smudgy freckles and a pigtail of golden curls watching them carefully, frowning. She had on matching moleskin trousers and an Akubra resting on her lap.

"In fact," he continued, his own frown suddenly developing, "that's the reason we're in this tin can. It was Fi's hair-brained idea, and she somehow talked Dad into it."

"You're not a fan of train travel?"

He brushed his chiselled jaw, tracing the line of a very faint scar. "Not a fan of tight spaces. I'm more your 'Give me land, lots of land under starry skies above' kind of fellow."

He was quoting from a Bing Crosby song, and Lynette was almost charmed, but she told herself to stop it. She had promised Alicia no more unavailable older men! This guy had to be fifteen years Lynette's senior, or at least that's what the scar suggested, not to mention the faint lines that were settling in around his eyes and lips.

Plus there was the minor matter of him residing on the polar opposite side of the country. Couldn't be *more* unavailable!

"There're worse places to be fenced in, surely?" she told him as he took the laden tray Agnetha was now offering.

Turning back, he smiled again, his gaze narrowing further. "I'm beginning to see that."

Then he gave Lynette a deep, lingering look that she felt

all the way down to her platform sandals. She was debating whether to return the look when his pupils suddenly dilated and his smile vanished.

"Oh, hey Dad," he called out to an elderly man who was approaching from the door closest to the bar, the one that led into an adjoining restaurant. "I... I was just sorting out drinks for tonight."

The men were clearly related—you could tell from the sun-scorched skin colouring, narrow, ice-blue eyes and strong, thick eyebrows—but their differences were stark. Flynn, the son, looked a little threatening. Those broad shoulders, that scar, that tense jawline. But mostly it was in the way he squinted, like he was staring into bright sunshine and didn't trust what he was seeing.

His dad had narrow eyes too, but his had that hooded, grandfatherly look, and while he must have been tall once, he was now stooped over, his broad shoulders skeletal below his green-and-white checked shirt, the red, whiskery skin dropping from his cheekbones and neck in craggy folds. Scraps of grey hair poked out below a dinged-up old Akubra, and he looked like a harmless old man, sweet too.

But as he approached, something remarkable happened. The younger man stooped, his eyes became more hooded, while the older man seemed to stand taller, stronger, and when he spoke, his deep voice belied his age.

"Yeah mate, I can see that," he said, watery eyes fixed to Lynette now.

Flynn glanced between them and offered Lynette a strange, almost apologetic wince before turning back to his father and saying, "I've also ordered some champagne for after dinner so—"

The soggy-blue irises darted back to the son. "It's not a party, mate. It's business. When're you gonna start taking this seriously, son?"

Flynn shrank even further under his father's words. "I was just—"

"Just order coffees and scrap the leg-opener. You won't be needing it." The older man shot another look at Lynette that made her bristle. Then he stared past them to the lounge and said, "Where're we gonna do it?"

"Oh, I thought we could grab a quiet spot here, after dinner—"

*"Quiet?"* He made a *pft!* sound. "Use your head, Flynn. It's a bloody circus in here. We'll do it back in mine. I'll arrange it like I arrange everything else."

He glanced around again. "Time to get this show on the road. Where're the others?"

Flynn pointed to the group seated halfway down the carriage, and for the life of her, Lynette was sure the younger man's finger was shaking—and it had nothing to do with the train track.

# CHAPTER 3
## The First Foreboding

As Lynette's new amour pointed at a group of four seated nearby, Alicia was also watching the foursome closely, wondering if they were on their way to a funeral. They looked utterly miserable, their expressions dour, their conversation nonexistent. They were clearly from the same gene pool, or at least three of them were.

The two men seated together could have been father and son, one of the women the daughter—all three of stocky build with matching golden-ginger curls, large, splotchy freckles and sun-etched skin. They also wore matching outfits, quite clearly country folk and posh ones at that, judging from the shine on their riding boots and the way their checked cotton twill collars were crisply turned up like their hats, one with a strand of pearls around her neck, the only real concession to her gender.

The fourth member of the group was the odd one out, clearly a ring-in—short and busty, with olive skin and luscious, long black hair. She was wearing a red-and-white gingham dress with a massive bow on one shoulder, the other shoulder bare, revealing doughy skin and a white swimsuit line. It was too short at the hem, her dress, and too tight around her bosom, her heels too high, her matching red resin earrings so chunky they almost clipped her shoulders as she swished her hair, which she did often.

"Country family, I reckon," whispered Perry, eyes following Alicia again. But she'd already guessed that from their wardrobe.

"Not the dark-haired one though," she whispered back.

He agreed. "Reckon she's the in-law and not thrilled to be

here. I overheard her in the café at Central. Not a happy camper."

"Unlike the others who look ready to *par-tay*?" said Alicia drolly.

He chuckled. "I know. Poor darlings, having to endure this dreadful journey. Could they *be* any grumpier?"

As he said it, all four sat straighter and yanked their lips upwards, and Alicia looked past them to see who they were fake smiling at. Another scorched-faced man, older than all of them and wearing an equally old hat, was making his way through the lounge from the bar. He was also in a checked shirt, a green-and-white one, but his was not crisp cotton with the collar turned up. It was a thicker, scruffier flannelette, like something you might wear mustering cattle.

Behind him was the handsome fella Lynette had been flirting with, but he did not look so handsome now, also smiling rigidly as he balanced a tray of drinks in his hands, and Alicia glanced back at the older man. There was something about him that was making them all uncomfortable. No, worse than that—nervous.

Whoever this bloke was, he had some kind of power over them, and she couldn't help wondering what. The two seated men sprang up as he approached, both offering their chairs, but he waved them off.

"We're not staying," his bone-dry voice boomed. "Let's head straight to tea."

"Actually, Clay," began the older of the two, who had to be the man's brother, they were just a few years apart. "I think we're scheduled for the later dinner sitting—seven p.m."

Clay turned his steely blue gaze towards him. "We'll eat when I say we eat, Phil. Let's go, people."

And with that they all jumped up and grabbed a drink each, then proceeded in single file back through the carriage, past Lynette who was now wielding a champagne bucket and six glasses, and on towards the dining room.

And that's when Alicia's sense of foreboding first took hold...

As handsome Flynn Dartmoor passed Lynette, he didn't smile this time, just gave her that strange apologetic wince again and kept walking. But that was not the look that made Lynette's skin crawl as she stepped aside so they could file past her and into the restaurant carriage.

The older man, the one he'd said was his father, also swept his eyes to Lynette, but there was nothing apologetic in the leer he was now offering. Lynette was used to such leers, but still, it made her nervous. Like she'd just been sized up for dinner.

"About time, woman!" said Perry after she glided her way smoothly back to their table, her waitressing skills coming to the fore as she managed to balance the ice bucket and glasses without so much as a ripple.

"Get his cabin number did you?" added Alicia.

Lynette rolled her eyes. "We were just chatting. It's what you do in a bar, sis. I'm allowed to chat."

"Of course you are, dear," said Ronnie, reaching for a champagne flute. "Ignore them, they're just jealous. I was quite the flirt in my day—as I think you all uncovered after my seventy-fifth birthday fiasco." They all paused to shudder at the thought of their last adventure together, which had turned into a deadly game of hide-and-seek. Ronnie waved a dismissive hand in the air and added, "And as I believe you also discovered, it never did my marriage any harm."

Perry snorted. "Is that your best advice for Alicia? Flirt to your heart's content, it'll make your marriage stronger."

She tsked as Missy clapped her hands and said, "Yes, let's hear *all* your marriage tips, Ronnie. You too, Claire. You're the only ones with any experience in the group. Of course I have a lovely new boyfriend now"—a grin towards Ronnie—"but we're not at that stage *yet*."

"Oh, I'd never stoop to offering advice," said Ronnie.

"And I've been married for five minutes," said Claire, readjusting the black off-the-shoulder Audrey Hepburn-style dress she'd changed into (not a swimsuit mark to be seen). "What would I know?" Then she leaned in and said,

"Although I will advise not to have your honeymoon on a superyacht."

That made them all shudder again, recalling yet another mystery they'd been embroiled in, before Lynette held her glass high and said, "To Alicia and Jackson. May their union be long and corpse-free!"

"Oh, now you've gone and jinxed it," said Alicia, half joking, half deadly serious as her mind darted back to the jittery family.

For the next ten minutes, the club settled into light conversation, mostly about the wedding dress Alicia had sourced through Claire's shop and was "to die for!" Before they knew it, it was seven p.m., their allotted time for dinner in the adjoining Queen Adelaide Restaurant.

Located in its own car, via two swishing, slightly scary, carriage doors, they were escorted in by a friendly maître d' called Marvin. He was officially the train's "Guest Experience Manager" and had a dimpled chin and a smile so infectious you couldn't help smiling along. The diner's art deco decor also brought a smile. It featured elegant, stencilled glass partitions, plush, intimate booths and stiff curtains drawn back so diners could view as they chewed.

The only drawback—they could not fit into one booth.

"Damn, it's just four to a table. Two of us will have to share with strangers," whispered Missy, expression bleak behind her black-and-white cat-eye frames.

"I'm sure we'll survive," Ronnie retorted. "We'll all take turns. Come on, Perry."

Then she nudged for him to join her on the other side of the aisle where there were two spare seats across from a thirty-something couple, who Perry instantly recognised.

They were the snarly duo from the café and part of the group he and Alicia had been ogling in the lounge. They'd also drawn the short straw and were separated from their pack, but they were not interested in sharing. As Ronnie went to take a seat, the dark-haired woman was already holding up her hand like a stop sign, eyes firmly on Marvin.

"We'd rather eat alone, thanks."

Perry looked offended by that, but Marvin simply waved a menu in the air and said, "Of course, Mrs Dartmoor, you've already started. I was going to direct them to a fresh table anyway," before ushering Ronnie and Perry down and across the aisle to an empty table of four.

Catching Perry's look, the woman's husband called after them, "No offence, guys!"

"All good," Ronnie called back.

But Perry was still smarting as he took his seat and then the menu Marvin was wielding. *Those two have no idea what fabulous conversation they were now missing out on*, he thought. *It certainly had to be better than the stony silence they'd been getting from their own group!*

"You really shouldn't take offence," came a craggy male voice, and Perry looked up to see a separate couple being ushered into the seats across from them.

They were in their late seventies or early eighties, the woman short and plump, her warm grey hair swept up into a messy beehive, the man twice her size in every direction, his own hair clipped short and brown in places where the grey hadn't yet reached, his mottled red nose enormous, his ears just as big and battered, like he might've played rugby for Australia once.

Yet he had the sweetest smile and a cheery, jocular way of talking. "That's the infamous Dartmoor family back there," he added with a whisper and a wink. "They think they own the country and everyone in it."

"That's 'cause they practically do," said the woman whose own voice was slow and expressionless, as "rural outback" as her get-up, which included a conservative Laura Ashley blouse (petite flowers, high neck, long sleeves) and drop-pearl earrings, which she was twiddling with now as she added, "They're the largest private landholder in the whole of Western Australia."

"Not quite," said the man. "But they're workin' on it."

Ronnie cocked her head to one side. "The Dartmoors?

Of Dartmoor Downs?"

They both nodded keenly, and Perry scoffed. "Trust you to know the wealthy landowners, Ronnie."

"I don't know them at all, Perry. I know *of* them. Wheat isn't it?"

"And the rest," said the woman, now whispering behind her menu. "They're our distant neighbours, the Dartmoors. One of the biggest players in WA's three-billion-dollar grain export industry. Last I looked they had well over thirty thousand hectares."

"But who's looking?" said the man, laughing. "Enough about them. I'm Jock Gleeson, and this is my better half, Iris. And I mean *much* better half. She's the light of my life this woman." Iris scoffed and rolled her eyes but she looked pleased by the comments, and not unused to it. "We produce our own crop," he continued, "right on their eastern border. Our farm's a very different scale of course, but it's all we need, isn't it, love?"

He smiled across to his wife again, but she didn't look so pleased now. Her reply smile felt forced to Perry, but he let it drop—could there *be* a more boring dinner conversation than farming? They finished introductions, then took some time to study the menus, all four of them swooning at the sound of the gourmet local cuisine.

"I'm not sure I can eat kangaroo though," said Perry, tapping on one of the mains. "Feels traitorous, you know. It is our national animal and all."

"Oh, don't be a dill," said Iris, her grey eyes twinkling back at him, her skin peachy, her cheekbones still plump and high. "It's the kindest thing you could do for the country. Because they're a native animal, they don't wreck the land like cattle do. Plus they can be a pest out here." She waved towards the grassy pastures that were now sweeping past their window. "Us farmers need to cull the buggers to keep them from nicking our grain. *And* they're one of the leanest meats, so they're good for you too."

She glanced at Perry's stomach, which was bulging a little now, it had to be said. It had been chaos trying to finish up at work in time for the holiday. Not a spare second for the gym.

She laughed. "Sorry, pet. Now *I'm* the one being offensive. And we can hardly talk, can we, Jocky?"

"Not me, that's for sure," he replied. "As I always say, good thing I produce so much high-grade wheat because someone's gotta provide the flour for all my cakes and scones!"

He bellowed with laughter as his wife tsked again and told him he was perfect "just the way you are" while Perry decided they were the cutest couple he'd ever met and discreetly pulled in his stomach.

Across the corridor, the rest of the book club were also arguing the merits of choosing the saltbush crusted kangaroo loin over a very delicious-sounding Pacific Ocean swordfish when the waitress appeared. She had a name tag that read CASSIDY and a beaming smile on her perfectly round face.

"Good evening, folks," she said. "Before you order, are they are any dietaries we need to be aware of?"

Missy blinked. "Dietaries?" Then she, too, stared down at her pudgy tummy, like she'd just been insulted. Missy had yo-yo dieted for years and was currently on the downward swing and super self-conscious about it.

"She means food allergies, intolerances, that kind of thing," said Lynette, the expert foodie in the group, eyes turning back to Cassidy. "We eat everything; nothing to worry about there. I'll start with the duck and green peppercorn paté, followed by the fish—*just* cooked, please, be sure to write that down—and then the apple-and-blueberry galette, thank you, but go easy on the cream."

The others ordered, a little less fussily, and very soon they were back to light conversation and laughter, and it wasn't until they were hooking into their dessert that the Dartmoor family was brought up again, back on Perry's and Ronnie's table.

Perry noticed that the wealthy wheat farmers had now finished and were making their way out. Except they weren't returning to the lounge bar. They were heading in the opposite direction.

"What's in that next carriage?" Perry asked Cassidy as she handed over cups of freshly brewed coffee.

"Oh, that's the Platinum Club, sir."

"And out of bounds for us peasants," murmured Jock, taking his cup with a wink. "Strictly first-class passengers only in there." Then he leaned forward. "Clay Dartmoor—that's the patriarch—he's booked himself in Platinum and shoved his brood into cattle class with us, including his baby brother. Poor Phil."

"This is hardly cattle class," said Ronnie, sweeping a hand across the linen tablecloth, dusting off some breadcrumbs. "And our rooms are just lovely. Although I must say you need to be a contortionist to use the tiny en suite bathroom."

"Oh, I have a tip for you," said Iris, tone conspiratorial. "My cousin Kate's been on this train a few times, says the solo cabins have communal bathrooms at the end of their carriage, and they're real roomy. You're welcome to use those if you like. Much easier for stiff old birds like us."

"See?" said Jock. "We share our facilities, while that lot"—his head pointed towards Platinum—"they're exclusive. We're not to go up there, apparently, but they can mingle down here anytime they please."

"And yet they're all heading that way," said Perry, watching as the last of the Dartmoors disappeared into the Platinum carriage.

Jock scoffed. "Yeah, well, it is the Dartmoors, mate, and the Dartmoors do what the Dartmoors want. Besides..." He tapped the side of his ample nose. "Rumour has it, Clay's announcing his successor on this trip; that's the reason they're here. Perhaps they're choofing off to his cabin now to see who gets the nod."

"Successor?" said Perry.

"We didn't think we'd live to see the day, did we, Jocky?" Iris blinked up at her husband. "Clay might be eighty, but we can't imagine him retiring. Must have something to do with Daisy." She turned back to Perry. "Clay's wife passed.

Last year. Very sad. I reckon it got him reassessing things, yeah?"

"You reap what you sow," said the husband under his breath. "Poor Daisy died of a broken heart she did. Husband was a ratbag, never could resist a young blonde." His eyes flitted down and towards the fair-haired Finlay sisters before glancing back at his wife who looked suddenly tense.

"Now, now, Jock, that's enough of the gossip," she murmured. "I can see we're making Ronnie uncomfortable."

And it was true. Ronnie also looked tense. She wasn't one for idle gossip, but Perry was in conversation heaven. He fluttered a dismissive hand in the air and said, "So why has Clay's wife's tragic death caused him to hand his farm to his kids?"

He felt like he was discussing an episode of *The Bold and the Beautiful.*

Jock shrugged his enormous shoulders and said, "He's not handing it to his kids. He's gifting it to just *one* of them."

"Ooh! There's a twist." Now it was more like that family drama *Succession*! "Why would he do something so divisive?"

Jock looked at Perry like he might be a bit dim. "Family tradition, of course. Clay's father gave him the property to run, and now he's giving it to one of his brood. Lord knows which one though."

Then he shrugged again and didn't sound quite so jocular as he added, "But that place is more trouble than it's worth. You ask me, whoever gets handed Dartmoor Downs will quickly find it's a curse."

Then Iris shivered beside him as though someone had just opened a window.

## CHAPTER 4
### The Fossil Hunter and the Barmaid

**B**y the time the club reunited in the lounge for a nightcap, the place had cleared out and all that was left were a few stragglers drinking alone and several lively groups who had clearly bonded over dinner and now seemed thick as thieves, not to mention half-drunk.

Which wasn't far off where the book club friends were at.

"Another champers? Really?" said Alicia as Missy returned with a fresh bottle. "You know we have to get up at the crack of dawn, right? For the first stop at Broken Hill."

"You're kidding?" said Lynette, who loathed early rises. "How early are we talking?"

"Around six, six thirty I believe," came a voice to one side, and they all glanced across at a man who was seated at the adjoining table. He held a hand up to wave. "Sorry, couldn't help overhearing."

He was a svelte fellow in his late fifties with an impressive Poirot-style moustache and slicked-back silvery hair, a shiny blue vest and bow tie to match. He introduced himself as Alan J. Taggart—"but everyone calls me Tag"—and then told them he was looking forward to the Broken Hill stop. "But it's Adelaide I'm particularly interested in. Their museum has one of the finest collections of fossils anywhere in the world."

The group glanced across to Perry, who gave them a subtle head shake as the man continued to tell them all about his work as a "fossil collector" and how he couldn't *wait* to hear the special talk by a leading expert in palaeontology, Professor Jonathan Miles.

"He's presenting on one of the few dinosaur bones ever

discovered in Western Australia, a toe bone would you believe? From the upper Cretaceous period. Discovered out near Gingin. Very exciting." Tag's eyes glinted. "You see, dinosaur fossils are *deliciously* rare in WA. There've been some remarkable discoveries around Broom and Kalbarri on the northwestern coast, up past Geraldton, but most come from the eastern half of the country, you know?"

"Oh, Perry knows," said Missy, not noticing Perry's head begin to shake harder. "He's a palaeontologist too. Aren't you, Perry?"

Perry tried not to groan. He was proud of his work, but this man was proving to be a bore and he didn't want to encourage him. Besides, they should be focusing on Alicia.

"Is that so?" said Tag, turning his eyes upon Perry. "Who do you work for?"

Perry smiled damply. "A museum in Sydney, and I'm not nearly as distinguished as Professor Miles, I can assure you."

"Then you'll want to come along on the tour and take notes," said Tag. "The story of the small pedal phalanx is absolutely fascinating. That's the toe, you understand?" A quick glance at Missy, who seemed the most in need of mansplaining. "The fossil toe was discovered by a young student by the name of Green—Michael Green I think it was—and he had the good sense to donate it to the WA Museum, and it's now on loan to South Australia. It's said to be around ninety million years old, but there's bound to be more remains, if we bothered to look."

Then his eyes darted towards the bar at the back and suddenly widened. "Or were *permitted* to," he added, a trace of bitterness in his tone.

Their gazes all followed Tag's, and they saw a group walking back from the dining carriage, just passing the bar. It was the Dartmoor family again, and Perry livened up considerably. Forget fossil hunting—or even Alicia— he wanted to know who had just scored the deeds to thirty thousand hectares. As they streamed through in a single queue, chins high, eyes ahead, sunburned faces blank, it was impossible to tell.

The patriarch, Clay, was bringing up the rear but didn't follow them into the lounge. Instead, he stopped at the bar and began talking to the bartender.

"What a coincidence," Tag said after the others had passed through, back towards the accommodation carriage. "If my eyes don't deceive me, that's Clayton Dartmoor up at the bar. His property borders the area of the find. Dartmoor Downs. Everyone's very keen to get in and have a bit of a fossick, but he simply won't allow it. Spoilsport." He smiled but there was an edge. "Perhaps I should use the op' and ask him myself while I've got him captive. See if he'll reconsider, for the sake of science, you understand? It's certainly more important than Weet-Bix."

"Weet-Bix?" asked Missy, looking completely lost.

Perry didn't blame her. He leaned in and repeated what the Gleeson couple had told them over dinner, how the Dartmoors were a wealthy wheat-producing family. "Is that why you're here?" he asked Tag. "To push your barrow with Clay Dartmoor?"

"Not at all," said Tag, hand patting his heart like it was wounded. "As I said, that's a coincidence. I'm here for the Adelaide stop."

"Well, I'm here to celebrate my friend's engagement," said Claire a tad curtly. "And all this talk of fossils is not exactly helping. I think I'll get more champagne and some water to keep us hydrated."

"I'll help you," said Perry, as much to get away from Tag as to steal a closer look at the Wheat Baron who seemed to have more enemies on this train than friends.

When they reached the bar, Clay Dartmoor had one more enemy to contend with. The young bartender was now giving him a dressing down, which he was taking with a dollop of delight, his watery eyes sparkling, his whiskery cheeks pulled into a cocky smile.

"As I just told you, Mr Dartmoor," said Agnetha, pushing a flat keycard back towards him. "That won't be happening. Not tonight. Not ever. Now if you don't mind..."

She turned to the book club friends, eyebrows high.

"Everything okay here?" asked Perry, glancing from the bartender to the man and back. A small group drinking nearby had also noticed the altercation and watched on, seemingly amused.

Agnetha smiled stiffly. "Of course, sir. Another bottle of sparkling wine and six fresh glasses?"

"We'll use the same glasses, thank you," he told her.

"And some cold water, too, if you don't mind," added Claire, who was glowering at Clay Dartmoor like she was the one who'd just been hit on.

He didn't seem to notice or care, just scooped up his tumbler of whisky and made his way out—away from their lounge, through the empty diner, towards what Perry now knew was the exclusive Platinum Club, the lounge for first-class passengers.

When Perry looked back, he noticed that Clay's keycard was still resting on the bar. "Is that his room key?" he asked, surprised Platinum cabins had secure keys, because the Gold cabins did not.

Agnetha misunderstood the question and snatched it up, dropping it into her tip jar like it was as irrelevant as loose change. "Don't worry, I'll make sure it gets back to him."

And if she happened to hurl it at him, Perry would not have been surprised. Nor would he have blamed her.

After the drinks were fetched, they thanked her, then carefully made their way back to the group, Perry relieved to see the fossil collector now deep in conversation with a woman on his other side.

"What have we missed?" Perry asked as he began refilling their flutes.

"We're still trying to drag marriage advice from Ronnie," said Missy. "But she refuses to cough up." Ronnie tutted and Missy whined, "But you were married to Bert for more than forty years! That's simply *amazing*. My boyfriend—Seamus—and I can only hope to last a fraction of that time."

"How about we each do a lovely toast to Alicia," said Perry. "Keep things simple. I'll start." He jumped to his feet again and raised his glass. "To Alicia and Jackson. May your eyes never stray"—a glance towards the Platinum carriage—"may your conversation never be dull"—now a quick peek at Tag, who was still droning on about fossils to the bewildered-looking woman—"and may your marriage be as smooth and fabulous as this—"

But he didn't get to finish that sentence as the train lurched suddenly and sent him flying straight into Tag's lap while the rest of the book club fell about laughing.

# CHAPTER 5
## Back to the (Other) Flying Man

Six hours later, the train was still doing its fair share of lurching, between crunching, screeching, clacking and rattling, but Alicia had long stopped laughing. It was now bang on five a.m. and her eyes were locked to the window in her cabin, wide and worried. Ten minutes earlier she had seen a man plummet from the train. Or at least, she thought she had. But as Lynette snored lightly in the bunk above her head, Alicia wondered if her sister was right.

Had she just imagined it? Was it all a dream? The work of her mad mind or one too many glasses of bubbly? Or was it the consequence of reading about old Mrs McGillicuddy and her view of murder through a speeding train window?

Yes, that's all it was, Alicia thought dreamily, her eyes beginning to droop, her limbs finally relaxing. It was all Agatha Christie's…

Bang! Bang! Bang!

Alicia sat up with a start. "What the hell was that?"

"Huh?" came Lynette's mumble from above just as a voice called out that they were approaching Broken Hill, before they heard a muffled bang on the next door down.

"Broken Hill? I'll give them a broken hill," grumbled Lynette as she turned over in her bunk.

Rubbing her eyes, Alicia peered past her feet and out the cabin window. It was their first official morning on the train, and the view was both mesmerising and surprising. It was now just after six a.m. The lush, mountainous outskirts of Sydney were long gone, as were the fertile agricultural tablelands beyond the Great Dividing Range. They had passed through those in the dark of night and were now officially in the outback. No other word for it. The earth swishing past the window was a thirsty ochre red, scattered with dusty mulga grass and saltbush, the odd yellow wattle or lurid purple native flower catching your eye. The sky above was a wispy blue and orange where the sun was rising, dipping and diving with the movement of the train. And they didn't need the wake-up call to know they were closing in on Broken Hill—there was an open-pit mine now creeping into the frame.

Alicia stretched her arms out and yawned widely. Had she managed *any* sleep last night? It certainly didn't feel like it. Groaning, she pulled herself from the covers, almost falling into the adjoining bathroom. She closed the door, slipped off her pyjamas and pulled a shower cap over her hair, then swished the curtain around her and began to take a shower.

As the hot water streamed down upon her, Alicia's memory kicked in and she gasped. That's right! She'd seen a man pushed from the train early this morning.

*Hadn't she?*

She tried to think back, clear the fog in her brain, but she was desperately hungover. Her head was thudding. Her memory murky. Wrenching the shower cap off, Alicia plunged her tousled hair under the water, trying to beat some sense into herself.

What *had* she seen exactly?

A flash of colour. Yes, that's right. Green and white, like a plaid shirt flying off the train. That's why she'd thought it was the farmer. He'd been wearing something similar last night.

Had she seen a body? She slowly shook her head. No... no... just the shirt... tumbling down towards the tracks, like the discarded clothing from the book Lynette had been reading.

She flung her eyes open and turned off the water. Lynette was right. Of course she was right! Alicia had dreamt the whole thing, but it wasn't *4.50 from Paddington* that had prompted her dreams. It was *The Girl on the Train.*

And this time Alicia was the poor, pathetic drunk.

Once the Finlay sisters had straightened themselves up and joined the queue of fellow passengers alighting the train via their assigned exit, the door closest to the bar, both women were feeling more human, although Alicia's doubts were beginning to creep in again, just nudging at the edge of her booze-soaked brain.

Their attendant Jacinta was on door duty, ticking each passenger off before they made their way across the station to the awaiting tour buses, and as there was a lull in the crowd, Alicia decided to take a punt, pulling her aside.

"Hey Jacinta. I wonder if I can ask a silly question."

"Fire away," she said, stifling a yawn.

"I'm just wondering... I mean, there weren't any, you know... *dramatic* incidents on the train early this morning, were there?"

The mousy-haired thirty-something just looked bemused. "Dramatic? How do you mean?"

"Don't mind Alicia." This was Lynette, back at her side, trying to pull her away. "She has an overactive imagination. Thought she saw something. But you didn't, Alicia, so just leave it."

"What did you see?" Jacinta asked, tone curious now.

Alicia shrugged. "Lynette's right, it's probably nothing. But if someone *were* to fall off the train, would there be some kind of alarm?"

Jacinta's eyes widened. "You saw someone fall from the train?"

"No! I mean, I'm not sure. I could've been dreaming..."

That seemed to appease the attendant, who smiled at the Gleesons as she ticked the tardy passengers off, then turned back to Alicia.

"I can assure you nobody fell off the train this morning. That's a very big deal, ma'am, and I think I would have heard by now. Besides, it's actually not that easy to fall from a train these days. Not like the rattlers from my youth, I can tell you! The Indian Pacific is fully air-conditioned, the windows and adjoining carriage doors all tightly sealed. Even if you managed to get a locked exit door open, an alarm would go off in the drivers' compartment, so they'd stop the train pretty quickly." She smiled warmly. "Had to be a dream. Or a nightmare really."

"*See?*" said Lynette, offering Jacinta a grateful smile as she pulled her sister away. "All in your mind, honey. Now let's just chill and enjoy ourselves."

Enjoy was not quite the right word for the tour they had selected from a list of five "off-train experiences" in Broken Hill. Since it was their first time in the frontier mining town, the club had chosen to visit the Line of Lode Miner's Memorial—a stunningly constructed tribute to the miners who had lost their lives extracting silver, lead and zinc from one of the world's largest bodies of ore—and there were a lot of them.

Dead miners, that is.

Slowly weaving their way through the open-air steel creation that floated like a rusty ship atop a mullock of mining waste, they read the many names etched into the glass panels inside and found themselves gasping at both the age and the manner of the deaths. Many were barely middle-aged when they died of heart failure and lead poisoning, younger crew were crushed by rocks and wagons, fell down shafts and into passes, or were entangled in falling ropes or machinery, including a fifteen-year-old "caught in belting".

That one produced a lot of wincing.

"It was a different time," Ronnie told them soothingly. "And we can thank our trade unions for changing all that."

Missy scratched her blue curls. "Gee, Ronnie, for a rich woman you're a real leftie, aren't you?"

"I am not a rich woman, Missy," she shot back. "I am a simple country girl who happened to marry a rich man. I am not my dearly departed husband's identity, thank you very much." Then she winked and said, "There you go, Alicia, that's my marriage advice. Never change for your husband. Always stay true to yourself."

Alicia nodded blearily and continued looking around, but she was already starting to flag. *Her* tongue felt like it had been caught in belting now, and she was hoping to locate a water bubbler when she spotted an elderly man standing out on a nearby viewing platform. He had a plaid shirt and a crisp, wide-brimmed hat on, his face gaunt and wrinkly below it.

"Oh, thank God," she said, her whole body relaxing as she crossed back to Lynette who was still studying the names with Perry. "He's here," she told her sister. "The old farmer. He's alive."

Lynette smiled. "Told you so."

"Told you what?" asked Perry. "Who's alive?"

So Lynette explained. "Silly goose had a nightmare, thought she saw that scary grain king fall off the train early this morning."

"Good Lord," said Perry. "That's dramatic even for you, Alicia."

Alicia nodded. "But it's okay. Crisis averted. Clay's out there alive and well."

Perry glanced out towards the platform and back. "I don't see him."

Alicia turned. "There, talking to that couple you shared dinner with last night. In the Akubra."

Perry looked again, then shook his head. "Sorry, honey, but I don't think that's Clay Dartmoor. I think that's his younger brother. Phillip, I think his name is. He's not quite as bony, a little shorter, certainly less menacing."

"What?" said Alicia, her heart dropping again as she whipped her head back around to take another look.

"So, it's not him," said Lynette. "That doesn't mean anything. There are other tours, Alicia. He's obviously on one of them."

"Yeah, that makes sense," said Perry. "He's probably on the drag queen tour with his super-fun family."

Perry was joking—about the family not the tour. There really was a tour of the main drag, conducted by a bearded, brightly clad drag queen who looked like she'd be better suited to mining. It was a homage to *The Adventures of Priscilla, Queen of the Desert*, a smash-hit, fish-out-of-water movie that had put this rough old town on the map.

Alicia said, "You know you didn't have to come on this excursion with me. You both would've loved that one."

Perry scoffed. "Honey, I don't need to come to the middle of Australia to see a drag queen. Some of my best friends... and all that."

"And I'm not leaving your side," said Lynette. "This is supposed to be a group holiday."

"Still..." Alicia's eyes were back on the look-alike brother. "Maybe I should go and have a word with this Phillip fellow. See if he knows—"

"Don't you *dare*," said Lynette. "The poor guy's trying to relax and have his own holiday. Come on, leave it."

Except Phillip didn't look so relaxed suddenly. Arms folded across his chest, the seventy-something was leaning his whole torso back while Jock Gleeson was pointing a fat finger inches from his nose, ranting about something. Jock's wife, Iris, was clearly embarrassed, glancing about with a stiff smile, then grabbing at Jock's thick elbow, trying to pull him away without much luck.

Eventually the rant came to an end and Jock dropped his finger and shuffled away, but Iris did not follow. She leaned in towards Phillip Dartmoor and said something that made him smile. And she smiled right along. Then he reached a hand up to her grey hair as though pushing a stray strand from her brow, and they stared at each other in silence for just a moment before she turned and walked off to join her husband, who was now listening to the guided talk.

The book club friends watched the whole thing with glee.

"I wonder what that was about?" said Perry as Alicia's eyes narrowed. "One minute there was fisticuffs, the next there was flirting. Very odd."

"Very none of our business," said Lynette. "Come on, we're missing all the grisly details."

And so they turned back to the memorial, but Alicia's mind was still on the missing man, and she wondered if his fate had been equally grisly.

~

Claire pulled her short-sleeved, fitted jacket closer to her chest, wincing at yet another ugly demise—this one a twenty-nine-year-old who "suffocated in ore"—and caught the eye of the man beside her.

"Sad, hey?" he said. "I always reckon farming's hard yakka, but I'm lucky my family wasn't in mining."

Claire's feline eyes narrowed further as she took in his splotchy freckles and reddish beard and realised he was part of the Dartmoor family they'd been gossiping about last night. A younger version of the irksome old man she'd seen at the bar.

"Wheat isn't it?" Claire asked, and he nodded, not looking at all surprised that a total stranger knew his business.

"But my real passion's vodka and gin," he told her, adding quickly, "Distilling it, I mean. I founded the Dartmoor Distilling Co." She stared back at him blankly. "The boutique distillery?" The blank look remained and *now* he seemed surprised. A little annoyed too. "Yeah, well, you'll hear about it soon enough. Gonna be huge. And a lot less stress than farming."

Then his eyes clouded over just as his dark-haired wife appeared, latest model iPhone in hand.

"Hey babes," she said, giving Claire the once-over. "I'm *so* done with this tour. I've taken enough shots to break Insta. Can we bail now?"

"Yeah, nah," he said, somewhat elusively. "Think we have to wait for the bus to take us all in one hit."

She groaned, pouted her lips, then blew a puff of air through them. "In that case, while we have a decent signal, let's give our children a call. Remember them, honey?"

As she spoke, her eyes were firmly on Claire, and the Eurasian beauty offered her a warm, unthreatening smile, but it didn't work. The other woman glowered now, before tapping her smart phone and pulling her husband away.

~

Back on the train, the attendants were all busily cleaning the cabins and storing the beds away while the passengers were occupied, but one of them was feeling guilty.

And it didn't make any sense.

Jacinta had every right to be in cabin number four—in fact, it was her *duty* to be in there, prepping the room for daytime—and yet she felt like a marauding intruder.

She glanced around furtively, then curiously, then, yes, angrily, because the anger was still there, as thick as the woolly green jumper she had just discovered scrunched in a ball under the bed. She glanced down at it and flinched.

The jumper was familiar. Very familiar. She'd seen it before, and she remembered now. It had been a birthday present. That's right. Hand-knitted by Mrs Dartmoor in a simple, rustic design—chunky, twelve-ply cable knit in pea-green Merino wool, a few stitches dropped along the way—and yet Jacinta would have recognised it in a box full of woollies at a jumble sale.

She draped it across the sofa, then glanced around and grabbed it back up. Brought it to her nose. Inhaled deeply. And that's when the cabin door swung open and she looked up with a start to see the one person she did not want to see.

There was a moment of stunned silence, then a voice that sent her barrelling back through time and tears and trauma:

"Well, well, if it isn't Jacinta McClaren. Fancy meeting you here."

# CHAPTER 6
## Food for Thought

By the time the guests returned to the train, there wasn't a stray jumper or unmade bed to be found, the cabins all back in travel mode with the lounges set up, the bathrooms cleaned out, and fresh bottles of chilled water on the reinstalled tables by the windows.

It was a welcome relief after the dusty excursion. While the day was still young, the temperature had heated up fast, and there were no complaints as the book club made their way into their air-conditioned carriage to continue onwards to Adelaide.

Although a decent cup of coffee wouldn't go astray.

So after freshening up, they reunited in the lounge bar for barista-made beverages before their late breakfast sitting. Agnetha was back behind the bar, and Missy felt sorry for her.

"Do you think the poor darling got any time off?" she asked.

"No need for violins," said Lynette. "This is a terrific gig, chugging across the countryside, serving coffee and cocktails to the well-to-do."

"Except when the well-to-do are hitting on you," muttered Perry, giving Claire a look.

He then described Clay Dartmoor's antics the evening before, and now they all felt sorry for the barmaid.

"Why *do* some men think that's perfectly acceptable behaviour?" asked Claire. "Next time I see him make passes at the staff, I'm going to speak up. Put him firmly in his place."

"Next time you see him, let me know," said Alicia.

"He's become a Houdini that guy."

Lynette's frown hardened. "Sis, seriously, let it go."

"Let what go?" asked Claire, eyes darting between the sisters. "What's going on?"

So, once again, Alicia described her early-morning "vision", how she thought she had seen Clay Dartmoor fall from the train, before Lynette quickly added, "But we checked with the attendant, and nobody's missing. Jacinta also said it's practically impossible for someone to fall—"

"Could've been pushed," said Alicia.

Lynette sighed. "Or it could've been a nightmare."

"You're reading *4.50 from Paddington*, aren't you, darls?" said Missy. "Maybe that got your imagination churning?"

"Or maybe I really saw something at four in the morning," she shot back.

"Four?" said Ronnie, pulling out some knitting from her recycled calico tote. "It would have been very dark then, dear."

"Might've been closer to five," Lynette conceded grumpily. She was the one who had checked her phone clock that morning. "I was exaggerating, Alicia, just like your mind's doing. You saw some checked material, and you're imagining it was a body."

Ronnie pulled her eyes from her wool and glanced out the window at the flying terrain. "Either way, I'm not sure how you would've seen it, Alicia." She crooked her neck this way and that. "You can barely see beyond this carriage, and we've been told Clay sleeps up in Platinum. That's several carriages away from yours. I hate to doubt you, dear, but I think it'd be impossible."

Lynette waved a hand at Ronnie like she'd just closed the case, but Alicia still wasn't convinced.

"So where is he?" she asked. "Clay's whole family's together again—I saw them go into breaky—but he's not with them. He's gone AWOL."

"Are you saying you think they *colluded*? To kill him?" asked Missy excitedly.

"Nobody's dead!" said Lynette, dropping moodily to the

back of her lounge seat.

Perry sat forward, addressing Alicia. "The fact that Clayton Dartmoor is not dining with his family is evidence of his disregard for them, I suspect, not of their doing him in. As Ronnie says, Clay's officially a Platinum passenger— our dining companions last night had all the goss. Said he booked himself into the better class and chucked his family into Gold with us. So he has his own bar and restaurant. He's probably chatting up the poor waitress who's serving him his Eggs Benedict as we speak."

"Speaking of eggs," said Missy, tapping her phone. "Time for breakfast, folks."

It was only after the club had finished their meal and were heading back to their cabins that something occurred to Alicia. Spotting the carriage attendant in the communal kitchenette, she pretended she wanted a fresh cuppa and waved Lynette on, then made a beeline for Jacinta.

The crew member was wiping down the benchtop and smiled as Alicia walked in.

"That was fun," Alicia said casually as she reached for a teabag.

Jacinta continued wiping. "Yeah, Broken Hill's one of our most popular stops."

"I can see why. Although not everyone got off, right?"

Jacinta glanced up from her cloth. Frowned suddenly. "Most did. Why do you say that?"

"I'm just wondering about Platinum—"

There was a rushed exhale. "Oh well, I wouldn't know about Platinum. My buddy Walker works the on-and-off sheet for that section. What's all this about?" Then she dropped her head to one side and said, "You're not still worried about that nightmare of yours, are you?"

Before Alicia could reply, Jacinta dumped the cloth and led her out of the tearoom and towards the exit door at that end of the carriage.

"See this here?" She pointed to the exterior door that was now firmly closed and rattling along with the rest of the train.

"This is the only way in or out. Like I said, all the windows are sealed shut, and these doors are securely locked during motion. But if you *did* want to open one, you'd need a set of these."

She reached for a key ring attached to her belt and held up a clump of keys, including a fob. "It's not a simple process. You really mustn't worry."

Alicia studied the keys. "Who has access to those?"

Jacinta laughed. "Just the staff!" She dropped the keys back to her belt. "Seriously, you have got to relax. Everyone on this train is safe and well. Now did you need anything else?"

She was staring at the teabag Alicia was still holding. Alicia offered a jaunty laugh and shook her head, then she returned to the tearoom and proceeded to make an unwanted cup as she thought, *I'll relax when I see Clay Dartmoor alive and breathing. Until then, I need to find this Walker fellow and his all-important on-and-off sheet...*

That was easier said than done.

Alicia knew that the relevant Platinum cabins were towards the front of the train, and so she dumped the cup at the first opportunity and retraced her steps back through their lounge bar and diner where the crew were now clearing away the debris from the final breakfast seating. She spotted the fossil collector, Tag, still lingering over his coffee and gave him a wave as she continued on, but that's where she came to a halt.

The door to the adjoining carriage had a very clear stop sign or, in this case, a polite placard that read: PLATINUM PASSENGERS ONLY BEYOND THIS POINT. THANK YOU.

She glanced through and could see that there was another lounge bar, this one decorated in shades of sepia, moss and gold, with a dining area incorporated in and not a soul in sight. Glancing tentatively at the automatic door opener, she went to push it when a voice said, "Hello there!" and she snatched her hand back like it was on fire.

Turning, she found Tag standing behind her.

"You going through?" he asked, glancing at the flashing green button.

Alicia hesitated, then asked, "Are you a Platinum passenger?" He nodded and held up a keycard as if for proof. "So how come you're eating and drinking with us Goldies?"

Tag glanced around and back before mock whispering, "Because I've been on this train a few times and have always found it's so much more fun with you plebs, but don't tell the VIPs that!" He chuckled, then gave her a sideways glance. "You after a sneak peek, hey? Want to see how the other half live? Or should I say, travel?"

She smiled. "Well, if it's not too much trouble?"

And with that he pushed the button and led the way through.

~

Lynette was wondering where Alicia had got to and was now poking her head out of her cabin door and peering down the corridor.

"All good, honeykins?" called out Missy.

The young librarian was standing outside her own cabin, watching the view from that side, and Lynette stepped out to join her.

"Seen Alicia?" she asked.

Missy shook her head. "I'm just waiting for Claire to finish in the loo, giving her some privacy and that."

"How's it going in there together?"

Missy grinned. "It's great!" Her grin faltered. "Claire was so generous, sharing her room with me. There's no way I could've come otherwise."

"She's sweet like that, Claire."

Missy's corkscrew curls bobbed about in agreement. "It's no fun being the povo in the group."

Lynette snorted. "Alicia and I are hardly loaded."

"Yeah, but she gets a decent package at the magazine surely? And you must earn good money in your new job, yeah?"

Lynette had now finished her business and hospitality course and was managing an upmarket seafood restaurant called FishFishChew. And it's true her salary had risen substantially since her days waiting tables at the cheap-eats Italian joint, Mario's, her responsibilities along with it. Lynette was now in charge. She was respected. She should have been happy, but for some reason she was not, and she couldn't work out why.

"I thought you loved it there, chookie," said Missy, catching her frown.

"I *do*," said Lynette, not sounding the least bit convincing. "Anyway, you have an obscenely rich new boyfriend now, don't you?"

"I do!" Missy echoed, laughing. Then she pulled her cat-eye spectacles off and gave them a clean. "But *he's* not rich. I mean, just 'cause he's Ronnie's nephew and he drives that lovely car she gave him, doesn't mean he's loaded. And sure, he'll probably inherit from her one day, but she's not going anywhere in a hurry—touch wood." She stopped to tap her brain as she did so. "And nor would he want her to! Any case, it's *his* money, isn't it? Not mine. We are just dating."

"Yeah, but I have a good feeling about you two. I reckon you have a very bright future."

Missy burst into embarrassed giggles at that, and Lynette thought about her own future and felt her stomach tighten. Alicia was getting married the following week and would be moving straight in with Jackson. That left Lynette all alone with Max, their beloved black Labrador (currently at home with a carer). She adored Max, but...

She sighed heavily.

Lynette had always thought of herself as a feminist, a thoroughly modern woman. Resisted the notion that she needed a *man* to complete her life. And yet, somehow, for some reason, she was feeling upended by the turn of events. She was happy for her sister—she really was—and yet it was so... well, *surprising*.

The truth is, Lynette was the one who usually got the guy,

certainly got all the attention. While Alicia had dated just two men in the past five years, Lynette's count was well into double digits. That's why she had always assumed *she* would be the one skipping off into the sunset first while Alicia was left snuggled on the sofa with Max, watching pitiful rom-coms...

Lynette sighed again and wondered how things had gotten so out of kilter.

~

Iris Gleeson closed her door gently and turned back to her husband who was sitting by the window, legs crossed out in front of him, a James Patterson thriller in his lap.

"Stop spying, woman," he said. "They'll catch you."

"I'm not spying," she retorted, dropping onto the couch beside him. "But you overheard that girl this morning. Said she saw someone get chucked overboard."

He held up a large, fat finger. "No, she *thought* she saw that, and the attendant—Jacky is it? Jessie? Anyway, she told her it didn't happen. That means it didn't happen."

"Yeah, but what if—"

"Iris, enough already." He reached over and grabbed one of her hands. "We're on holiday, right? Let's just relax, or you'll ruin everything."

"You weren't so relaxed this morning, love." A sharp eyebrow upwards. "Why go off at Phil in Broken Hill today? What was that about?"

"Hey, he started it, going on about Dartmoor Downs and how they could rescue us, like we're on the ropes. We don't need his handouts."

"He was being polite."

"He was being a boofhead."

"But he's right though, isn't he? You're not getting any younger, Jock, and you know what the doctor said—"

"I'm fine, Iris!" He squeezed her hand tighter. "And even if I'm not... well, you promised me."

She stared back at him. Hard. "Yes, I did promise you,

so why the carry-on?"

"No carry-on, it's all good. Drop it now please, or you really will give me a heart attack."

Then he let out a small chortle, trying to lighten the mood as he returned to his book while Iris reached for her wedding band and began to twiddle it, her gaze drifting outwards. Her mind drifting back…

She remembered an elegant homestead. A brass four-poster bed. Shiny, antique furnishings and heirlooms at every turn. The hundred-year-old grandfather clock that she'd loved at first sight. The enormous cedar dining table. Waterford crystal glasses. Wedgewood dinnerware…

She had it all in her grasp once. Every little bit.

And yet she'd let it slip through her fingers. Smash to the floor. And now she could barely afford kitchenware from Kmart, let alone the repairs to their ramshackle old homestead! And how they were going to pay off this train trip was a whole other kettle of fish.

It had been a folly. A very stupid idea.

She glanced back at her buffoon of a husband and thought, *Oh God, what have I done?*

# CHAPTER 7
## The Vacant Cabin that Wasn't

Alicia was trying to work out what was different about the Platinum accommodation carriage as she strolled along behind Tag. And then she saw it. There were several differences in fact. For starters, there were half the number of compartments, which meant the rooms were clearly much larger—if only she could see in. Every door was closed. So, too, the blinds on all the internal windows that looked out into the corridor, allowing them a dual view—another difference from Gold.

Unlike the constant coming and going in her carriage, this one felt abandoned. Unoccupied, although Tag told her all the cabins were full. The first-class passengers weren't soaking up the view from their own private Platinum Club lounge either, the one they'd just passed through. Its leather banquet lounges were empty, its elegant quartzite tabletops bare of any suggestion they'd ever even been used.

"So which cabin is Clay Dartmoor's?" she asked.

Tag stopped and spun around. "Wouldn't have a clue."

*Really?* Just a handful of passengers in this carriage and he really didn't know? After his rant last night? She didn't believe it for a moment and was about to call him on it when the door to cabin two swept open and a man in a staff uniform and a finely shaved head stepped out. He had a lopsided smile that dimmed when he caught sight of Alicia, who was peering in to check out the lovely interior. The double bed had morphed back into a plush living space, complete with silk cushions, coffee table and two ottomans. On the table she could see a bowl of fruit, a stiff, tan-coloured Akubra with a pair of spectacles beside it, and

51

on the table by the window a stack of papers and an unopened bottle of champagne. The French stuff this time.

She sighed wistfully as the attendant secured the door behind him and nodded at Tag before giving Alicia a second look.

He drew his lips back into his wonky smile and said, "I'm sorry, ma'am, I think you might be going the wrong way."

"Oops, that's my bad," said Tag, stepping closer. "Walker, this is Alicia. She's from Gold. I was just giving her a quick tour."

"That's very kind of you, sir, but unfortunately Gold-class passengers are not permitted in this section. You are, of course, welcome to join your friend in the Outback Explorer Lounge at any time."

Tag gave a little shrug, and Alicia said, "Thanks anyway, Tag. But actually I wanted to have a quick word with you. Walker, yes?"

The attendant nodded warily, and Tag said, "I'll leave you to it."

He gave them a curious look before continuing on to cabin one, while Walker waved her back down the corridor and towards the Platinum Club, back in the direction she had come.

They had tea and coffee facilities too, but theirs were fancier, with a coffee pod machine and iced cookies the size of Alicia's fist, and she glanced at them longingly.

"You're welcome to have one," Walker told her. "It'll be our little secret."

She laughed but tapped her stomach. "Not sure I can fit another thing in, but thank you. I won't take much of your time. I just wanted to ask about one of your passengers, a man called Clay Dartmoor. You remember him?"

He tidied the cookie pile and said, "Of course."

"Did you happen to see him this morning? As we were getting out at Broken Hill?"

Walker didn't answer that time, just looked up from the pile blankly, so she quickly added, "It's just that I know you guys check everyone who gets on and off, and I'm just wondering if you ticked Clay's name off. Fact is, I didn't see him on the tour and I'm hoping he's okay."

Walker's lopsided smile was back, but there was a hint of something else in there too. Annoyance? Anxiety? She couldn't tell, and nor would he.

"Sorry, I can't discuss my passengers' movements with you. I hope you understand."

"Oh, of course, I get that. It's just—"

"Excuse me!" came a shrill call from behind Alicia, and she swung back to see an elderly lady holding up one hand. "Yes! You, young man! Do you think you could make me one of those lovely cappuccinos you made for me earlier? It was just delightful!"

Walker gave her a hearty wave, then glanced back to Alicia. "I have to get on. If you don't mind…"

He escorted her into the lounge to a mini-bar where, apart from a variety of top-shelf wines and spirits, there was a glistening espresso machine that left the pod looking second-rate, then nodded towards the door that led back to the Gold diner.

Alicia took the hint and left him brewing coffee, but she wasn't yet done with Walker or the first-class carriage.

~

Missy was kicking herself or would have done if she wasn't busily trying to stay upright, swaying from side to side as she strode towards the Explorer Lounge. She'd suggested they reunite before lunch to discuss their respective books but now worried it was premature.

At least it was for Missy.

Despite holing away in her cabin for the past few hours to focus on her short stories, Missy had struggled to keep her eyes from the view. Weird, really, considering they were passing little more than endless red plains scattered with native grass and mulga shrub, the occasional hillock, the odd Acacia tree looking oh so lonely out there by itself.

Yet there was something about the vista that not even the Queen of Crime could distract from.

It almost lulled you into a stupor…

She wondered, too, if they'd bitten off more than they could chew. The club usually studied one murder mystery at a time. Had broken the rule just once and compared two. But now they had *six!* Eight really if you counted her extra short stories. Add to that a busy train schedule and a hen's party, and Missy couldn't imagine what on earth she was thinking.

And when she aired her concerns at their impromptu book club, they all concurred.

"We've been consuming too much and reading too little," said Ronnie, who was clicking away at her knitting as she spoke, balls of wool wedged beneath her book. "In mine, Poirot hasn't come across the corpse yet. He's still being propositioned by the evil Mr Ratchett."

"Oh, he *is* evil, isn't he?" said Claire, clapping her hands together. Then she held up her book and said, "I haven't gotten very far either, I'm afraid, even though I'm loving *The Sleeping Car Murders*. It's very gripping. And quite different to my usual reads. I think this club is teaching me that it's not Agatha Christie I adore—although of course I do—but it's a riveting whodunnit. And this one is right up there." A wistful glance at Perry then. "Speaking of riveting, how're you going with the *Blue Train*? You realise it's the book Christie was struggling to write when she vanished in real life?"

"Yes, but you'd never know it," said Perry. "It's a terrific read, or I think it is. I'm with you lot—can't seem to find the time. Perhaps we should go straight to our rooms after lunch and focus."

"But where's the fun in that?" groaned Lynette.

"Not enjoying *Girl on the Train*?" asked Missy. When Lynette assured her she was, she blew out a quick puff of air. "I was worried it wasn't 'cozy' enough for this group, but I really want to compare it with my Christie short story *Girl in the Train*. See if there are any similarities at all, apart from the title, of course." She chuckled. "Of course, I can't imagine the protagonist in my book getting quite so sozzled on her train... *Not* that there's anything wrong with getting sozzled on a train!"

She giggled now, thinking of all the sparkling wine they'd been knocking back for Alicia, but when she glanced across, the other woman seemed lost in thought, her eyes glazed over.

"Alicia?" Missy prodded.

She blinked. Blinked again. "Hmm?"

"You okay?" asked Perry now.

"What? Oh yeah... It's just..." She stifled a yawn. "I think I need a nana nap. Had a bad night's sleep."

"What a pity," said Ronnie, needles still clicking away. "This nana slept like a log. Nothing like a rocking train to nod you off."

"She was too busy imagining bodies flying," said Lynette, rolling her eyes.

"I did *not* imagine it," said Alicia.

"Still worried about that?" asked Claire. When Alicia nodded, she said, "So let's work through it logically, like your fiancé would do."

"I'll play Detective Jackson," said Lynette, scratching at her groin and lowering her voice. "Who did it, babe?"

Alicia smirked back at her and shrugged. "No idea. But if he was pushed, it *has* to be family. Most murders are done by loved ones, as paradoxical as that sounds."

"Okay then, why? What possible reason could they have?"

Alicia shrugged again. "Nobody knows what really goes on in families, but... they did seem very scared of him."

Lynette scoffed. "So they push Daddy off a moving train because they're a pack of cowards? That sounds more like a brave move to me, brazen even. That takes guts." Lynette held up a finger. "And *how*? Hmm? I mean, how did *you* manage to see a guy fall from a distant carriage?" She waved her hand out the window. "We can barely see the next carriage, so it's hardly—"

She stopped dead, her eyes wide, and they all looked out to see the train was rounding a wide bend, and there they were—the front cars well within view. It was like they were watching another train entirely as it snaked its way back towards them, and Alicia gave her sister a smug look as Ronnie stopped clicking and started tutting.

"I've had enough of this Spanish Inquisition," she said, folding her knitting away and into her calico bag, dropping her book in behind it. "There is a simple way to sort this out, and we should have done it a lot earlier. I'll ask the staff."

"I tried that," Alicia told her. "They're not telling."

Ronnie tutted again as she stood up. "If someone has vanished from the train, we need to know about it."

Gripping the tops of the chairs as she walked, Ronnie strode to the bar area where Guest Experience Manager Marvin was standing at a podium, ticking off names for lunch. They watched as she spoke with him for several minutes, then returned to their section, where she remained standing, hovering over them.

"Right, well, Marvin knows nothing about any missing passenger and seemed more amused by the idea than alarmed—even when I mentioned your early-morning vision, Alicia. Tells me it simply could not have happened but was happy to look into it further. I'm quite sure he thinks I'm being a silly old goat but was far too polite to say so." She winked. "One of the perks of aging. People tend to humour you. Just ask Miss Marple." She winked again. "Anyhoo, he assured me he'd double-check with the Platinum attendant after lunch and report back to me pronto. Happy?"

Her eyes were on Lynette when she asked that, and the younger woman looked offended.

"Hey, I'm not the one who saw a flying human!"

"No, but you are determined not to believe your sister this time, and I can't help wondering why. *That*, to me, is the real mystery here."

Then she pointed back to the diner and added, "But enough mystery for now. Our table's ready, and Marvin tells me there's a camel curry on the menu that sounds particularly tasty."

The curry was indeed tasty, and the book club tried their best to savour it as they swapped small talk, but Perry, for one, was struggling. As before, they were spread across two tables, but there was no one opposite him and Ronnie this time, and he was glad of it.

All he could think about was this potential new mystery, another real-life one, and he was wracked with guilt, knowing he shouldn't want it yet wanting it just the same. He recalled a line from the book he'd only just started, a line Hercule Poirot utters to a fellow passenger:

*'I think that you have a yearning in you for interesting happenings. Eh bien, Mademoiselle… You may get more than you bargain for.'*

That was just fancy speak for "Be careful what you wish for", and it was a lesson Perry knew only too well, so when Marvin vanished for ten minutes during dessert, then returned with another crew member, both wearing relaxed smiles, he heaved a very audible sigh of relief, followed quickly by a silent—shameful!—tug of regret.

"This is the attendant from the Platinum carriage," Marvin told them, introducing Walker to the book club before kneeling down between their tables.

They were now the only guests left in the diner, yet Marvin kept his voice hushed. It was also upbeat, surprisingly upbeat as his eyes turned to Ronnie and he added, "And you are quite correct, Mrs Westera. Clay Dartmoor is no longer on this train."

Then he offered a dimpled grin as her jaw dropped towards the table, while Perry blinked back feeling happy, guilty and incredibly confused.

# CHAPTER 8
## So Where the Hell is He?

There was a collective moment of confusion as the book club stared between Marvin and Walker, waiting for some kind of explanation.

If Clay was no longer on the train, where the blazes was he?

Ronnie said something to that effect, and Marvin suddenly blushed beetroot red and said, "Oh, no, no, it's okay. *He's* okay. He got off in Broken Hill this morning."

"Really?" said Ronnie.

"Oh, thank goodness!" said Missy.

"And you saw him get off?" asked Alicia, eyes firmly on Walker.

The attendant opened his mouth as if to say something, then shut it again just as Marvin said, "I checked the on-and-off sheet myself, Alicia, and Clay Dartmoor was definitely ticked off."

"I didn't realise you could disembark at Broken Hill," said Ronnie. "That's a very short trip."

The guest experience manager looked sheepish now. "We don't *normally* allow it, that is true. But Mr Dartmoor informed us late last night that he'd be departing the train in the morning and, well…" He coughed discreetly.

"Ah," said Ronnie. "I see. It was Mr Dartmoor, and the Dartmoors do—"

"—what the Dartmoors want," said Perry, echoing Jock from the evening before.

The carriage manager smiled slimly but did not reply.

"But isn't that a bit weird?" asked Missy now. "Why would he bail so early? We're only a third of the way through. He's going to miss all the fun."

Both attendants did not respond to that, but Alicia's eyes were still narrow.

"So he was *definitely* seen getting off the train this morning, alive and well?" she asked Walker directly.

He did not hesitate this time. "That is correct."

"Great," said Marvin, standing up and reaching for their empty dessert bowls. "That's sorted. Thanks for your time, Walker."

The attendant began to turn away, but Alicia couldn't stop the soft thudding she now felt in her chest. She had a terrible hunch that Walker was lying, and she couldn't work out why he would do such a thing.

"What cabin was Clay in?" she called after him. "Wasn't cabin number two was it?"

It was an educated guess—there hadn't been a soul in Platinum's communal lounge when she passed through earlier, and yet cabin two had been empty, so where were its occupants? When Walker swung around, she could tell from his startled expression that she had guessed correctly.

"Okay," she said, "so why are all his things still in his room? I saw his hat, his reading glasses, some important-looking papers—"

"You were in his room?" asked Marvin, his voice slightly alarmed.

"No, your man Walker was coming out when I happened to pass by. Look, that's not important. Right now I'd like to know why Clay Dartmoor left his stuff behind if he really did jump off happily this morning."

All eyes were now on Walker, including Marvin's.

"Is that correct?" he asked, and Walker seemed suddenly offended.

"But I'm not lying, Marvin. He told me he was getting off—"

"I'm not suggesting you're lying," Alicia cut in. "I'm just saying you might've been mistaken, that's all. I remember what it was like getting off our carriage this morning— we were all bustling out, everyone bleary-eyed. And there are a few Dartmoors on this train."

"I can assure you my team and I are never bleary-eyed," he replied. "And we only have one Dartmoor—Mr Clay Dartmoor—in our section, so we could not have been confused. His name was ticked off. He was not ticked back on. He officially disembarked this morning."

"Okay, so explain the left luggage," Alicia shot back.

He blinked. Glanced at Marvin. "I can't speak for Mr Dartmoor, but I can only assume his family will take care of it."

"*Assume?*" said Alicia.

"Okay, let's all take a deep breath," said Marvin, trying to bring the tension down. "There is another way to confirm all of this. I'll speak to the family directly."

"*We* would like to be present for that, thank you," said Ronnie now, sitting forward.

"Is that really necessary?" Walker asked of Marvin. "I mean, this all feels like a gross overreaction."

"Young man!" Ronnie boomed, making the club almost recoil along with him. "We are not a bunch of nosey parkers conjuring up drama. We have a terrible tendency to stumble into deadly mysteries, so you're going to have to take us seriously, and we're going to have to speak to the man's family in person. If you'll just humour us, that would be tickety-boo. Then you can return to your work, and we can return to enjoying our holiday. Is that fair?"

"Of course it is," said Marvin, eyes boring into Walker. "Happy to arrange it. If you'd like to remain here, I'll see if the family are available."

"Thank you!" Alicia called after him before giving her sister a smug look that said, *This ain't over, baby. Not by a long shot.*

It took fifteen minutes to corral the Dartmoor family, and they did not look happy to be corralled. Although, to be fair, happiness was not exactly their strong suit.

They arrived en masse, Clay's eldest son, Flynn, leading the charge, Clay's younger brother Phillip rounding out the group. While the others sized up the book club, seemingly confused, Flynn offered Lynette a smile of recognition.

"Lynette, isn't it?" he said, and she smiled back.

"What's going on?" blurted Flynn's younger brother, staring from him to Lynette and then to the rest of them. His eyes rested on Claire, and he looked even more confused. He clearly recognised her from the Miner's Memorial where they'd had a very brief conversation. His wife remembered her, too, because she was back to glaring. "Who are you people and what's this about Dad going missing?"

"Oh, they're the Murder Mystery Book Club, Patrick," said Flynn, a note of mischief in his voice.

"I don't think that's relevant," snapped Ronnie, tsking at him. She leaned forward and explained the situation just as she had explained it to Marvin.

When she had finished, they all stared at her like she had lost the plot.

"Hang on, are you saying you saw my father fall off the train?" This was Flynn, the mischief now gone, his thin blue eyes boring into Lynette, as though waiting for the punchline.

She held up two palms and said, "I didn't, no. But my sister thinks she might have, and well, we're a suspicious lot. Just need to double-check."

"Double-check what?" asked Flynn's sister—the one with the pearls and the golden ponytail. "Of course Dad didn't fall off the bloody train. He's perfectly fine. More's the pity."

"*Fiona,*" came Phillip's voice, and she shrugged her lips downwards as the book club swapped a look.

"Sorry," she muttered, not sounding at all contrite.

"Anyway," said Flynn, frowning at his sister. "I'm not sure exactly what you saw, but it can't have been Dad. He got off the train this morning." Then he looked across to Walker, who was lingering at the back, behind Marvin. "Didn't he?"

Walker assured him he did, but there was something about the darting of his eyes and the crinkle of his brow that caught Alicia's attention again. It was like a flashing beacon above his head, and yet no one else seemed to notice.

"There you go," said Flynn breezily. "Dad's done a runner. Abandoned us again. Which, by the way, he'd already warned us he'd do. Told us last night he was clearing out. Said he'd hire a car in Broken Hill. Make his own way home."

"Is that normal?" asked Alicia.

He shrugged. "Dad doesn't do *normal*. Plays by his own set of rules. Plus he is a grown man, yeah? Can do what he wants."

"I did explain all that," said Walker, sounding apologetic.

"Okay, so what's the big deal?" asked Patrick's wife now, producing some lip gloss from a pocket and dabbing at her lips, like they were just shooting the breeze.

"Well, it's just his luggage, you see," said Walker. "He left it all in his compartment."

"Typical," said Patrick. "Leaving it for us to clean up."

"*Us?*" said Fiona, bushy eyebrows wedged tight. "What do you mean *us*? I'm the one who'll be doing the cleaning. I'm the only one who ever cleans up after Dad." She flashed the book club women a weary look.

"Hey, I help out when I'm home," Patrick spat back.

"Yeah, but you're never home, are you? Always flitting off to the big smoke with your pretty wife and your poncy kids while I do all the hard yakka—"

"*Poncy kids?*" said the pretty wife, now stepping forward at the same time that the uncle said:

"Just leave it, Posey. Come on, Fiona, cut it out."

Fiona turned her fiery gaze upon him. "Hey, stop telling us what to do, *Uncle Phil*. You're never around either. We could've used your help over the past few years, especially when Mum was dying."

Phillip stepped back like he'd been slapped, and now Flynn was stepping forward.

"That's enough, Fiona!" he boomed. "What is wrong with you this arvo?" He nudged his head at the book club as if he was trying to tell her to shut her big mouth.

She folded her arms and glanced away moodily.

He turned to Alicia. "I'm sorry if we've given you a scare,

and I'm not sure what it is you *think* you saw, but I'm positive Dad's alive and well and happily driving without his bickering kids towards Dartmoor Downs as we speak."

"How positive?" asked Alicia. "Have you heard from him?"

They all went mute except for Posey, who shook her glossy black locks back and said, "He's hardly the type to send selfies from his road trip, sweetheart."

"That may be so," said Ronnie, "but we can sort this out once and for all if you could just call him and confirm he's okay."

She shrank back. "No, thank you."

"Can't call him," said Patrick, chin high. "There's no Wi-Fi."

"Actually," said Marvin, holding up a hand, dimples deep. "We're closing in on Adelaide, so there should now be decent Wi-Fi coverage in this carriage, sir."

Patrick's chin dropped, but he did not reach for his phone. None of them did. Then eventually Flynn said, "Oh for Pete's sake, I'll do it."

Like they were being asked to wrangle a deadly brown snake.

Flynn pulled out his smartphone and tapped a number in. Then he listened for a moment and looked relieved as he clicked it off again and said, "No dice. Sounds like he's out of range."

Patrick gave Marvin a smug look while Perry cocked his head to one side.

"How long does it take to drive from Broken Hill back to your property?" he asked. "Must be quite a haul."

The family looked at each other. "Three solid days of driving, depending how much you muck around," said Flynn. "And Dad's not the muck-around type."

There was a snort then from Patrick, and they all looked at him as he glanced towards the ceiling.

Perry said, "Why wouldn't your father fly? Surely there's a decent airport in Broken Hill. He'd be home in a fraction of the time."

It was a good question, but the Dartmoors looked like it was absurd. Then Phillip explained: "My brother hates flying. Had a near-miss in a crop duster when we were young. Lucky to be alive. He'll do anything to avoid getting back in a plane."

Now Claire's head was cocked. "How was your brother, really? I mean, isn't it worrying that he wanted to leave the holiday early?"

Phillip stared at her like he didn't understand the question, so she added gently, "Could he be depressed?"

That got them *all* snorting. They didn't bother answering. Flynn just glanced at his watch and said, "As fun as this is, we're not far off Adelaide and I need to get ready. As soon as we make contact, we'll let you know. Good enough?"

His words were directed at the group, but his eyes were thin slits, boring into Lynette again, and his smile, while present, was far less playful. She nodded quickly, and he motioned for his siblings to follow him out of the diner, which they did, while their uncle remained.

Phillip really was a younger version of his brother. The same thinning, greyish-red hair and splotchy, drooping skin, although less ruddy, with more reassuring smile lines around his mouth and eyes. He was better dressed, too, his riding boots recently polished, his red-white-and-blue plaid shirt clearly new, the folds from the packaging still obvious across the front.

"Sorry about all this," he said, offering a warm smile. "I'm sure my brother's fine." Then a quick look at Claire. "Including his mental health."

"But why would he desert his kids and do such a harrowing drive alone?" she persisted.

He shrugged. "Like Flynn said—he plays by his own rules, old Clay."

"So there's no chance he..." Claire leaned closer. "You know? Threw himself off?"

Phillip's smile evaporated. "Definitely not! Not in a million years." He made a Cor! sound. "Clay's probably happily chewing on some beef jerky, driving across the

Nullarbor, oblivious to all this. But if you don't believe me—or his ratbag kids—we've got the attendant here to vouch for him, isn't that right, mate?"

Walker nodded again, but it was even less convincing than before, and for one very brief moment he glanced at Alicia, and she would now swear on a stack of Agatha Christie books that he was lying.

~

Tag was bristling with intrigue. *What were they all up to in there?*

The amateur palaeontologist had just asked the bartender for a Pimm's and lemonade and was loitering by the adjoining doors when he noticed the two groups at loggerheads in the dining carriage. Something was up; he could sense it. Just like he could sense when a dinosaur bone was lurking, buried beneath millions of years of sand and silt, waiting to be freed.

His excitement dissolved. Bloody Clay Dartmoor. They'd had such a laugh in the bar last night. It had been rather surprising! Of course, Clay hadn't known who Tag was at first. He'd been very drunk. And surprisingly frank, ranting about this, ranting about that…

And that's when Tag had struck.

But he'd misfired. Badly. Turns out Clay wasn't quite as drunk as he'd appeared.

Tag glanced back towards the group now. They weren't discussing *him* in there were they? Had someone overheard his altercation with Clay in the Platinum Club?

The dining car's adjoining doors suddenly swished open, and he saw the Dartmoor children making their way through, so he scuttled back to the bar, snatched up his drink and turned his whole body away, hoping they didn't notice him.

Hoping they didn't know just how ugly things had turned last night…

# CHAPTER 9
## An Experience to Remember

The Indian Pacific had long left the red desert behind, weaving its way through the scenic southern tip of the ancient Flinders Ranges and across the golden fields of South Australia's rich food bowl and vineyards and was now closing in on its capital city of Adelaide.

Once again there were six off-train experiences to choose from, and while the group had pre-booked the same tour as Tag—the natural history museum in the heart of the city—Perry was now regretting that choice, fretting that the fossil hunter would cling to them like red dirt.

But his fears were misguided. Tag kept his distance for most of the tour, acting like a virtual stranger, while the tour itself was excellent and the talk by the guest palaeontologist riveting—even for heathens like Missy and Lynette, who didn't know their minerals from their meteorites.

Of course, it helped that the tour group were fed glasses of sparkling wine during the lecture, followed by a private dinner right in the middle of the museum foyer. It felt a little like *Night at the Museum* with intimidating skeletons and taxidermic beasts watching over them, a once-in-a-lifetime opportunity, and Perry thoroughly enjoyed himself. Although, truth be told, he genuinely wished Tag was beside him when an elderly lady pulled Professor Miles aside and asked how Adam and Eve fitted into all this "natural selection nonsense".

The accomplished scientist answered the question with tremendous equanimity, and Perry wanted to swap eye rolls with Tag, but he was on another table, his eyes staring into his deconstructed native ooray plum cheesecake like he was trying to bore a hole through to the plate.

Perry went to comment to Alicia, but she, too, seemed distracted, so he tucked his claws away and let it drop.

When they eventually reboarded the train for the next leg of the journey, he was surprised to hear her suggest they dump their gear and head to the Explorer Lounge for a nightcap.

"You've changed your tune," he said. "I thought you'd be dragging your feet and heading to bed."

"Oh no. I've got my second wind," she said, winking.

Alicia was lying.

She was utterly drained, and the mere thought of more alcohol made her gag, but she was hoping to run into the Dartmoors again, see if they had any news on Clay.

When they arrived in the communal carriage, however, there was not a single Dartmoor present. The Gleesons had taken possession of a long, circular lounge, however, and invited the club to join them. As Perry completed the introductions, Missy offered to do a bar run.

"Make mine a scotch and soda," said Ronnie, offering Perry a defiant look.

"I'll come with," said Alicia, but it wasn't the bar she was interested in.

While Missy gave Agnetha the orders, Alicia said, "Be back in a mo'."

"Where are you going, possum?" Missy called out.

But Alicia didn't respond. Just tucked her head down and made her way as swiftly as she could towards Platinum.

She wanted to have another chat with Walker.

Back in the lounge, it took just one round of drinks for the conversation to return to the Dartmoors. During the last stopover, the Gleesons had selected a tour of Adelaide's central market, keen to get a feel for the region's local produce and were surprised the Dartmoor clan were all there *sans* Clay.

"Not like the kids and Phil to go their own way,"

mused Iris. "They're getting brave in their old age."

"Actually, it's Clay who's gone his own way," explained Ronnie. "We've been told he jumped ship in Broken Hill."

Iris sat forward suddenly, spilling a splash of white wine down her linen shirt. "What? Really? I mean… Wh-why would he do that?"

Jock handed her a serviette and gave her an obscure look. "Does it matter, love? We can all breathe easier now, or at least those poor kids can."

Because it clearly wasn't lost on anyone how miserable the three siblings were around their father.

"Bloody odd though," persisted Iris as she dabbed at her blouse. "So unlike Clay." Jock flashed her another look, and she said, "Sorry, but it's true. He may be a grumpy old bugger, but he's not a quitter. He's a stickler. That's why it was so strange he was handing the farm to one of the kids so soon. And I'm struggling to accept he'd now desert the trip mid-journey."

"Oh, his children were very nonchalant about it all," said Ronnie. "Insisted it was typical of their father, and I guess they'd know. I have to say, from what I can see, they're a rather odd bunch."

"That's one word for it," said Jock, chortling.

Perry leaned forward. "Yes, you seem to know them quite well. Tell us more. Born and bred WA I assume?"

Iris now blew out a dismissive puff of air. "Oh, everyone knows everyone in our neck of the woods."

Then she sat back and gave them quite the dossier on the Dartmoors. It turns out the family were amongst the first white settlers in Western Australia, back in the early 1800s, logging the thick, native woodlands and utilising the freshwater lakes and streams to plant their seed—in every sense of the word. As the family grew, so did the farm, slowly amassing more and more acreage, not to mention wealth.

"Clay's granddad was one of a bunch of kiddies—fourteen I think," Iris told them. "Most of them took off for greener pastures, so to speak. He stuck around and inherited the farm, doubled it in size, then passed it on to Clay's father who did the same thing, then passed it on to him."

"And so the cycle continues," said Jock, sounding utterly bored.

"And Clay's children?" prodded Claire now. "They're all still on the farm?"

"But it's not what you think," said Iris. "Massive estate. Several homesteads, plenty of space. Flynn's the eldest, no kiddies of his own. Recently divorced." She glanced at Jock. "That silly girl was never going to last." Shook her head and added, "City slicker."

Like that explained everything.

"Youngest boy, Patrick, chose better," she continued. "His wife's more robust. They've got a bunch of kids, so Clay'll be chuffed—they'll keep the Dartmoor name going. He's setting up a distillery, Paddy is. Or at least that's what Mable down at the CWA told me." She was referring to the Country Women's Association, a community group for women in regional and remote Australia. "Said he was testing his brew in some of the local establishments. Not half bad they reckon. Still… such an ambitious project. Can't imagine Clay approving."

She flashed another look at her husband, who still seemed thoroughly disinterested. "And then there's the daughter, Fiona. Well, she's the troubled middle child I guess you could say. Never married, no kids, and there's plenty of reasons for that."

"Plenty of gossip," muttered Jock.

"Oh come now, Jocky," she said, playfully slapping his arm. "The fact is, Fi's married to that farm. No one else would get a look in even if they tried. Besides you have to be one tough nut to join that family. I don't know how Posey does it. That's Patrick's wife."

"So who did he hand the farm to then?" asked Perry. "Clay, I mean. Do we know?"

The Gleesons both shrugged, and Iris said, "We hit the sack early last night, didn't we, Jocky? But I've got my fingers crossed for Fiona."

"The daughter? Really?" said Perry.

She slapped him with a frown. "Now, now, no need to be sexist. Fiona'd make a real go of it I reckon. I hope she got it anyway."

"I'm afraid she didn't," came a jovial voice, and they looked up to see Tag listening in again. He smiled. "Sorry, couldn't help overhearing. This lounge bar really is quite narrow."

Perry smiled too, surprised how happy he was that Tag had reached out again. Besides, it sounded like he had some gossip! "So who was it then?" he asked, waving him closer. "Who got the gig? And how come you're up on the latest?"

Tag scooched along so their knees were almost touching. "I ran into Clay last night, just after I left here. He was drinking alone in the Platinum Club. Looked positively miserable. So I grabbed a whisky and sat with him for a bit. Had a natter."

Perry tried not to snort. "Natter about the dinosaur toe, did you?"

Tag smiled stiffly. "Didn't come up. We simply chewed the fat. Clay wanted to moan about his children. Called them lazy hippies or some such." He glanced around, looking worried they'd suddenly materialise. Lowered his tone considerably. "That's when he said he'd just handed over the keys to the farm and that it didn't go as well as he'd liked. Said he was thinking of changing his mind and leaving it to his favourite kelpie. Said the dog worked harder and had more sense." He chuckled, then just as quickly sobered up. "I assumed he was joking. Any case, he said Flynn was his chosen heir."

"*Flynn?*" said Iris, her brow like a rippling wave pool. "He really gave it to Flynn?"

Tag nodded. "I'm sure that's what he said. The eldest son, yes? The divorced one?"

She nodded, but her eyes were dark and staring at her husband. "Poor Fiona! She'll be spitting chips. She put everything into that place, lived and breathed Dartmoor Downs. Even went off to that fancy college, do you remember, Jock? To study agriculture. I just can't believe he'd do that to her."

"I can," her husband grunted. "He was always an old chauvinist, you know that. Can't have his pretty daughter taking over the farm."

"She's hardly pretty, love," said Iris. Then she winced, glancing across the group. "Sorry, that sounded meaner than I meant it to. But I think Fi'd agree. She's not into makeup and all that palaver. Salt of the earth she is, laser focused on the farm. And now it's been wrenched from her."

"How will she react?" asked Claire, suspicious.

"She'll have to lump it," said Jock. "It is the old man's farm. Handed to him by his old man. His younger brother Phil never got a look in, had to accept it back then, and Patrick and Fiona'll have to accept it now."

"Oh, but Phil never wanted the farm, nor does Patrick," said Iris. "Paddy'll happily focus on his brewing. Nah, Dartmoor Downs was always Clay's passion, and I know Flynn worked hard—I'm not saying he didn't—but it was *Fiona* who was the most passionate. Doesn't seem fair somehow. Such a cruel blow."

Jock nodded. "We've got two daughters. And we look forward to the day they both take over the farm from us."

"Oh, Jock, they don't want the farm," she replied lightly. "I wouldn't lump them with it. They have careers of their own."

"They'll change their minds." He winked at the group. "Few more years in the big smoke and they'll be begging to come home. It's a beauty our place. Prime bit of land too." He chuckled suddenly. "Clay wanted it, didn't he, love? But we wouldn't sell."

"Really?" said Perry, tone teasing. "So Clay Dartmoor doesn't always get what Clay Dartmoor wants then?"

Jock chuckled along. "Dead right he doesn't. Nah, the girls'll take it over eventually— *both* of them, like I said. None of this sibling-rivalry rubbish. And we'll happily let them, won't we, love? Not like old Clay." He looked at his wife then, his brow suddenly furrowing. "Truth is, I don't think it matters who he named as his successor. Clay's not handing over the reins. It's not in his DNA. And it's something Flynn'll have to learn if he hasn't already. Clay's there for the long haul. Won't be going anywhere. Not while he's still breathing."

*If he's still breathing*, thought Alicia, who had just returned to the group, trying to mask her concern as she took the drink Missy was offering.

She hadn't managed to find Walker down in Platinum, but she did bump into another attendant, a younger man with a name badge that read ARLO. He'd looked at her curiously as she approached.

"I know," she told him, "I'm not meant to be in this section. It's all very taboo. I'm just looking for Walker. I need to speak to him urgently."

"Walker?" His curiosity turned to concern. He glanced up and down the carriage, then back at her. "Why do you need to speak to Walker?"

"Just tell him I want to talk to him about Clay Dartmoor, or more specifically, Clay's look-alike brother Phillip. Just tell him that, okay?"

The younger man reached for a blemish on his skin and began picking it. "What do you mean?"

"Just tell him exactly what I said please."

He dropped his hand, looking oddly defiant. "I can't. He's not here. He's in a meeting with the JM."

"JM?"

"Journey Manager. Hana. She's the boss."

*Interesting*, thought Alicia, chewing now on her lower lip. "Why is he meeting with the boss?"

Arlo gulped. "I don't know. Why would I know? It's nothing to do with me."

Then he'd squinted and asked which cabin she was in, and so she had scurried back to the group in the Gold lounge, but as she listened to Jock's words, her mind wandered from Clay to another character from her Christie novel *4.50 from Paddington*. It was the cantankerous

Mr Crackenthorpe, also über-wealthy with a massive estate and a bunch of needy kids breathing down his neck.

*"You won't get me out of here until you take me out feet first,"* he'd told Miss Marple's young spy, Lucy. *"And I'm not going to die to oblige anybody."*

Alicia wondered whether Clay Dartmoor had any choice in the matter.

# CHAPTER 10
## Meanwhile, Back in the Cabins

"**S**o where'd you disappear to during drinks?" asked Lynette as she slipped into her silk pyjamas, ready for bed.

It was now ten thirty. The drinking party had disbanded early, everyone exhausted after their excursions, and even gossiping about the Dartmoors couldn't sustain them. The only ones remaining in the bar were Perry and Tag, who had got into a lively banter about "the ethics of selling dinosaur bones to private collectors" and were about to order more drinks.

In the Finlay compartment, Alicia was having first dibs in the bathroom, busily brushing her teeth, one foot holding the door open when Lynette posed her question, so she finished the job before rinsing her mouth.

"I tried to find Walker," Alicia said. "You know, the attendant in charge of Platinum?" She then told Lynette what she had been told by an oddly gulping Arlo.

Lynette swapped positions with her sister and then held her chin up to the mirror, inspecting her reflection. "So?" she called back as she pulled at the skin under one eye. "Walker's having a meeting with his boss. Why is that suspicious?"

"Because *Walker's* suspicious. He's lying about Clay. I can feel it. And maybe he's finally fessing up to the JM."

"JM?"

Alicia sniggered. "Get with the lingo, Lynny. That stands for Journey Manager."

Then she turned away before she could see Lynette's eyes roll back at her in the mirror.

~

Three doors down, Ronnie was catching up on her reading. At last, the odious Mr Ratchett had been murdered on the Orient Express, stabbed twelve times in his bed, and that got her thinking of their missing man, Clay Dartmoor, and how, if he really was dead, it was such a pity his body hadn't been located. That was the problem with missing people (she'd know; she'd experienced something similar only recently). With a corpse you can look for evidence—in Ratchett's case, knife wounds that point to whether the suspect was strong or weak, left-handed or right. But a missing person provided no such opportunity.

Pity really, she thought, as she continued reading.

Very soon she was chortling as Poirot kept tripping over clues in the loathed victim's compartment. Because yes, the Belgian detective was quite correct. There were far too many clues lying about. It did seem very suspicious. Far too contrived. It was one thing to find a smashed watch, but a pipe cleaner, a burned message and a monogrammed handkerchief—

Ronnie sat up with a start, almost banging her head on the panel above. Oh, what a silly billy she'd been! Why hadn't she thought of it earlier?

She needed to get into Clay's cabin, and she needed to do it tonight!

~

"Where are you going now?" Jock asked, staring hard at his wife.

Iris glanced back from the cabin door, bath bag in one hand, the other holding a fresh towel. "To the bathroom of course."

"We have a bathroom." He nodded to the en suite.

Shaking her grey beehive at him wearily, she said, "We discussed this, Jock. I want to use the communal bathrooms. I don't believe that's taboo."

"But—"

"But I'm too old and too plump for that tiny shower, and I won't do it. I told you that already. Did you think I was lying?"

He gawked at her. Tugged hard at one of his enormous ears. "Should I have booked us in Platinum? Are their bathrooms larger?"

Iris glowered at him now. "And how would I know that, Jock?"

His eyes slid away, and she shook her head at him.

Then she turned and reached for the door handle, yanking it open before turning back. "I really wish you'd trust me, you silly old goat."

She humphed her way out, and he was left sitting on the lower bunk, feeling both anxious and befuddled.

~

Posey Dartmoor stepped back into the shadows of her cabin, holding her breath as a vaguely familiar old lady swished past, towel in hand, and then glanced back at the top bunk. She held her breath again, waiting, watching, until she heard Patrick's guttural snore, and exhaled.

Good. Her husband was asleep. Although how he managed it with all the chaos going on, was beyond her.

She thought of Clay then. Of the last time she saw her father-in-law. She felt a shudder, then a prickle of guilt, followed quickly by a burst of red-hot contempt. That old bastard did not deserve her sympathy. And he was not going to bring her little family down. Not if she could help it.

And she could. She had a plan. But first she had some cleaning up to do.

Grabbing her own towel, she secured her dressing gown tightly around her ample bosom, then slipped out of her compartment and into the corridor, heading in the opposite direction from the old bag.

~

"My God it's like Times Square out there," said Perry, pulling the cabin door back into place. "Still need to wait a bit."

Ronnie frowned. "I haven't got all night, you know. I'm on a mission."

"One you'd have to abandon the minute you got to Clay's cabin. How did you think you were going to get in? By chanting Open Sesame?"

She tutted as she sat back on his bed.

Ronnie had re-dressed and was en route to the Platinum carriage when she bumped into Perry returning from the bar. Having ascertained her purpose—to rummage about in Clay's cabin—Perry had quickly steered her back and into his own, insisting they lie low for a bit.

"I agree with you, Ronnie," he had assured her. "Something is rotten in the state of Dartmoor. I don't think Clay got off willingly at Broken Hill either."

While neither of them had noticed the anxious look on Walker's face, as Alicia had, both had come to the same conclusion that he might have got it wrong. After all, the family looked ominously alike. With a hat worn low on your head and your collar up, it wouldn't be that hard to impersonate old Clay disembarking.

That left some doubt, and neither of them liked doubts. Nor did they like the way the Dartmoor siblings had behaved during that exchange in the dining room before Adelaide. Fiona was more angry than worried, and Patrick and Flynn were far too dismissive. It was all rather odd. Certainly not how you hoped your loved ones would react if they were told you might be missing.

And the way *none* of them wanted to call their dad's mobile was especially telling.

They were hiding something. Ronnie and Perry were sure of it. Although what they were hiding was less clear. And perhaps a quick peek in Clay's cabin would shed some light.

The problem was getting in, Perry told her.

"Unlike Gold-class cabins that only lock from the inside," he informed her, "Platinum passengers have a secure keycard, so the door automatically locks when they leave."

That had stopped her in her tracks until he told her he had a solution, but first they had to wait ten minutes in *his* cabin. "Tag and I were the last to leave the bar, so they're cleaning up now. Should be out of there soon, and we can sneak in after that."

"But what's the point without a key?"

He smiled wider. "Oh, I can get the key, madame. Or at least I hope I can."

After a few more minutes, the coast was clear, so they made their way down to the end of their carriage and into the lounge which was—blessedly!—empty. Perry headed straight for the bar and plunged his hand in the tip jar on the counter.

"Going to bribe your way in?" asked Ronnie.

He smirked and pulled out a room card. It was just as he expected. Agnetha, the bartender, had dumped it in there last night, and that's where it had remained.

"So if that's Clay's room key," said Ronnie as they snuck on towards Platinum, "how did Clay get into his own cabin last night?"

Perry shrugged. "Maybe they gave him a spare or he never went back in? Who knows? Any case, let's hope this still works. Now shhh!"

That was the tricky bit, sneaking into the out-of-bounds Platinum Club and on to the compartments. Luckily that lounge was also empty and there was not an attendant in sight, but they put their heads down and raced through anyway, then breathed a sigh of relief when they slipped through the adjoining doors and into the accommodation carriage.

So far so good.

Perry poked his head around the corner and suddenly stepped back, finger to his lips. "Someone's down there," he told a surprised-looking Ronnie.

Then he carefully peered around the corner again.

There was a woman lurking in the corridor. She was short

and curvy, her body hidden within a thick terry towelling bathrobe, her hair lost behind a white towel. Perry couldn't see her face. She was not staring in their direction, but she looked like she had stalled between cabins number one and two—the one Walker had all but confirmed belonged to Clay.

"What's going on?" whispered Ronnie, and Perry turned back with a finger at his lips.

But it was too late. The woman must have heard them and suddenly darted off, in the opposite direction, to the other end of the carriage where she vanished around the corner.

"Who was that?" Ronnie asked as they both stepped out.

Perry lifted one shoulder. "But it looked like she was trying to get into Clay's room. And why was she walking around in her dressing gown? These compartments must have very roomy en suites. Maybe she was one of Clay's conquests and was trying to rendezvous with him and didn't realise he was missing?"

"Or maybe she was just passing and we're reading into it," Ronnie hissed back. "Come on, she's not coming back. Let's go."

They continued along until they got to compartment two. Perry pushed the card into the door slot, and for a dreadful moment it did not work. But then there was a reassuring click, and they were in. He closed the door quietly behind Ronnie, then checked the internal blinds were drawn before reaching for his smartphone and swishing the torch on.

"Best keep the lights off," he whispered.

But Ronnie already had her torch on and was shining it about.

They were relieved to find it empty and still set up for daytime, the bed tucked away, the hat on the table, the spectacles beside it. Ronnie stepped across to check those out, noticing a small picture tucked beneath. She picked it up and saw that it was an old, slightly faded Kodachrome photo of a couple, standing side by side, slim smiles on both their faces, squinting into the sun. She instantly recognised a young Clay—his ginger hair shaved at the sides with an unruly curly mop on top, his skin tighter yet still creased around the eyes, his shoulders still bony but broader, stronger beneath a buttoned-up dress shirt. Beside him was a young woman with Shirley Temple-style ringlets, long and golden blond like Goldilocks. She was wearing a sixties-style shift dress and had a sweet button nose, which was dusted with brown freckles, the same freckles that were now smattered across her children.

She turned the photo over and saw someone had scribbled *Clay & Daisy, 1974.*

"The dead wife?" asked Perry, glancing over her shoulder. Ronnie nodded.

Perry continued glancing about. "So what exactly are we looking for? A cracked watch? A monogrammed hanky?" He was recalling clues from *Murder on the Orient Express.*

Ronnie chuckled quietly. "Not exactly," she told him, popping the photo back. "But Alicia said something about important papers. I wondered whether they might tell us something. Ah yes, here they are."

She stepped across and reached for the file, careful not to upset a small silver cigarette case as she did so. While she carefully flipped through, Perry inspected the room further.

"Lovely rich wood panelling," he said. "I wonder if it's Tasmanian myrtle?"

She tsked now. "We're looking for evidence of a crime, Perry. Not of good styling." She waded through the pages, then dropped the file back with a disappointed sigh.

"Nothing salacious then?" Perry looked up from a copy of *Farm Weekly* he'd found in the magazine holder.

"Just some stuff about wheat prices from what I can see. Hmm, how dull. I was rather hoping it was the deeds to the land, something that proved who he was leaving it to."

"But we already know that. Tag told us it was going to Flynn." She made a strange strangled sound, and he glanced back. "Why would he lie?"

"Oh Perry, you've experienced enough mysteries by now to know not to trust a single word that comes out of a suspect's lips."

"You think *Tag's* a suspect?"

"Shh." She glanced across to one wall, like he might be asleep behind it. "And sure, why not?" she whispered. "He had the best access, admits to being with him late last night. By my calculations that makes him the last person to see Clay alive."

"But... but *why?* He barely knows the guy."

"Ah, but he knows his dinosaur bones and how there could very well be more under Dartmoor Downs."

"Are you saying he wanted Clay dead so he could dig?"

"Well, he was doing a lot of boohooing about it all last night, so yes, I do, and you would too if you weren't quite so smitten."

"I'm not *smitten*." Perry looked utterly offended. "That's ridiculous; he's not even my type."

"Shh," she said again, lowering her tone further. "Then perhaps you need to do a Lynette and try for a different type, or you'll end up as lonely as she is. Now we're not here to talk about your love life, so keep searching."

He scoffed again and stepped into the adjoining bathroom while she turned to inspect the glasses, bringing them up to her eyes. They had a steel, rectangular frame, definitely an older-man's style, she decided, and multifocals, judging by the lenses.

"I think these might be transition lenses," she said, holding them up as he reached for a small, purple-striped bath bag on the sink. "You know, the ones that darken in the sun."

"So?" He began wading through the bag, finding basics like toothpaste, deodorant, nail file and clippers and, oddly, women's perfume. He scooped it out. Black Opium by Yves Saint Laurent.

"The dead wife's?" He held it out to Ronnie.

But she was more interested in the glasses and the Akubra hat, which she was now inspecting. "Why would Clay drive off into the blazing desert without these?"

"Good point," he said. "And why wouldn't he take his

deodorant? It's a long, sweaty drive."

"Not everyone's a metrosexual like you, Perry."

He held up the perfume and the nail file. "I think this rather suggests he is."

Then he placed it all back and stepped out of the bathroom before suddenly swivelling towards Ronnie. "Show me that hat!"

It looked brand-new with a perfectly round brim and smudge-free exterior.

"Oh Ronnie," he gushed, barely able to contain his excitement. "I think we just found our monogrammed hanky, and I also think I know who dropped it."

# CHAPTER 11
## Day Two Dawns

Phillip Dartmoor seemed lost in thought when Ronnie spotted him, his cheeks softly stubbled, his eyes staring out one side of the Explorer Lounge windows.

It was their second morning on the train, and they'd now covered so many kilometres and time zones they'd been asked to switch their clocks to the magical-sounding "train time", which was ninety minutes behind Adelaide. That city had long vanished, and they were hurtling through vast, uninhabited territory again, the land stretched flat, adorned with a patchy sheet of red and green, above it a billowy quilt of grey and orange from where the sunrise was beginning to show its hand.

It was simply magnificent, but Phillip was frowning.

Ronnie ordered a tea and glanced about. The day's first stop was not until lunchtime, so the lounge was virtually empty, most of the passengers having a welcome sleep-in after yesterday's punishing wake-up call. Or perhaps they were just confused by the time!

But not Ronnie and not, as luck would have it, Clay's younger brother. He had ordered an espresso coffee from a bartender Ronnie did not recognise (looks like Agnetha was getting a sleep-in too), but it remained untouched as he chewed on one thumbnail instead.

"Morning, Phillip. I hope I'm not disturbing," said Ronnie, cup in one hand the other behind her back, her hip leaning against a seat for support.

He glanced up, surprised. Took a moment to work out who she was and then smiled warmly. "Ah, you're one of the book club people. I'm sorry. I've forgotten your name."

"Ronnie," she told him, and he invited her to join him.

She placed her cup down on the table in front of him and produced her other hand, holding out the hat they'd pilfered from Clay's cabin last night. "I think you mislaid this, yes?"

He looked at her, surprised, and then at the Akubra and shook his head. "Not mine, no. What makes you think it is?"

"Oh, just an educated guess." She sat down and placed the hat by the window. "It's quite new, and I thought I saw you wearing a new one yesterday."

In fact, Ronnie hadn't noticed Phillip's headwear at all, but Perry had, and he was certain the man had been wearing a brand-new Akubra earlier in the trip. He'd noticed it because it was the antithesis of his older brother's. Clay's Akubra was very old and very battered, the centre caving in, the rim split and a dirty-brown colour. Nothing like the one they'd found in his compartment last night.

Ronnie had not been quite so enamoured by the clue, suggesting that Clay was a very wealthy man, probably had multiple hats—Claire had brought along three herself—but Perry had then swept open Clay's cupboard to reveal a meagre selection of clothes, including two flannelette shirts, a moth-eaten jumper and a pair of stained moleskin trousers.

Then they'd found his small leather carry bag, and that sold it for Ronnie. Had the man taken anything with him at all?

So they'd both agreed the hat might very well have been left in Clay's compartment by somebody else. The question now was who? And why? Was it left inadvertently by the killer? Or was it a red herring, like the clues in Ratchett's cabin?

As passengers began to trickle into the lounge, making their way to breakfast, Phillip had been studying the hat with interest and now returned it to her.

"Whoever owns this will want it back. It's spanking new. Unlike mine, although it sure looks it. Clay says it's soft, like me." He pulled at the skin drooping from his neck. "He's not wrong though. Me and my hat don't get much of a workout, stuck inside all day in Perth. But nope. Mine's hanging up in my cabin. Good luck finding the owner though." Then he waved a hand towards the barista and said, "Every second person on this train's got an Akubra, including the staff, in case you hadn't noticed."

And he was quite right. The Indian Pacific's official uniform included the iconic Aussie bushman's hat. She kicked herself internally, then gave Perry a mental kick too. *Monogrammed hanky indeed!* There were about forty crew members on board, and this hat was more like a bog-standard Kleenex tissue that told them exactly nothing. For all they knew, Walker could have left it while cleaning the cabin.

She sighed and glanced out at the view. "Lovely way to wake up, isn't it?"

He followed her gaze and nodded along. "Can't believe Clay's missing it." His eyes shot back. "And no I haven't heard from him, but I'm sure he's fine."

"Except you can't be sure, can you? Did you see him get off? Manage to say goodbye?"

He shook his head. "Wish I had now. Last time I saw Clay was the night before, at the family meeting. Didn't see him after that, but that doesn't mean he didn't get off."

She watched him keenly. "So you were never in your brother's cabin that morning?"

One eyebrow shot up. "Why would I be, Ronnie? I'm in a completely different carriage. Just down from you, as I think you know." Then he shifted in his seat to face her and said, "Why are you lot so interested in my brother? What's all this about?"

"It's not your brother we're interested in, per se. It's the fact that he's missing. That worries us, and I suspect it worries you too. Is that why you're up so early?"

He released a dry, humourless chuckle. "Not at all— no offence, Clay." He glanced out at the barren landscape as he said that. "I've always been an early bird. Plight of the farmer. Not that I've been a farmer for many decades. But old habits die hard, I guess."

"Yes, Perth you said. You're still working?"

He nodded. "Got a farm machinery dealership. Should be winding it up but I'm not sure what I'd do if I retired. It's not like I have a wife and land to keep me busy."

Ronnie could swear he glowered at that. But then she was probably projecting.

He added casually, "Nah, I've always been a lark. Daisy used to say you can take the boy out of the country but not the country out of the boy." He smiled apologetically. "That's Clay's wife. Gone now, sadly."

"Cancer?" Ronnie asked, because it almost always was these days.

He nodded. "Too far gone by the time they found it. Problem with rural living—you die early. Not enough doctors, hospitals, specialists. It was a four-hour drive just to get chemo..." His brow crinkled further. "Poor Daisy, lasted three months, from diagnosis to death. The children were torn up, of course. She was their whole world. Very sad. Just turned seventy when she passed."

"Oh, that is young," said Ronnie, who was on the slippery slope to eighty. "What was she like, Daisy?"

Phillip's face lit up. "Lovely. Sweet. Straight as uncooked spaghetti. Cutest little freckles you ever saw. Beloved by all, not just the kids. No one had a bad word to say about Daisy. Bonza cook too. Made the best lamb roast this side of Kalgoorlie, and her sponge cake? Well, that was heaven on a plate."

"Oh, I do love a country woman's sponge cake. My mother's were award-winning. She entered them every year at Sydney's Royal Easter Show."

"Good on her. Clay'd never let Daisy do something so flashy." Then he held up a hand. "Sorry, no offence to your mum."

She laughed. "None taken."

He smiled. "Anyway, he kept her too busy on the farm. Wanted things just how he wanted them. That was just Clay. He couldn't have achieved half as much without Daisy holding down the fort. She was the real dynamo, kept the home fires burning, was what you might call the good wife.

In every sense of the word."

"*The good wife?* Sounds more like a doormat," said Lynette when Ronnie repeated the conversation to the group soon after.

Phillip had headed off for breakfast, joining the younger Dartmoors who filed in as they always did—as a collective, eyes ahead, expressions neutral, like they didn't have a care in the world. Whatever was bugging Fiona yesterday was now resolved, or perhaps she'd been read the riot act by her brother. She too looked unfazed, and Ronnie wondered about that as she waited for her own collective to join her (expressions rarely neutral, especially when you factored in Missy).

They were scheduled for a later breakfast sitting again and had enjoyed the lie-in but were now helping themselves to hot beverages from the bar before spreading out around her.

"It also sounds suspiciously like coercive control to me," Lynette added, squeezing some lemon into her black coffee.

"Oh dear girl, couples were very different in my day," Ronnie told her. "Husbands still ruled the roost, and wives deferred to them. Right or wrong, it's the way it was."

"Not in my family," said Claire, delicately spooning some chocolatey froth into her mouth. "My Chinese mother was very much the boss, and when she said jump, my English father got out the pogo stick."

She smiled, but they knew there was some angst in there. Claire's childhood had not been easy. She wasn't as close to her mother as she'd like.

"Well," said Missy. "I can't imagine my lovely new boyfriend—*Seamus*—bullying me and vice versa. If there's one thing I can't stand it's bullies—of any gender."

Alicia heartily agreed and added, "If Jackson ever tried to bully me, he wouldn't survive the hour. Lynette would be round with a baseball bat."

They all laughed at that except for Lynette, who barely cracked a smile.

Then Perry said, "Okay, this is all very interesting,

but what did Phillip have to say about the hat, Ronnie?"

"What hat?" asked Missy, also spooning some froth into her mouth and spilling most of it down her bumblebee-yellow blouse as she did so.

Ronnie winked at Perry, then said, "We might've done a little sleuthing of our own last night."

Five minutes later the group were gawking at them both.

"Why didn't you tell us you were sneaking into Clay's compartment?" asked Alicia.

"Shh!" said Ronnie as several passengers glanced their way. "We're telling you now."

"Hang on, so does *everyone* agree with Alicia?" asked Lynette. "Am I the only one who believes the family and thinks he got off?"

"Oh, he got off this train, Lynny, but not by his own means," said Perry.

"But... but what about that conductor, Walker? He saw him with his own eyes. He ticked him off."

"Could be mistaken; could be lying," said Ronnie.

There was no way a wise old farmer would head off into the great outdoors, she told them, without taking his clothes, his glasses, a photo of his dead wife and his carry bag, not to mention his bath bag and all its sundries.

Then there was the minor matter of the shiny new Akubra.

All eyes turned to the hat beside Ronnie, which they'd assumed belonged to her.

"You should not have pinched that," Alicia said with a hiss. "If Jackson was here, he'd—"

"Oh, your dishy detective fiancé would forgive us in a heartbeat, just like he always does," Ronnie hissed back. "Besides, this is important evidence, and I don't trust that family to keep it safe." She frowned. "I really did think it was Phillip's. But apparently not."

She went on to explain why and Claire asked, "You believe him?"

She thought about it, then said, "I'm afraid I think I do."

"And I absolutely do," said Alicia. "Don't you remember,

Perry? When I thought I spotted Clay at the Miner's Memorial, you said it was Phillip. And as far as I recall, he was wearing his hat then. That was *after* Clay had vanished."

Perry slapped a hand to his forehead. "Damn, yes, he was indeed. Sorry, Ronnie. I've given you the bum steer."

"Not at all," she replied. "Gave me an excuse to chat to him, and while this mightn't be his hat, it doesn't mean he hasn't got a motive." Then she waited a beat before adding, "I think Phillip was madly in love with his brother's cutely freckled, sponge-cake-baking wife."

# CHAPTER 12
## Games of Hide and Seek

It wasn't like Ronnie to be so soppy, and Perry was telling her exactly that. "The spirit of this trip is getting to you, Mrs Westera." Then he turned to the others, adding, "She even tried to hook me up with…" He quickly glanced around then whispered, "Terribly boring Tag."

"Oh, you'd be *perfect* together," said Missy, making him glower. The younger woman flung two well-chewed nails to her lips and said, "Soz! I didn't mean *you* were boring. Just that… you know, he's into old bones and things."

"Really, Missy? I hadn't heard," he shot back. "I can assure you all, just because we both have a penchant for palaeontology—it has a name, Missy, repeat after me: *palaeontology*—does not make us a perfect match. Now can we get back to the issue at hand please?"

"You're the one who brought it up, dear," said Ronnie.

"So Phillip had a crush on his brother's wife," said Claire, steering them back on track. "What has that got to do with his disappearance? She's deceased, isn't she?"

"Ah, yes," said Ronnie. "But the way Phillip was gushing about Daisy. The way he inferred her life hadn't been easy with Clay, makes me wonder whether he was bitter on her behalf. Perhaps he was avenging the poor woman."

"Ooh that sounds like a plot twist from an Agatha Christie novel!" said Missy, jiggling in her chair excitedly.

"It sounds like a long bow to me," said Claire, adjusting her black trademark chignon. "And wouldn't that also apply to the three children? Wouldn't they be even more bitter?"

"Yeah, but children don't always see that stuff," said Lynette.

Perry scoffed. "The Gleesons saw it all, and they're just the distant neighbours. Jock said Clay had a wandering eye. I do wonder—"

"Is that Walker?" Alicia suddenly interrupted him, peering above their heads, back towards the bar. "I think that's Walker."

They followed her gaze and saw a crew member with a buzz cut reach for a jug of orange juice from the bar, then glance directly towards them before suddenly turning and walking in the opposite direction.

Alicia jumped up. "I need to speak to him!"

She raced after him, only to be thwarted by a large group streaming out of the restaurant dining carriage at the same time.

Lynette watched on, sniggering as Alicia struggled to squeeze past them and then told the others, "She's been playing Where's Walker? since our meeting yesterday. Wants him to confess he didn't see Clay get off in Broken Hill." Lynette growled. "I can't believe we're wasting so much time on this."

Then she leaned in and added, "While Alicia's not here, we need to talk." They raised their collective eyebrows as she glanced around and then back again. "Guys, I know we're fixated with mysteries; it's our *thing*. But is this really how we want to spend these few days? I mean, this is our last chance to enjoy quality time with Alicia."

"Your sister's getting married, Lynette, not joining a nunnery," said Ronnie.

Lynette shrugged a tanned shoulder and sat back. "I'm just saying, it's a hen's party. There's a lot of clucking going on but not much partying."

"Normally I'd agree with you," said Claire, "but Alicia's the one leading the charge here."

"She's giving in to her darkest imagination," said Lynette. "You know what she's like, and we're all just following like a pack of lemmings. Might be time to call it. Get back to the fun."

"And we do still have our books to discuss," added Missy.

"But what's the point of discussing a *fictional* mystery when a real one has landed in our laps?" countered Perry. "I mean, whether he got off alive or was thrown off in the dead of night, it's still a mystery. No one has proven either at this stage."

And nor would they. At least not yet, Alicia told them when she returned looking sulky. Because Walker had vanished.

"I swear to God that man's avoiding me," she said. "Took off like a rocket the minute he saw me."

"He's *working*," said Lynette. "Leave the dude alone."

Alicia sneered at her. "Anyway, Marvin just told me we can file into breaky if we're ready."

The group were ready—all of them surprisingly hungry considering how much eating they had been doing—but they also knew they'd be split up again, so they agreed to defer any discussion of the missing man until they could reunite in Ronnie's cabin.

This time Alicia and Lynette had opted to sit with strangers, but the Swiss couple across from them were harder to crack than the wood-fired artisan toast they'd both ordered.

"Yes, we are enjoying the trip," was about all they could drag out of them, and so they sat in stiff silence, focusing on their own meals instead.

As her lips sank into a creamy buttermilk pancake, Alicia noticed the young attendant, Arlo, enter the dining room from the Platinum carriage. She watched him, eyebrows raised, hoping he had news on Walker, but when he caught her eye, something very strange happened. The colour drained from his cheeks and he picked up his pace, rushing past, eyes now averted.

That turbocharged her curiosity.

She glanced across to Lynette to see if she'd noticed, but she was still trying her luck with the Swiss, now attempting to ascertain their views on Australian cuisine.

"Cuisine? Yah, is okay," the Swiss woman said, glancing

down at her dry toast, and Lynette looked like she wanted to thump her.

Alicia wiped her mouth with her napkin and stood up. "I'm sorry," she said vaguely. "I... I left something in the room."

Then she hurried after Arlo.

~

Sipping tomato juice at a nearby table, Iris Gleeson watched as one of the book club members dashed out of the carriage like she'd seen a ghost, and she frowned across to her husband, but Jock hadn't noticed, was waxing lyrical about the youth of today and their "gluten-free, dairy-free, *taste-free* fads" to a Dutch man who was nodding along fervently, while his partner, who didn't appear to speak a jot of English, just smiled benignly beside him.

Iris tried to smile too, but her nerves were jangling. She felt on edge, troubled, and she wasn't quite sure why.

"Isn't that right, dear?" came her husband's voice through the fog, and she blinked, realising that all three were now staring at her expectantly.

She produced a swift smile, a playful eye roll, and said, "Oh Jocky, you sound like an old fuddy-duddy!" Then she leaned in and asked the couple if they had any young people of their own. That improved the woman's English enormously, and she began to rattle on about her "grandbabies" as Iris sat back and pretended to listen again.

It was something she was very good at. Pretending. She'd had decades and decades of practise.

~

Jacinta secured the bunk bed and plumped up the cushions on the newly re-formed couch, then glanced around, smiling. The hospitality attendant was feeling lighter for the first time in years, like she'd finally unburdened herself. And she wondered, as she worked, why she hadn't thought to do it earlier. Why had it taken so long? She had a sudden flash of an angry man, his blue eyes glinting, his red beard almost bushranger like, his hand clutching hers like a vice.

*"You ever say a word—one little word about this—and I swear to God, girlie, I will destroy you."*

The memory alone sent shivers down her spine, and she knew that was why. He'd scared the bejesus out of her! Scared the truth from her lips too. That's why she didn't speak up for fifteen years. Probably still wouldn't have, not if she hadn't crashed into Fiona Dartmoor.

Or, to be more precise, Fiona Dartmoor hadn't crashed into her.

Oh, they'd played a good game of tic-tac-toe at the start of the journey, keeping to their own squares, pretending not to see each other. But that was never going to last. It felt almost inevitable when Fiona finally busted in on her. Was certainly a relief when they got talking and Jacinta spilled the truth. Every ugly detail.

What *was* surprising was Fiona's reaction.

She was sceptical at first, then shocked, then suddenly, gobsmackingly furious. It had taken Jacinta a good twenty minutes to calm her down. But she was secretly glad to have shared her burden, like dumping a weight vest she had been lugging about without even realising it. She felt freer, lighter—

"Jacinta?"

She glanced up from the basin she was scrubbing and out to the corridor. It was Arlo, and he was as white as the fresh towels she'd just hung up.

"We need to talk," he told her as he stepped inside and secured the cabin door behind him. "It's about the Dartmoors. I think I might've stuffed up."

And suddenly she felt the weight of fifteen years settle upon her again…

# CHAPTER 13
## Getting Ticked Off

Back in the dining carriage, Ronnie was struggling to focus on her Croque Madame. What on earth was going on? First Alicia jumps up mid-breakfast, chasing after some young attendant she'd never seen before, and now she could see two more crew members striding in the opposite direction like they'd been called to a fire. They weren't exactly wearing uniforms these two fellows, but they looked suspiciously like security guards, keys dangling at their hips, walkie-talkies in hand, grim expressions across their faces. If she weren't in her mid-seventies and stuck in the window seat, she'd make chase, but they were through the dining room in seconds, heading for the Platinum carriage.

And besides, it probably had nothing to do with Clayton Dartmoor.

Still… it made her wonder, and she wasn't the only one. Claire caught her eye and was now raising her black, exquisitely plucked eyebrows.

~

Alicia had just entered her accommodation carriage when she spotted Arlo slip into cabin four. It was one of the Dartmoor family compartments, she was sure of it, and she scratched her shaggy blond hair, wondering what he was doing in there. She knew the staff caught up on housekeeping while the guests were at breakfast, but she also knew Arlo worked Platinum. Did they help each other out, or was something else going on?

Chewing on her lower lip, she lingered outside the door,

hoping to eavesdrop, but the clacking and crunching of the train put paid to that. Should she knock? Mind her own business? Go back to those delicious pancakes?

Suddenly Alicia heard the door click and she panicked, pulling open the nearest cabin door and throwing herself inside. Fortunately, the room was empty and had already been made up for the day, and she glanced around hurriedly trying to work out where she was.

Ah. This had to be Patrick and Posey's room. She recognised Posey's enormous red resin earrings resting on the table by the window. She noticed two hats, too, both Akubras, and mentally checked them off her list. Then imagined Posey suddenly storming in, horrified to find her there. Imagined her grabbing one of the hats and slapping Alicia about the face with it...

She took a deep breath. Time to get out. She quickly pulled the door open a smidgen to check if the coast was clear and spotted Jacinta striding further down the corridor, Arlo close behind. What were they up to?

She watched as they reached the end of the carriage, then vanished into the tearoom.

"What's going on?" hissed a voice in Alicia's ear, and she jumped.

"Oh Jesus, Claire, you scared me!"

"And you scared us, running off like that. What are you doing snooping in this room?"

"I'm not snooping. I just..." She waved her off. "I'll explain later. Come on."

She stepped out and led the way down to the kitchenette. There they found Jacinta inspecting a clipboard, Arlo beside her, picking at his skin, his eyes wide.

Jacinta's eyes also widened as she glanced up to see the book club friends watching. She dropped the clipboard like it was molten lava and said, "Hey guys. You want to grab some teas, or is there anything else you need?"

"The truth would be good," said Alicia, stepping in.

~

Flynn Dartmoor could hear movement in Patrick's room next door, but now everything had gone quiet. He hoped that didn't mean his younger brother was on his way to see him, and if he was, he hoped even harder that Posey wasn't tagging along. He didn't know what to say to her. She was so damn demanding, and it was all such a mess. Nothing had gone as intended.

They had a plan. A bloody good one. But it hadn't quite worked.

He thought of Fiona then. Was that why his sister was so moody? Was she losing patience? Forgetting the promises he'd made? Or was there something else going on? She'd refused to say, had gone all sulky like she does, after that blasted book club had given them all the third degree. She'd barely said a word since, except to tell them *she* wasn't clearing their dad's crap out. *"They can burn it for all I care."*

He didn't blame her. They were all angry, but they had to keep a united front. They had to get through this, together. It's where their strength lay. It was their superpower.

And Clay's kryptonite.

He almost smiled. They'd certainly caught their dad by surprise that night. He never knew what hit him. So why wasn't Flynn feeling victorious? Why were they all so stressed and anxious? Like adolescents again, sitting around the enormous cedar table at the old homestead, heads down, shoulders hunched, praying he wouldn't single them out over the lamb roast. Hoping their mother would speak up and then hoping to God she wouldn't, or things would get even uglier. (For her, not them, and he couldn't bear that.)

Something prickly caught at the back of his throat and he coughed, cleared it away. *Get your shit together, Flynn*, he told himself. *You're not twelve anymore; you're a grown man. Act like it!*

Hell, he was now older than Clay was when he first took over Dartmoor Downs. And yet Clay didn't trust him. Didn't accept that he might know better, might have his own grand plans. Like they were stuck in the 1960s and nothing was ever allowed to change!

Well, he would show him. All of them. He would prove

his father wrong, and he would do it his way. The right way. And not even bully Clay would stop him.

Not now, not anymore.

He leapt to his feet and gave himself a shake. He needed to get out. Blow off some of this steam. He marched for the door and reached for the handle. Then glanced back.

Now, where had he left his Akubra…

~

The attendants swapped a worried look as Alicia and Claire stepped into the tearoom.

"We know something strange has happened on this train," Alicia told them. "You can't keep fobbing us off. We want the truth, and we want it now."

Jacinta rubbed her neck and darted a glance at Arlo, who was back to picking at his skin. "Go on then," she said. "Tell them."

Arlo paled again. "Really?"

"They won't say anything. Promise you won't repeat any of this to anyone, or Arlo here will lose his job."

"Repeat what?" said Claire now. "What's this about?"

Jacinta took a slow breath. "You've been worried about Mr Dartmoor, yeah? Well, we're a little worried now too." Then she added with a whisper, "We're not one hundred percent sure he did get off at Broken Hill."

That didn't surprise Alicia in the slightest, and she nodded at Arlo. "You think Walker's lying too? About ticking Clay's name off?"

"W-Walker?" he stammered. "No… I mean, it's not his fault… I…"

He stopped, blinked at Jacinta, and she sighed wearily again. "Look, Walker wasn't doing the roll call that morning. Arlo was. He's the one who ticked Mr Dartmoor off, at least—"

"I thought it was him, honest I did!"

"Shh!" said Jacinta, a finger to her lips.

He thrust his own hands to his lips and tried to quell his

nerves. "It looked so much like him. I... I saw him get off through the Platinum carriage and then get on the bus for the Memorial tour, which he was booked in for. That's why I know he got off."

"Okay, that's good then, isn't it?" said Claire.

Alicia was shaking her head. "But Clay wasn't on that tour. We know because we were."

Both attendants blanched now. "That's what we feared," whispered Jacinta. "You see, Arlo mostly works Platinum, right? So he didn't realise there was a look-alike brother until you mentioned it, Alicia."

"Oh no," said Alicia and Jacinta nodded.

Arlo said, "Jacinta'd told us how you thought you'd seen someone go overboard real early that morning. That cracked us up in the staff room—" He stopped as Jacinta flashed a frown at him. "Sorry. No offence or anything. It just seemed so crazy, you know? Now... well..."

"Not so cray-cray?" said Alicia, enjoying his discomfort.

"Now Arlo's freaking out that maybe it was Phillip Dartmoor he saw getting off the train and on that bus, not Clay," said Jacinta. "I mean, he just can't be certain."

"I did ask!" he said, Jacinta hushing him again so he lowered his voice. "I said, 'It's Mr Dartmoor, right?' and he said, 'Yep,' and so I ticked him off."

"Well, he would say that," said Claire. "If it was Phillip."

He nodded, digging at his skin again.

"Did he have a hat on? The guy you ticked off?" Alicia asked.

He stopped digging. "I... I'm not sure; can't remember. Does it matter?"

Alicia shrugged as Claire held up a hand. "But I don't understand. Why would Walker tell us that he ticked Clay off if he didn't?"

"He's just covering for me," spluttered Arlo. "He's a good bloke. But he wasn't feeling great that morning, so I said I could handle it by myself. Said I'd be cool. Shit!"

"Shh!" said Jacinta again.

Alicia's mind swept back. No, she realised, Walker never

actually said he'd ticked Clay's name off. That's what had niggled at her. He'd been clear that Clay's name was ticked off but never said he was the one who'd done it. Now his shiftiness was making more sense. And no wonder he'd looked doubly shifty when he'd met the entire Dartmoor clan and realised for himself that there could very well be a mistake.

"But I thought he got off, honest I did!" Arlo was saying, head in one hand. He looked up. "Mr Dartmoor wasn't in the lounge or his room when I cleaned them during the stop, so I just figured… I mean, he should've been in his room at least, right?"

"Hang on," said Alicia now. "You cleaned Clay's room? It's just that I saw Walker doing it later that morning."

Arlo looked confused, almost annoyed, like it was irrelevant, but Alicia felt her stomach tighten. What was Walker doing in Clay's cabin two hours after Broken Hill, and long after Clay had gone missing? Just checking his protégé's work? Or something more sinister?

Claire was more interested in what Phillip was doing in his missing brother's carriage when they arrived in Broken Hill that morning. "He's a Gold passenger. He should've been getting off in Gold, through the bar door like we did. Shouldn't he?"

And that's when Alicia understood exactly why Arlo had come to see Jacinta and why they were scanning that clipboard. There was a way to confirm all this, and it rested with Jacinta's on-and-off sheet.

"You never ticked Phillip Dartmoor off in Broken Hill, did you, Jacinta?" Alicia asked.

She winced, giving Arlo a sympathetic look. "My Mr Dartmoor—Phillip Dartmoor—never exited through my section. At first I figured he'd stayed on board. It's very rare, but like I told you, some people do sit the excursions out. Two of the Dartmoor siblings didn't get off either. But then he returned via my door after the excursion."

She picked up the clipboard. "I definitely ticked him back on. But I never ticked him off." Then she quickly explained.

"Some passengers do alight through other doors—they're not supposed to—but we have a system for checking. There's a call button they can use to access another door, and the SOM would have a record of that."

"SOM?"

"Safety Operations Manager."

"Okay, so we need to check with this SOM," said Claire, "because they'd also know if Clay used another door, right?"

Both attendants nodded, Arlo's nod slow and wary, but Alicia was frantically shaking her head. "Too much mucking about," she said. "It's all too confusing. It's time to take it straight to the top. You need to alert your boss."

"But I can't!" wailed Arlo. "I'll get the sack! I'll probably get Walker sacked too. He trusted me. He shouldn't have. I've stuffed up everything."

Jacinta had a hand around his shoulders now. "Shh. It's an innocent mistake. You'll be fine." Then she looked back at the book club friends, eyes imploring. "We don't even know if it is a mistake yet, right? Just because Arlo can't say for sure that Clay Dartmoor got off in Broken Hill, doesn't mean he didn't."

"But it also doesn't mean he did," said Alicia, shaking her head at both of them.

~

It did not take long for the book club to come searching.

After Alicia and then Claire had vanished mysteriously from breakfast and failed to return, the group had swapped suspicious glances, then gobbled down their own meals and followed in fast pursuit. That's when they ran into Arlo scuttling back the other way. He stood aside to let them pass, but they waved him on. He seemed in an almighty hurry.

Once in their carriage, they spotted the two women at the furthest end, staring out of the exit door, deep in conversation. Jacinta had vanished.

"What the blazes is going on?" asked Ronnie, wobbling up.

And so Alicia explained what they had just learned from the two attendants.

"So that was young Arlo dashing past us like he was fleeing for his life?" said Perry. "Is he fessing up?"

"Hope so," Alicia replied. "He didn't want to, but he should be on his way to see the JM now."

"Journey Manager," explained Lynette for the benefit of the others.

"Poor chookie," said Missy. "He wasn't to know. Those two older Dartmoor men do look really similar, and it wouldn't have been hard to mistake Phillip for Clay. Of course they're not identical twins, not like my boyfriend and his brother."

"Really? You have a boyfriend?" said Lynette, tongue firmly in cheek. "You never mentioned it."

Missy blushed and Ronnie growled, but it wasn't their banter she was angry at. "If all this is true, then Phillip Dartmoor owes me an explanation. Before breaky, I asked if he'd seen his brother that morning, and he reminded me, almost smarmily I might add, that he's in the Gold carriage with me, suggesting, quite clearly, that he never entered Platinum."

"Could've been lying," said Perry. "I bet he lied about the Akubra too. I bet that was his hat we found in Clay's room. He probably threw Clay off the train just before five, then hung in there until Broken Hill, switched to his brother's bunged-up old hat, and slipped out. Then tossed the old hat in Broken Hill. We never found that in Clay's compartment, did we, Ronnie?"

"Except Phillip was wearing his Akubra at the Memorial, remember?" she replied.

"How do we know that was his?" he shot back. "Maybe he pinched someone else's or bought a new one or something so he'd look like himself again?"

"Okay," said Claire, "but let's back up a bit. Why would Phillip push his brother off and then hang around in Platinum for an hour or more? If he'd done it, wouldn't he keep his distance? Slink back to Gold; leave from there?"

"Not if he wanted to properly impersonate his brother," said Perry. "Could've been part of his plan—to deliberately confuse the attendants so everyone would think Clay was still alive an hour and a half later when we got to Broken Hill, if only to buy himself more time. And who better to impersonate Clay than his brother? When the attendant knocked on his door for the wake-up call at six, he would've called out, pretending to be Clay, thus making it seem like Clay was still alive then."

"Ooh, that sounds like a Christie plot again," said Missy.

It sounded like good sense to Alicia. At least… some of it did. She pointed to the exit door handle. "Problem is, it still doesn't tell us *how* Phillip managed to push Clay off while the train was still making its way to Broken Hill. Jacinta told me these doors are securely locked during motion. You need a set of staff keys and a special fob to open them."

They all stared down at the door's bright yellow sign— DO NOT OPEN WHILST CAR IS IN MOTION—then Alicia said, "Or *do* you?"

Suddenly she reached for the handle and gave it a good yank.

"Don't!" screamed Missy as Lynette stepped quickly back, smashing into a panel high above the wall. Mercifully the door did not open, and now Lynette was cursing as she rubbed the back of her head.

"Sorry, occupational habit," said Alicia, fact-checking like the good journalist that she was.

"You might've given us some warning," moaned Lynette, shooting cranky glances at the wall behind her.

Alicia apologised again and said, "So he definitely needed keys. Any thoughts on how he got hold of them?"

"Maybe he was in cahoots with a crew member?" suggested Missy. "Or bribed one. Or maybe stole a set when they weren't looking. There's no other way."

"Oh, yes there is," said Lynette, who was now staring up at the small red box she had slammed her head into. She was no longer grumbling. "In fact…"

She turned around, eyes glinting. "Any one of us can get

the keys any damn time we like."

Then she pointed up towards a small glass box with the words EMERGENCY KEY BREAK GLASS printed across the front.

# CHAPTER 14
## The Key to It All

The book club stared at the red box, feeling both gobsmacked and stupid. Nestled safely inside was a set of keys, including a fob key, the very one Jacinta had told Alicia she'd need to open the exit door.

She said, "No way. Can it really be that easy?"

"It's not the tightest security in the world," conceded Ronnie.

"Doesn't need to be," said Lynette. "Who'd want to open a door mid-journey? Apart from a deranged killer that is." She gave her sister a pointed look. "But you'd have to allow for it, right? In case there's a fire or a run-away engine or something."

"Touch wood!" said Missy, tapping at the panelling by the door.

"Plus Jacinta said the door sets off an alarm when it's opened, so that would be their security," added Alicia. "The question is, why did the train driver ignore the alarm? Why didn't he stop the train?"

"I think a more pressing question is, how many of these little red boxes are there," said Perry. "And—"

"—are any missing their keys?" squealed Missy. "Yes, Perry! We need to start looking. If we find a broken one, then they'll *have* to take us seriously. This is so *exciting*. We're getting close, kiddoes. I can just feel it. Shall we split up and start hunting?"

"No need to split up," said Alicia. It had to be one of the carriages towards the front. That's where she saw the body go flying. She grimaced. "I'm just not sure Walker is going to let us into Platinum."

"Fiddlesticks," said Ronnie. "We have a right to find out, and if we have to, we'll barge our way in."

Turns out, no barging was required. There wasn't an attendant in sight when they made their way into the first-class carriages, and it was only when they got to the accommodation section that they saw some at the furthest end, gathered in a huddle by the adjoining door.

They were all staring up at a red box. The front glass had been shattered, and the keys were missing.

"Well, what a surprise," said Ronnie, tone haughty as the group turned to look at them.

There was one woman—tiny with a bleached-white, pixie hairdo—and four men. One of them was Arlo, one was Walker, the other two had keys rattling at their belts and walkie-talkies in hand.

The woman's black eyebrows shot upwards as she glanced across at them, but instead of holding up her hand as a stop sign, as Alicia expected, she held it out to wave and said, "Hello there. You must be the Murder Mystery Book Club I've heard so much about!"

The woman might have been petite, but she was the big kahuna on the train. Her name was Hana Sato, and she introduced herself as the Journey Manager. But they all knew that meant the buck stopped with her, and it filled them with relief.

"I am sorry this has been such an unsettling few days for you all," she told them, her voice as sweet and smooth as maple syrup. "And I appreciate you bringing your concerns regarding Mr Dartmoor to my team. I believe you have all met the Platinum attendants, Walker and Arlo?"

Walker looked sulkily back at them while Arlo just looked sheepish.

"And these two gentlemen?" asked Ronnie of the two men with keys. "Security, I presume?"

"Not exactly," said Hana. She introduced one the Safety Operations Manager, Bray, the other as "train tech

Tom", then promptly excused them.

"I'll call if I need you," she told them, then smiled slimly at Arlo and added, "You can get back to work too."

Arlo looked both relieved and worried in equal measure and scooted after them while the book club looked at Hana.

"So you finally know about the missing man," said Ronnie, pointing up at the broken panel, "and are taking it seriously?"

"Oh, I can assure you I have taken this very seriously since I first heard." Hana's eyes darted to Walker, and there was a very subtle crinkle of her brow. She then glanced up at the smashed box and added, "This, er, new development does, of course, add extra gravitas."

"And you accept he was thrown from the train?" added Alicia.

Hana's right hand did form a stop sign now. "I never said that, ma'am. I just need to get all the facts—"

"*All the facts?*" repeated Ronnie, not letting the big kahuna off the hook. "The fact is, young lady, my friend Alicia here saw a man fall off the train at an ungodly hour and no one has taken her seriously, including—I'm ashamed to say—us! Then, lo and behold, we hear that very same man has vanished from this train, not so much as a peep, and we're all expected to believe his family when they tell us he happily skipped off into the sunrise to drive half the length of Australia. Alone! It's utterly absurd. The man was elderly. He left his sunglasses behind, not to mention all his belongings, and that, taken with what Alicia saw, is grounds for a proper investigation."

When she had finished, Hana was still smiling politely, as if she were accustomed to cranky passengers and they didn't faze her in the slightest.

"Of course, madame," she replied. "And I can assure you I have begun investigations and am getting to the bottom of it. In fact"—her eyes turned to Alicia—"Alicia Finlay? You were my next port of call. If you've got a moment, I'd like to ascertain what you saw that first morning, outside of Broken Hill."

"Happy to help," said Alicia.

She was just compiling her thoughts when the adjoining door cranked open and two women burst through, chatting and laughing. They stopped short when they saw the group, and one gasped.

"Oooh this looks a wee bit serious!" The woman had a strong Irish lilt. "Everything all right then?"

Hana smiled warmly at her. "Absolutely. How was breakfast, ladies? Those buttermilk pancakes are a bit deadly, aren't they?"

The second woman giggled. "Deadly delicious! You'll be rolling us off the train at this rate!"

"Not to worry, ladies. You'll get a lovely walk this arvo when we stop at Cook," Hana told them, and they laughed some more as they continued on.

Only once they were out of earshot did Hana turn her attention back to Alicia. "I'd like to do this in private." Then she glanced at the book club and added, "I promise to have her back to you safely in time for the next stop."

Lynette looked ready to object, but Alicia was already nodding. "That's fine," she told her, then gave them a confident wave as she followed Hana down the corridor towards the front of the train.

As they walked, the Journey Manager called out, "Walker, I think you'd better join us, don't you?"

Walker did not look quite as confident as he turned and followed.

Hana led them through several accommodation carriages, offering hearty greetings to passengers they passed and stopping to respond to random call-outs on a walkie-talkie strapped to her belt.

They soon reached a set of doors prohibiting all guests from going further, and yet she swept on, guiding the way through carriages with luggage, linen and roaring power generators, before finally stopping at what she called the "staff room". It was a tight space, furnished with a small desk, several chairs, and various equipment, including a laptop, printer, and a worryingly large first aid cupboard.

She directed Alicia into the spare chair and then took the seat at the desk, pulling the laptop open and tapping something into it while Walker stood looking ill at ease beside the entryway.

"Once again, my sincerest apologies," she told Alicia as she tapped. "Our aim is to give our guests the best experience possible, and I'm hoping we can clear things up soon and you and your friends can return to enjoying yourselves." She glanced up. "You're celebrating your engagement I hear?" Alicia nodded, and she smiled warmly. "That's so exciting. Congratulations."

Alicia tried to match her enthusiasm, but all thoughts of celebrating had gone overboard with the body.

Sensing this, Hana glanced at her watch and then at Walker and said, "Let's get straight to it, shall we? So you thought you saw something unusual very early that first morning? Can you describe what you saw?"

Alicia nodded and told her about the unsettled sleep, the green-and-white checked shirt. "I'm almost a hundred percent sure it was Clay Dartmoor."

"But *not* a hundred percent?"

Alicia frowned. "I saw his shirt. For some reason I can't seem to picture a body. I don't understand why, but it had to be him. It had to!"

Hana held a petite hand up again. "I'm not saying you *didn't* see something, Alicia, but I have spoken directly with the family, and they assure me it could not have been Mr Dartmoor, that he was alighting the train that morning and hiring a car to drive home, which apparently is not out of character. They've also adequately explained his remaining luggage—again, not out of character to leave such things to his daughter. We also had a first-hand witness who saw him alighting the train that morning. However"—a crinkled glance at Walker now—"that has recently come into dispute."

Walker flushed bright red at that and said, "I'm so sorry, Hana. I had no reason to doubt Arlo—"

"And we still don't," she said, cutting him off, eyes back on Alicia. "My team saw a man resembling Mr Dartmoor—Mr *Clay* Dartmoor—exit the train via the Platinum carriage in Broken Hill yesterday morning. We ticked him off, assuming, as one would, that it was the same Mr Dartmoor who was booked in that carriage. Had we known that his brother—*Phillip*—had also exited through that carriage the same morning, we would have checked that more closely."

Alicia nodded, noticing her use of the words *team* and *we* and thought that boded well for the two crew members involved. She especially hoped sweet young Arlo didn't lose his job over this, particularly if he'd been deliberately duped. But she couldn't worry about that now.

As if reading her mind, Hana said, "Walker came to me with his concerns last night, and we've since spoken with Phillip Dartmoor, who has confirmed that he did indeed get off via the Platinum carriage in Broken Hill that morning, so we can no longer say for sure that *Clay* Dartmoor did. Which is why I need a few more facts."

Alicia already knew this but felt vindicated nonetheless and sick to her stomach—the thought of Clay flying from the train now churning it up. "So what was Phillip doing in Platinum that morning?"

She crossed her arms. "At this stage I'm more interested in learning what it is you think you saw the night before."

Now Alicia's arms were crossed. "Not *thought*, Hana. I *know* I saw it. And you should be talking to the police about this."

She blinked rapidly. "What police, Alicia?" She freed a hand and waved it out to the dusty landscape sweeping past the window. They were in the heart of the Nullarbor Plain now, a vast, barren plateau almost twice the size of England and a damn sight hotter. "No police out here I'm afraid. And I really don't want to sound the alarm if we don't have to. After all, Mr Dartmoor—Clay—did inform his family he was getting off so—"

"They could be lying."

She shook her head firmly. "He also informed my

attendant here. Didn't he, Walker?"

Walker nodded equally as firmly. "He mislaid his room key that first night, and as I was helping him in, he told me very clearly that he was disembarking in Broken Hill. He said—"

"It's not important what he said," said Hana. "The fact is, he was unequivocal on that point. He was leaving us in Broken Hill first thing. That was his intention. He told Walker that directly." A quick, slightly worried glance at Walker, who was nodding again. He was not lying now; Alicia was sure of it.

But intending to get off willingly and being thrown off earlier were two different things.

Hana misread her frown. "We don't normally allow early disembarkations, but we do try to be accommodating."

*Yeah, yeah,* thought Alicia, uninterested in the rules. "The fact is you can't say *for sure* that Clay ever did get off."

She stiffened. "Our problem is while his brother, Phillip, has conceded that he exited through Platinum in Broken Hill, he can't recall whether Arlo called out to him or ticked him off." She held up a hand. "He agrees Arlo might have called out to him, but he was preoccupied. Hence the reason we can't be absolutely certain that Arlo got it wrong." She sighed heavily and sat back in her seat. "It's a bit of a mess. I'm sorry you've been caught up in it. But we are attempting to get some assurances now." A quick glance at her screen. "I've put a call out to all the hire car companies in Broken Hill to see if anyone has a record of hiring a car to Clay Dartmoor, and that should hopefully clear things up."

"So the broken glass?" asked Alicia. "The missing keys? How do you explain that?"

"That was only just noticed this morning and was immediately brought to my attention. It does rather throw a spanner in the works." Hana looked unsettled for the first time since they had sat down, rubbing a hand through her glacial hair. "But it's not exactly proof that the door was opened. Just that the keys were taken."

*Stolen*, Alicia wanted to tell her, but it was clear Hana was determined to see her guests in the best possible light. Instead, she said, "Can I ask why the alarm didn't go off? I mean, if that door was opened, our attendant told us that an alarm should have sounded in the drivers' carriage." Hana winced at that, and Alicia said, "Ah, it did."

Hana held up two palms. "Another thing we can't be sure of. Both drivers were replaced at Broken Hill. We have put in calls to them to confirm if it did go off and at what time."

"But shouldn't they have alerted you when it happened? Why wouldn't they report that? Apply the brake? Something?"

"We're not sure. If an exit door had been opened for a few seconds, it might have been missed." Her brow crinkled again, and she glanced at her phone. "But I'm waiting for confirmation on that. They certainly didn't alert our night managers—"

"You have night managers?"

"Yes. A Service Operation Supervisor and her Assist."

"And they didn't see anything themselves?"

"It is a very long train, Alicia, and they don't just stroll around willy-nilly. Apart from communicating with the drivers, they also do stocktakes, handle staff call buttons, help set up the diners for breakfast and, most importantly, confirm our ETA into Broken Hill so the staff know what time to start door knocking. That ETA can shift depending on freight traffic."

"They sound busy."

She nodded. "And both sleeping now as you can well appreciate, but they confirmed to me earlier that they received no worrying alerts of any kind, from the drivers, the staff, any of the passengers. Nor did the regular staff who clocked on at five thirty."

"So no one saw or heard anything?"

She nodded. "I'm also heartened by the fact that there have been no reports of a body spotted along the track— and this track is well used; it's a major freight route through the desert—so someone should have seen something. But it would help if we could narrow down exactly where it might—I stress *might*—have occurred. Which is why I really need you to focus, Alicia. Can you tell me exactly what time you saw... what you saw?"

Hana was clearly struggling to come to terms with the idea that a body had fallen off her beloved train, and Alicia felt for her but, unfortunately, couldn't be specific.

"Although my sister could," she told her, and Hana reached for her walkie-talkie.

Ten minutes later, they were all staring at the laptop screen, including Lynette, who informed Hana that she'd been woken by Alicia at around 4:55 a.m.

"I can't recall exactly," said Lynette, who'd been escorted to the staff room by an attendant, "but there was definitely still a four in front of the time when I checked my phone. But only just. That's why I was so cranky." She offered her sister an apologetic grimace.

Hana was grimacing along because while the track to Broken Hill was relatively straight, it did have the odd bend, particularly as they narrowed in towards the mining town. Which means Alicia might very well have seen the front of the carriage from her own window at that hour, especially if she was sitting up, reaching for a water bottle.

"It still would've been pretty dark at five," said Walker.

Hana smudged her lips to one side. "Yes, but the sun was starting to come up, and there would've been residual light from the train."

"I didn't make this up," said Alicia. "I know what I saw."

Lynette's eyes narrowed. "So you guys really are taking this seriously?"

"Until we can prove otherwise, of course we are," said Hana. "However..." She sat forward and clasped her hands together on the desk. "I have a very big favour to ask. Until we know for certain, we'd like you and your group to keep this under wraps. Please let's not upset our fellow passengers, especially if it does turn out to be a false alarm."

"But you can't honestly believe that?" said Alicia. "I'm sorry, but shouldn't you be calling it in? I know we're miles from a copshop, but can't you at least get a search party together?"

Hana blinked back at her again. "It's not as easy as that. Even with a more precise location, that's still an enormous span of track, a very rugged landscape. And to make people go out and search under such hot and harsh conditions without knowing for sure…"

She held up another placatory hand. "Your recollections have helped narrow things down considerably, and I will be asking all freight trains to make a concerted effort to check the area once I've done more calculations." She glanced back at her screen. "In the meantime, we may still get proof of life from one of the car hire companies or his family."

*Proof of life?* Alicia shivered a little at that.

Hana noticed and stood up, reaching out a hand to brush Alicia's arm. "Let's all hope this is wrapped up very soon and you can get back to celebrating. Until then, I thank you for your time, ladies, and again ask that you keep this matter private. No point alarming the others."

Then, seeing Alicia's burgeoning frown, she quickly added, "I can assure you, Alicia, if we still have no answers by the time we arrive in Perth, the police will be ready and waiting. That goes without saying."

That was also a good twenty-four hours away. Alicia glanced at her sister, and they read each other's minds. That meant twenty-four hours for the Murder Mystery Book Club to do what the Murder Mystery Book Club did best— and keep sleuthing.

# CHAPTER 15
## Separating the Wheat from the Chaff

**B**y the time Walker escorted the Finlay sisters back to the start of the Gold section, their dining carriage was bustling with life again. The seats were all occupied, cutlery clicking, guests laughing and chattering.

As they waited for the waitress to clear some plates before they could pass through, Lynette ogled a roasted cauliflower salad and said, "How can it be lunchtime already? Didn't we just have breaky?"

"Time flies when you're having fun," said Alicia.

Lynette grabbed her hand. "*Are* you having fun? Really? It's supposed to be your prewedding party, honey. And now the suits are in charge, we can hand the whole thing over, right?"

Alicia scoffed. "Have you met me, Lynny?"

"That's why I think we should let it go. This is supposed to be a break from all your dark, scary thoughts. It's supposed to be fun."

"Again, have we met? This *is* fun. I mean... I don't wish the poor man dead—" The waitress gave her an odd look as she passed, so Alicia lowered her voice and added, "But I'm enjoying the mystery. And my thoughts are going to get even darker if we don't solve it, so we're in it now, Lynny, whether you like it or not."

She pouted. "Fine, come on."

They proceeded through the Queen Adelaide Restaurant, noting that the Dartmoors were not amongst the diners. That was probably just as well. If Alicia had spotted Phillip, she might have demanded to know why he was in his brother's carriage the day he vanished. But they'd promised

Hana they'd stay out of it, so accosting the man in a busy diner would not be ideal.

Once in the next carriage, they spotted their group huddled at the other end of the lounge, so they grabbed soft drinks from the bar on their way through.

"We've asked Marvin to serve our lunch in here," said Claire as they dropped into spare seats. "They're so very accommodating, don't you find? That way we don't have to split up, and you can tell us all about your chat with the JM."

"Good thing you've chosen this far corner then," said Alicia, noting a few couples further up, "because we have to do it on the sly. Hana doesn't want us startling the horses."

She clocked Perry's expression, and that's when she realised. Ronnie was missing.

"Oh no," Alicia said.

"Oh yes," he replied. "She's on her high horse and off and galloping!"

~

Phillip Dartmoor looked surprised to find Ronnie at his cabin door, but he managed a smile that was quickly deflated when she burst out with: "You lied to me."

He blinked. "I beg your pardon?"

"May I come in?"

Before he could answer, she was striding through.

His compartment was tidy, everything in its place. There were several books on the window table. Biographies by the look of them. And two teacups, both drained.

She waved towards the couch and said, "May I?" not waiting for a yes as she sat down, scooping up a bright yellow notepad that was in her way. There was a list of names scribbled on it, and she glanced across it before Phillip snatched it from her and shoved it in the magazine tray.

"Can I get you a cup of tea? Something to read? A blanket perhaps?" he asked when he turned back.

He was being facetious, and it rankled her further.

"I'm not sure why you find this all so amusing, Mr Dartmoor. Your brother is missing, and the only people who appear to be taking it seriously are my book club and me."

"About that. I appreciate your concern, but I'm not sure it's any of your—"

"It *became* our business the moment one of us witnessed a man falling from the train that looked suspiciously like Clay."

He shook his head. "I just can't accept that was him."

"Why? Have you heard from him? Had a delightful phone call telling you all about his travels?"

He plunged his hands into his pockets and looked away. He was still standing, now leaning up against the closed bathroom door, keeping a respectful distance.

She sniffed. "That's what I thought. Did you push him off?"

"What?" Shocked eyes darted back. "Of course not! That's bonkers. Why would I want to hurt my brother?"

"Perhaps you got into an argument. About his wife, say?" She was fishing, and all it was bringing up was a craggy scowl. "We're hearing from all and sundry that he wasn't the best of husbands. Perhaps your crush on Daisy—"

"My *crush*? What are you talking about? I didn't have a crush on Daisy. Loved her like a brother. That's all. And I loved my brother too. I promise you."

*Loved.* He'd used the past tense, and not for the first time. "So why did you lie to me then?"

"When?"

She sighed irritably. "Before breakfast this morning. I asked you very plainly if you were in the Platinum carriage yesterday, and you told me you were not. I have just learned from the staff that they saw you there."

He thrust his chin high. "I didn't lie. As I recall, you asked if I had seen my brother that morning and I told you no. Because I hadn't. The fact that I was in the Platinum carriage is irrelevant."

"Oh poppycock!" she spat back. "You're being tricky with your words, and that has me alarmed. The only people who are tricky with their words are sleazy politicians, real-estate agents and criminals. Which one are you, Mr Dartmoor?"

He blinked. "I…" He shook his head. "I wasn't trying to be tricky, Ronnie. I was trying to be discreet. Yes, I was at my brother's cabin, but I didn't go in. That's what you asked."

"Tricky!" she said again, and he held up one hand.

"I knocked on his door and he didn't answer, so I assumed he'd already cleared off—as he said he would—and so I jumped off and joined the Broken Hill excursion. Apparently the attendant called out my name; I honestly can't recall. I was deep in thought. Lots on my mind. But I never entered my brother's room. Never."

"So *that* you do remember?" She tsked. "So why not just tell me that?"

"Because I didn't feel it was any of your business, quite frankly." Now he looked rankled. "Look, the evening before we'd had a family meeting. It had been… well… *intense* I guess you could say."

"So there was a fight?"

"What? No!" He shook his head firmly. "It was all very civil. Nothing personal, just business-related, to do with Dartmoor Downs. But Clay was a bit drained by it all, and I didn't blame him. None of us did. He's getting on in age. Just lost his wife. Needed a bit of alone time is all. Said he was hopping off the train in the morning. Wanted to get some fresh air, make his own way home. In his own time."

She must still have looked sceptical because he added, "Look, Clay's done stuff like this before. It's not that unusual. We had a family holiday in Singapore a few years back. Daisy organised it. Supposed to be five days, he left after two. It's what he does. But sure, we probably should've objected, insisted he stay, but…" He offered Ronnie a weak smile. "It's not easy to tell Clay what to do."

"Clay Dartmoor does what Clay Dartmoor wants?" she suggested.

He frowned. "Like Flynn says, he's a grown man.

Has every right to go his own way. But I did worry—about his exhaustion levels. Whether he should be driving across the desert by himself. *That's* why I stopped at his room yesterday. To see if I could convince him to stay, or failing that, I was going to suggest I tag along. But… well, he'd already left by the time I got there. I knocked but he didn't answer."

"And you never went into his cabin?"

"How could I? Didn't have a key."

"Of course you didn't have a key; you're not a young blonde," she shot back, and he looked surprised.

Then he rubbed a hand across his craggy cheek. "Ah, you've been reading the gossip mags."

"I most certainly have not!" She was scandalised by the very suggestion. "We witnessed it for ourselves. Your brother tried his luck with a young barmaid. Very inappropriate behaviour."

"But that's just Clay. He's always been a flirt. It's harmless."

"I think the barmaid would beg to differ. Just because my generation of women put up with such nonsense, doesn't mean the next ones will take it lying down—and don't you dare snigger at that appalling pun."

He swallowed back a smile, and she decided she liked him, despite herself. She stood up and stepped towards the door. "And if your brother has come to harm at the hands of an angry young blonde, I'm sorry to say, I'm not a hundred percent sure I'd have much sympathy."

Then she brushed past him and out, leaving the man blinking rapidly behind her.

~

When Ronnie joined the group in the lounge, they were digging into an array of colourful salads and a large ploughman's platter. She took a plate and helped herself as they watched her warily.

"Still in one piece, is he?" Perry ventured.

Ronnie looked up. "He'll live, but he won't lie to me so easily next time, I'll grant you that." Then she sighed with exasperation. "I'm not sure he's the culprit. He's ticking all the boxes, but... I just can't see it. And he had a reasonable explanation for being in the Platinum carriage. Says he was worried about his brother. Admits the family's business meeting the night before had been intense, and Clay was exhausted by it, told them all he was clearing out, so he was just checking up on him."

"That fits with what the Gleesons and Tag told us," said Perry. "It would be intense if he was announcing his successor. Could've ended in blows?"

Ronnie dabbed her lips with her napkin and nodded. "Except Phillip says it was all very civil, nothing personal. But I do wonder. I mean, their business *is* personal. Two of his three children were about to be officially ousted from the family farm, not to mention losing a multimillion-dollar enterprise. How can you not take that personally? There must have been a fight, otherwise why would Clay feel the need to go?"

"Sounds more like a tantrum to me," said Missy. "My sister, Henny, used to do that when we were kids. If she didn't get her way or was snippy about something, she'd threaten to leave home. Sometimes it was just bluster, but sometimes she did go. For hours! Freaked the parentals out, as you can imagine. Luckily she grew out of that nonsense. I guess it was her way of cooling down."

"But what was Clay cooling down *from*?" asked Ronnie. "The man had just handed over his life's work to his eldest son. A time for celebration, not sulking, surely? But listen, there's something else..." She glanced around and back. "While I was in there, I saw a notepad with some things scribbled down. Freshly scribbled I might add."

She produced a blue-smudged thumbprint as proof. "I'm not sure it has anything to do with this, but I thought I should mention it. Now let me see if I can remember..." Her face scrunched up tight. "There was the name Andrew or Andrews, I think it was... James someone or other, and then the words barber and gardener of all things."

"He's worrying about his *hair* and his *lawn* at a time like this?" said Alicia.

"I wouldn't put it past that family," said Ronnie. "They're shockingly blasé. Keep saying 'Oh that's just Clay', but how dreadful would it be if one of your group suddenly announced they were deserting a holiday early? Imagine if it was one of us."

"Missy'd be clinging onto our legs, not letting us go," said Perry, winking at the young librarian.

Missy giggled.

Claire said, "What if Clay was testing them and they failed? Was hoping they'd beg him to stay, and he was left feeling unwanted. Perhaps it wasn't a dummy spit so much as deep depression. I know his family scoffed at the idea, but you don't always know, do you?" She looked at Alicia. "Could it have been suicide? Could Clay have jumped?"

It was a good question. One they should not dismiss so easily, given their history.

Alicia's eyes slid across to Lynette. "At the time, I was positive he'd been pushed, but to be honest I'm not sure how I would've known that. All I really saw was that flash of green and white, which we now assume had to be Clay. I guess he could've pinched the keys himself and taken a leap. Aussie farmers do have a high suicide rate."

But Ronnie was not convinced. "Clayton Dartmoor wasn't your average Aussie farmer struggling with isolation, debt, droughts… I didn't know him, sure, but I knew *of* him, and he was so much more than a farmer. He was an astute businessman, ruthless too, I'd suggest. You don't amass all that land and wealth, not in the harsh outback, without being a true survivor. An Aussie battler."

"And why would he?" added Perry. "Even if all that land was causing him grief or stress or whatever, he'd just lightened his load, handed it to his eldest son. No more battle, surely?"

"But that's a risk in itself," said Alicia. "Retirement can be hard for men of that generation—losing their sense of purpose. And maybe he misses his wife? I know he was a bad husband, doesn't mean he didn't love her."

Ronnie recalled the old photo she saw in Clay's compartment and conceded the point. "Why would he bring along a memento of his wife if he was really that callous?" she asked them. "Perhaps he was softer and more sentimental than anyone acknowledged." She also wondered why you'd throw yourself so dramatically from a train when you had thirty thousand hectares of your own in which to end things, should you feel the need.

"Could've been an accident," suggested Lynette. "Maybe Clay nicked the keys so he could open the door and have a cheeky ciggie and stumbled out. I caught my sous chef standing on the loo the other day, smoking out a high window."

Ronnie chuckled at that and reminded them she did find a silver cigarette case in Clay's cabin. But then they all shook it off, agreeing that if Clay Dartmoor wanted to have a smoke, he'd have a smoke, and he'd do it any damn place he chose.

"We're getting distracted," said Perry. "We've got less than twenty-four hours until Perth and the police take over, so let's stick to the assumption it was murder." Then he leaned across and grabbed Alicia's hand. "Unless you'd rather we didn't. It is supposed to be your—"

"Arrggh!" Alicia growled, cutting him off, catching them all by surprise.

She leapt to her feet and stormed off towards the bar, causing the club to swap worried frowns and other passengers to look across inquisitively. While she was up, the waitress appeared to clear their plates, and so they didn't say a word until Alicia returned, a souvenir Indian Pacific pen in one hand and a blank journal in the other.

She slapped them down and said, "Okay people, once and for all: There is no way we are going to lounge about, swapping marriage advice while there's a baffling mystery staring us in the face. Are you all *insane*? So no more fretting about me and my silly little hen's do! Got it?"

Her eyes danced across the group, who looked suitably

chastened. Except for Lynette, who was pouting again.

"I want to do this," Alicia told her sister firmly. "And I think we *need* to do this, so let's get on with it. But let's get on with it *quietly*." Then she sat down and opened a fresh page. "Okay. So. We've already worked out *when* and *how* it happened; let's see if we can come up with *who* and *why*." Alicia turned to Ronnie. "We know the family had a meeting the night before, and we know it was *intense*. Soon after, Clay says he's deserting. You don't bail for no reason. That sounds like a fight to me. They must have squabbled over the inheritance."

"Agreed," said Perry. "Don't forget, Tag got drinking with Clay soon after that meeting. Said Clay was grumpy, called his kids ungrateful hippies or some such. I think all the Dartmoors should be on the suspect list."

Alicia scribbled the names down as Lynette said, "Except Flynn, right? He was just handed Dartmoor Downs, so he'd have no reason to kill his dad."

"Oh, *that's* the reason you think he's innocent?" said Perry, twiddling his diamond stud earring. "What if Clay really was about to renege, leave it all to his favourite kelpie—"

"According to who? *Tag?*" Lynette scoffed. "He's a troublemaker, that dude. He said it himself it was clearly a joke. What we know *for sure* is that Patrick and Fiona had just lost a squillion-dollar farm. They must have been enraged. Might've acted on it. And Flynn did tell me this trip was all Fiona's idea. Maybe she'd been plotting this for a while."

Claire sat forward and gasped. "Yes! Now I think about it, Fiona definitely had something on her mind, right at the start of the trip. The very first time I saw her, she was walking to her cabin just after we left Central Station. And… I don't know how to explain it, but she looked… well, *murderous*. Although, to be fair, Flynn did too."

"Oooh that's revealing!" said Missy. "I can believe it of Fiona and Flynn. Not sure about Patrick though. Didn't the Gleesons say he only cared about his distillery?"

"Except distilleries are massive money pits," said Lynette.

"He'd want his share of Dartmoor Downs, if only to use as collateral to build his business. A properly capitalised small whisky distillery, for instance, would set you back at least a million. Maybe two." They all stared at her wide-eyed, and she shook her hair from her face. "I did learn some stuff in business school you know."

Perry said, "Sorry, Lyn, but I still think we need to consider Flynn. It's something Jock said about how Clay might hand over the reins, but he'd always be in control. Maybe Flynn realised that, and once he was officially named the successor, he got rid of him. For good."

"Or maybe Flynn doesn't want the place at all," suggested Claire. "With his father gone, he can now sell it. Imagine how much he'd get if he sold to a large Chinese conglomerate or the like. And now he gets to keep all that money to himself."

Lynette wasn't smirking now. "But he seemed so scared of his father. I just can't imagine him having the guts to do it."

"Does it take guts though?" asked Missy, twiddling one of her blue curls. "To throw an old man off a moving train? I don't think so."

That shut them all up for a moment. Because she was right. It felt like such a gutless act.

Perry said, "You need to have another chat with Flynn, Lyn. Suss all this out."

"Oh *sure*." She smirked as her voice turned coquettish. "Hey, Flynn, have you got a sec? It's just that we think you might've shoved your dad off the train so you can make a lot of money." She rolled her lovely green eyes.

Perry laughed. "I'm sure you can be a little cooler than that."

"Oh, I am cool, but *seriously*?"

"You're right, pork is seriously uncool for a wedding," said Alicia, speaking suddenly very loudly. "Chicken's a much safer choice." She shut her journal and tapped the cover. "Now what do we all think about the flowers? Lilies or tulips?"

As they frowned back, trying to grasp exactly why Alicia

was talking gibberish, a familiar group approached. It was the Dartmoors on their way to lunch, and now they understood, clamping their lips shut as the family swished past.

This time Uncle Phillip was leading the charge, Patrick, Posey and Flynn in the middle, Fiona bringing up the rear. As usual they didn't acknowledge anyone in the bar, let alone the book club, their eyes ahead, expressions deadpan.

Except for Fiona.

Her eyes suddenly swept down towards the book club and narrowed, glancing at Alicia's journal and back, her pace slowing, her brow furrowing.

"Oh, lilies are *much* more elegant," gushed Ronnie suddenly. She'd also noticed Fiona's expression and was hoping to ward her off. "Tulips are so common, don't you think?"

It worked. Fiona kept walking and Ronnie exhaled. So did Alicia.

Only when they had cleared the carriage did she speak again. "That was close. We need to move this to one of our cabins before we get busted."

They all agreed and began to get up, but Alicia grabbed her sister by the elbow. "Not you."

Then she gave a subtle nod towards the bar. One of the Dartmoors had split from the pack and was perched on a corner stool. This was Lynette's chance.

Her eyes lit up, then she frowned at Alicia as if to say, "Really?"

Alicia nodded. Just once. It was absolute. Then she gave her another look, a longer look that said, "But stick to the program. *Behave*."

Flynn had his back to the crowd, leaning across the bar when Lynette sidled up. He was just being handed a glass of what looked like soda squash but didn't look up as he began to open a manila folder crammed with papers.

Lynette ordered a beer from the bartender, waited until she had it, then slipped onto the stool beside Flynn.

"Hey Man of Mystery," she said, and he glanced around,

surprised. Then he smiled, which was a positive sign. Lynette was not sure how she'd be received, considering they had all but accused the man of bumping off his dad.

"Much better idea," he said, pushing his soft drink aside and signalling to the bartender for the same.

"Not going in for lunch?" she asked, indicating the next carriage.

He shook his head. "Too much food on this trip." He tapped the papers in front of him. "Besides I have work to do."

She had a feeling it was a hint, but she wasn't going to take it. Not yet. She glanced down and saw the words *biodiversity* and *nutrient management.*

He caught her looking and his narrow eyes turned to slits. "I'm not a greenie you know. Not trying to save the planet or anything." Like that would be a sacrilege. "It's just there are some on-farm sustainability practises that will actually save us money in the long-term if we bothered to implement them. It's a win-win. Things like better water management and crop rotation, reduced tillage, robotic sprayers that could bring our chemical use right down..." He stopped, smiled sheepishly. "Sorry, I get carried away."

"No, I love that," she said. "Good on you. And I don't think there's anything wrong with trying to save the planet. We need more of it. What does your dad think about that?"

He rubbed the soft scar on his chin with his thumb and shrugged like it didn't matter, but she knew it would. Taking a deep breath, she raised her beer and said, "Anyway, I hear congratulations are in order. You're officially the boss now."

An immediate frown quickly morphed into a smile. "Aah the old gossips have been at it, have they?" He glanced past the bar, into the diner. "It's all still being worked out, but yeah... that's the idea." His frown returned, his eyes narrowing so much you'd swear they were closed. "So Dad better bloody show up because I still need his help with all this." His eyes widened again. "We are worried, you know. Still haven't heard anything."

"That *is* worrying."

He took a good swig of his beer.

Lynette did the same, then said, "Look, I'm sorry we were all so full-on before. When my book club are together, we're like Miss Marple on steroids." He laughed at that, another good sign, so she added, "You know we're really hoping we've got this wrong and he'll show up?"

"Sure, why wouldn't you be?" He took another gulp. "You're wrong to blame us though."

"We don't—"

"Lynette, I didn't come down in the last shower. Doesn't take any kind of Miss Marple to know if something's happened to Dad, us kids are the prime suspects. But we shouldn't be. We all love him. We do. He can be difficult at times." He rubbed his scar again, offered a dry chuckle. "Well, *most* of the time, but that's also what makes him such a success. He's driven. And I've gotta respect that. I want to learn from Dad. He knows that. And… you know?" He nodded down to the report. "I think there's some stuff he can learn from me."

He didn't sound quite so convincing then. He cleared his throat and gathered the papers together. "Anyway. Fact is, Dad's fine. So he got off early. He's just having some well-earned downtime, and why shouldn't he?"

Lynette tried not to frown at that as she glanced around at the happy revellers lounging and laughing, sipping cocktails after a gourmet three-course lunch. Wasn't *this* downtime?

He read her mind and smiled. "Downtime from *us*, I mean. We can be a handful when we get together, us kids."

Except again, she recalled a bunch of shaky wimps when she saw them in Clay's presence that first night. Not so much as a raised objection or a hair out of line. Once more, he must have read her mind because his smile dissolved and his eyes were squinting again.

"Dad's fine, Lynette. Just getting some space is all. So you can tell your fellow Miss Marples none of us bumped off the old man to be shot of him."

"I don't mean to—"

He held up a hand. "Again, last shower. Didn't come down in it." He closed the folder and stood up. "I think I'll go and join my *family*." He emphasised that word, like he was putting her in her place. Then he leaned down, very close to her ear, and growled, "If you really believe my dad has come to harm, then you're looking in the wrong direction. There is one arsehole on this train who wished him dead. You should be talking to him."

Then Flynn gave Lynette a hard look, and for a fleeting moment she saw Clay's ferocity in his icy blue eyes before he blinked it all away...

# CHAPTER 16
## Moving Things Along

Jock Gleeson clocked the handsome couple hunched together at one end of the bar as he escorted his wife through to the dining room. They had their heads together and looked, well, *impassioned*. He wondered about that as he helped Iris into their allotted seats and then passed her a menu.

Couldn't pretend he wasn't feeling regretful.

Had he made a mistake, keeping his own daughters away from Flynn? He was once a ratbag, that fella. A so-called "eligible bachelor", breaking hearts across the state just like his dad. But he had settled down of late, young Flynn. Barely in the papers anymore, other than the odd vacuous story about his short-lived marriage. She'd been a blow-in, his wife, some startled-looking city string bean who was never going to settle down in the sticks.

His girls were true-blue country stock, would've been happy out there despite what Iris said. Louise and Belinda were born and bred right next door to Dartmoor Downs. Had soil and wheat in their veins. Would have made a decent match, especially his Billie. She had it hardest for Flynn. Wept like a baby when Jock refused to let her ask him to her formal school dance. He didn't think Flynn deserved her, but now he knew it didn't matter.

If he had let Billie try her luck, she might now own half of Dartmoor Downs.

It was pride that stopped him. Pride that always got in the way. But gee it would've been fun to see the look on Clay's face if Flynn *had* fallen for his Billie. Imagine if they'd married! That would've been priceless. That would have turned old Clay to stone, and that alone would have made Jock one very proud papa. He smiled sadly and peeled his eyes from the menu he hadn't read, to the view outside the window, wondering where the old bastard was now.

~

Down in Ronnie's carriage, the gang was tightly wedged in, four across the lounge, Perry leaning against the cabin door, Alicia's journal now bursting with notes. They agreed each member of the Dartmoor family had a viable motive. If they weren't avenging Daisy, Clay's downtrodden wife, it likely had something to do with the inheritance.

And if you believed the neighbours, Fiona was top of the suspect list.

"Except who made her the official biographer?" asked Ronnie now. "We need to be careful who we listen to. Sometimes one person's idea of the truth is very different to another's."

Alicia agreed. "And even if the younger son—what's his name? Patrick? Even if he didn't want the hassle of the farm or need the money for his distillery, he still might've taken the rejection personally."

"Or his wife did," added Claire. "Posey's pretty formidable. She could be involved. And I can't imagine her letting her hubby get away without his share."

"Who wouldn't want a slice of the pie though?" said Missy. "I mean, my folks haven't got much to leave, but if they died"—she tapped on the wood table now—"and went and left the house to Henny, who's got kids and maybe they think she needs it more... I'd have to confess, I'd be a little bummed out. We should both get it, sell it, and split it between us. You gotta be fair about this stuff, right?"

"It's not always that simple," Ronnie replied. "The family tradition was to hand it down to one child—usually the eldest son by what I can glean."

"Crap tradition," said Missy.

"Not necessarily," persisted Ronnie. "Unlike your

parents' house, Missy, Dartmoor Downs is a working enterprise. So, along with the land, Flynn was inheriting all the work and costs of running that enterprise. And it also makes sense to hand that to one child, otherwise they may be inclined to split it up or squabble about its direction or do exactly what you suggested and sell it entirely, sharing the proceeds. Thus ending a long family legacy."

"And here's another thing," said Claire. "If handing the farm to the eldest son was their tradition, then it shouldn't have come as any great surprise to the younger ones, so I can't imagine them suddenly erupting with anger and tossing their dad off."

They all stared at her, frustrated. Because she was right. None of it was sitting straight.

"Okay," said Alicia. "Let's just agree that all three siblings are suspects, as is Uncle Phil—because of all that dodgy business about being in Clay's carriage and crushing on his dead wife. But I think we need to go back a step to the *how*. We know how they got the keys, but how did they get Clay to not only meet them at an exit door just before five in the morning but then open it and throw him out?"

"Might've been spontaneous," suggested Perry. "They're country folk. Don't they wake before dawn? So Clay's already up, and so's the killer. They bump into each other, a fight ensues. They spot the emergency keys, and Bob's your uncle, off he goes."

"Except that all takes time," said Alicia before putting on her own fake voice: "*Hey, Dad, can you wait there a minute while I smash this box and scoop out the keys, then open this fiddly exit door, then wrestle you to it and off...*"

They all laughed at that and not insensitively. The truth was it felt good to release some pent-up tension. As much as they revelled in mystery, a man had likely been murdered, and that sat like a knot in their stomachs. Sometimes it needed to be unwound.

Eventually Missy said, "I'm back to thinking it was all planned. Don't forget, munchkins, that Fiona suggested this trip. Maybe she's been on the train before and knew how everything worked. Or had pinched the keys earlier and then asked to meet her dad at an exit door. As he got there, she opened it and said, 'Hey, look, there's a kangaroo!' And as he's peering out, she gives him a shove."

"*Hey, there's a kangaroo?*" said Perry, sniggering. "Like Farmer Clay hasn't seen his share of roos?"

She smirked. "Just trying to work out how he got close enough to be chucked out."

"Perhaps he didn't," said Claire now. "He could've already been dead or unconscious. Drugged or killed, say, in his compartment and then carried to the door and thrown out. Easy enough to do when everyone's asleep, including the staff."

"Not everyone was asleep though," said Alicia. "Hana says there're two night managers. They keep themselves pretty busy, but it still would've been a risk. Plus the day crew started work at five thirty, so they were cutting it fine. Could easily have been caught."

Claire shivered. "So it's likely at least two people were involved. One was on lookout, the other did the deed. Hauling a body through a carriage requires strength. I'm not sure Fiona could do it alone."

"Oh, I am," said Perry. "I thought she was going to tear our heads off back there. I reckon she's as strong as an ox that one. Probably tackled a few in her time."

They all laughed again just as the intercom in the corridor crackled to life, informing them they would soon be stopping at Cook. Perry opened the door so they could better hear the lively description of the tiny ghost town they were approaching.

As the speaker (who sounded a lot like Hana) finished her lively spiel, the Gleesons strolled past on their way back from lunch.

"Grab your sun hats and waters, folks!" Jock sang out to them. "It's gonna be hot and dusty."

They all smiled and nodded, then Perry closed the door, leaned up against it and whispered, "What do we think of the Gleesons?"

"As suspects?" asked Ronnie, surprised.

"They knew Clay; weren't his biggest fans. And there's definitely a connection with his brother. Do you remember in Broken Hill, Alicia? We saw the Gleesons talking to Phillip. Jock looked like he wanted to rip the guy's throat out, and then Iris looked like she wanted to smother it with kisses. Very suspicious."

"So what would all that tension be about?" asked Ronnie. "What would be their motive?"

He gave it some thought. "They share a border with Dartmoor Downs. Must all know each other. Maybe Phil and Iris were having an affair, and it all came to a head that morning. There was a fight, a struggle. Clay got in the middle? It was an accident. They had to dump his body...?"

They all stared at Perry like *he* was now talking gibberish, so he said, "What about this: Jock said Clay wanted his land. Badly. Maybe he'd been hassling them for it and that's what they were fighting over."

"Still doesn't make any sense," said Ronnie. "Jock is under no obligation to sell to his neighbour. It's absurd. Besides, he made it very clear he's leaving it to his daughters. Like it wasn't even an issue."

"Okay, so what about these daughters then?" continued Perry. "What if there's some dark past there, some bad blood? I mean, if Clay tried his luck with a bartender on the train, why wouldn't he have a crack at the young fillies next door?"

"Fillies? Are we really calling them fillies?" asked Alicia, mid-scribble.

"The point is," he shot back, "are they sexy blondes?"

Ronnie's eyebrows shot up. "Now you're thinking clearly, Perry. Yes. I'll chat with the Gleesons on the stopover. Make some discreet enquiries. And, Perry, perhaps you should tackle our fossil fanatic again, see if he knows anything more. I'm not sure if he's a 'troublemaker', but he was the last one drinking with Clay in the bar."

"Happy to," said Perry, "and not because I'm *smitten*."

A glare at Ronnie now who chuckled back at him and

stood up, stretching. "Speaking of old fossils, I'm looking forward to Cook. I need to move about before my bad back fossilises. It might also air out our little grey cells."

"That's not all it might air out," said Missy, thinking of ghosts now. "But hang on, Lynny's flirting intel out of Flynn. Perry'll do the same with Tag. Ronnie's chatting to the Gleesons. What about the rest of us?"

"I want to speak to the staff some more," said Alicia, "especially the night managers—see if they saw or heard anything suspicious. But I'm not sure they'll let me."

"You'll find a way," said Ronnie. "That still leaves Patrick and Fiona."

"You take Patrick," Claire said to Missy, remembering how threatened the wife had acted in Broken Hill. "And I'll tackle Fiona."

"Good luck with that," sniggered Perry, staring down at Claire's slim, perfectly groomed facade. "She's one tough broad, that Fiona. I think you'd come off second best."

Fiona didn't look so tough when Missy spotted her two minutes later, loitering at the furthest end of the corridor. The book club were finishing up in Ronnie's cabin, and Missy had ducked away first to use her own facilities when she spotted Clay's daughter. She was talking to someone concealed around the corner, one hand out as though imploring.

Missy knew this was Claire's suspect, but there was something about Fiona's stance that had her intrigued, so she took a few steps closer.

Fiona sounded sad, a little whiny. "I'm so, so sorry," she moaned. "I told him to leave you alone. I promise I did. I never knew he'd do that. If I'd known, I would have—"

That's when she sensed Missy and glanced around.

Missy gulped and offered a silly wave before turning and making a beeline for her cabin.

"Oi, you!" Fiona called out.

Missy stopped, kicking herself for not being more subtle, memories of schoolyard skirmishes fraying her nerves.

Steeling herself, she turned back to find Fiona's bushy eyebrows wedged together.

"You're from that group, yeah? The one asking about my dad?"

Missy gulped again, and now *she* was sounding whiny. "I'm really, really sorry about that. I mean, we weren't trying to be nosey. It's just that we've been worried—"

"Yeah, nah, don't worry about my dad. He'll be fine." Fiona's tone showed a care factor of zero. "Listen, did I hear my brother say you're also a book club? Like a crime fiction club or something?"

"Oh! Yes!" Missy exhaled. "We're the Murder Mystery Book Club. But we're not here for that. Not really. It's our friend's hen's party."

"Bummer. I was gonna ask if I could be an honorary member."

Missy was doubly surprised now. "Really?"

"Yeah, mate. I'm hard up for entertainment. My brothers are heathens, never read anything outside of a tractor manual, and Posey thinks *Vogue* magazine's a book." She laughed, a deep, dark chuckle that ended with a snort through the nose. Laughed again, then said, "Oh well, pity you're not in session, so to speak. I've just finished an Agatha Christie novel. Bloody loved it. Would've been good to have a chat."

"*Have a chat?*" said Perry, scoffing after Missy scampered back to Ronnie's room to relay the news.

They were sharing her sunscreen, lathering their arms and legs, and Lynette was still absent. Alicia hoped she was making progress and not of the romantic kind.

Perry was appalled that Fiona wanted to discuss a fictional mystery while starring in a real one of her own, but Alicia saw it as a gift. A chance to imbed themselves in the family. Prod Fiona for more details.

"That's a relief," said Missy, taking the tube now and squeezing out a giant dollop. "Because I told Fiona we were meeting up later to talk books and said she could join us. I told her between Cook and the dinner stop, Rawlinna.

Four thirty in the lounge. Hope that's okay?"

"It's brilliant. Well done!" said Alicia.

Missy beamed and handed the tube to Perry, who shook it away.

"It's a quick stop," he told her.

But she pushed it back. "It's the middle of the Australian desert, Perry. The guidebook says it can be really harsh. Just do it!"

He rolled his eyes and took the cream as Missy turned to grin at the rest of them. "But that's not the exciting news." She slapped her oily hands together as she described the incident by the tearoom. "Fiona was apologising to someone for something *a man* did. Someone she felt responsible for. She said something like, 'I'm so sorry. I never knew he'd do that.' And I reckon she was referring to her dad."

"How can you be sure?" asked Perry, now applying a very thin layer to his forearms, his nose twisted up in disgust.

"Because after she left, guess who popped their head out from the corner?" They all stared, waiting. Missy was beaming so much now, she could have powered the overhead lights. "Our attendant, Jacinta! And yes, peeps, just like Clay's past conquests, she too has long, blond hair."

Jacinta's hair was really more of a light mousy colour and currently tucked up beneath a red baseball cap when the group found her, preparing to tick names off again at the exit door. They were just pulling into Cook, and she was chatting to a group of waiting passengers, including the Gleesons who had matching wide-brimmed straw sun hats on, Jock's large nose smudged with white zinc, a clumsy glob stuck to one cauliflower ear.

Alicia warned Missy that now was not the right time to ask about Fiona, suggesting she put it off until after the tour, then she excused herself to turn back and search for Lynette.

It did not take long.

Her little sister was back in their cabin, also applying sunscreen. She winked when Alicia raised her eyebrows and said, "We have a new suspect, Alicia, and it's not Flynn.

I'll tell you all about it later, but suffice to say, Perry is going to be *very* disappointed."

# CHAPTER 17
## Exorcising Ghosts

The tiny town of Cook was a dusty, desolate place, and the missing man was on the book club's mind more than ever as they stepped off the train and glanced about. Forget Clayton Dartmoor. It felt like this entire community had vanished overnight, leaving nothing but empty carcasses of buildings and random, hand-painted signage that suggested it once had life.

The place seemed utterly deserted. A true ghost town.

Created as a railway stop in 1917, there was a two-storey school, now ramshackle and condemned, a small bush hospital that must have brought life into the world once but that life had long cleared out, as well as a public swimming pool that would have been a welcome reprieve out here in the heat if it wasn't filled up with dirt and weeds.

They must have been a lively crowd, too, full of good humour, because the hand-painted signs said things like OUR HOSPITAL NEEDS YOUR HELP. GET SICK. And IF YOU'RE CROOK, COME TO COOK.

The group found them mildly amusing although Ronnie sighed. "It's sad how these old towns died out. Such a pity everyone wants to live on the coast these days."

"I think there's still like, four residents here," said Missy. "They provide the train with fuel and water. But I guess the rest of them all moved away."

"Can you blame them?" said Lynette, pulling on dark shades as she stared at the glaring horizon. "I wouldn't last a day out here. Talk about Snoresville."

"Better not get too attached to Flynn then," quipped Perry. "I'm guessing Dartmoor Downs doesn't exactly have a teeming population and a shopping mall."

Smirking back, she said, "Speaking of Flynn…"

Lynette waited until a group of travellers strolled past, then outlined her earlier conversation with the Dartmoor heir over a beer. She told them of Flynn's plans to go green, which they all agreed would be a good motive if his father was against it.

"But would you kill someone to save the planet?" asked Missy.

Lynette said, "Hell yeah! At least, I would. Starting with some of those mining magnates who couldn't care less about anything but their share price. But anyway, that's not what I wanted to tell you." She glanced quickly at Perry. "Flynn says we should be looking at Alan Taggart. Says he's the perfect suspect."

"Who's Alan Taggart?" asked Claire, looking confused beneath an enormous floppy black hat with a long white sash, à la Breakfast at Tiffany's.

"You mean Tag?" said Perry.

Lynette nodded. "Flynn said Tag's been hassling his dad for years to let him dig, and I mean hassling. Endless letters, petitions, even went to state government pushing his case. And Tag did speak to Clay that first night, shared a drink, remember? There's no way he didn't try his luck again. How often would he get access to the one person who can make it happen?"

She held up a hand as Perry's brow furrowed. "I'm not saying Tag meant to do it, but maybe things got out of control. The Platinum Club is also their dining room, right? So there must be sharp knives about. Maybe Tag stabbed him in the heat of the moment and then had to dispose of the body?"

Perry looked beyond incredulous, yet she ploughed on. "Here's the thing though. If it did happen that way, it was a waste because Flynn told me he firmly agrees with his dad, and there is no way he's letting Tag rip up his land for fossils. He said, and I quote: 'Our job is to feed half of Asia and the Middle East, not provide a bloody scavenger hunt for boys who won't grow up.'"

"Ouch," said Missy, also looking worriedly towards Perry.

His expression had now morphed into one of amusement. "Indiana Jones sure has a lot to answer for." He tipped the top of his Fedora. "We're not talking gold-plated arks, people. I can't imagine anyone—least of all Tag—killing a man so he can dig up a few bones." He shook his head and looked about. "Still, if I find him, I'll be sure to ask about it. Until then, should we take some happysnaps? No one will believe we were ever on this trip if we don't."

He turned and beckoned the group closer as if he had nothing more on his mind than a selfie.

~

Iris Gleeson was holding her smile, rigid as a cast-iron bathtub, while her husband snapped photos with his mobile phone. The couple were standing at the front of the engine carriage, also taking mementoes of the trip. This was a popular vantage point, the iconic train behind them, the even more iconic desert hugging it on both sides.

The book club had now dispersed to track down their respective suspects, and it didn't take long for Ronnie to find the Gleesons. It was a searing forty degrees Celsius, the hot, dry wind slapping at their straw hats, mocking their attempts to stay safe.

Ronnie watched them for a few minutes, her own wide-brimmed Cancer Council hat tied firmly around her chin so it wouldn't fly off, before stepping forward and offering to photograph them together.

"That'd be tops," said Jock, handing over his phone and then placing an arm around his wife's waist. "We'd do one of those selfies the young 'uns do, but I'd take up too much of the frame."

He patted his enormous stomach, and they laughed as Ronnie snapped off a few shots.

Then she handed the phone back and said, "Yes, young people are so very versatile, don't you find? You have two daughters, I believe?"

She was happy with the segue, and they did not seem to notice the subject change.

"Not so young now," Iris told her as Jock began snapping more images of the train. "Belinda's forty-five and Louise is nearly fifty! Goodness, makes me feel very old."

"Ah, but you must be so proud," Ronnie persisted. "I'd love to see a picture. I never had children of my own."

"Oh of course." Iris pulled out her own phone and brought it to life.

As she scrolled for images of her girls, Ronnie thought it marvellous the way some parents naturally assumed the world was interested in their progeny. It would not have occurred to her that Ronnie had ulterior motives.

Might as well use the opportunity…

"So do you ever see the Dartmoors socially? Neighbourly barbecues, that kind of thing?"

Iris snorted as she kept scrolling. "Strewth no! They don't want a bar of us. Mostly keep to themselves and that's as we like it. Ah, here we are. The girls together. That's a few years old, that shot, but yeah, we're so proud."

Ronnie took the phone she was being offered and studied the image on the screen. The "girls" looked in their late thirties here, also arm in arm, standing on a coastline somewhere, beaming from ear to ear, and she smiled too. Because while both were short and plump like their mum, the rest was pure Jock—large ears, wide noses, and lovely dark brown locks.

Not at all to Clay Dartmoor's taste, as far as Ronnie could tell.

"They're beautiful," she told Iris, and of course Iris nodded along—just as all parents do—but this time Ronnie meant it, if only because it saved the poor darlings from the blonde-seeking lecher next door.

~

Claire peeled a black strand of hair from her eyes as she

stared into the derelict swimming pool. She was supposed to be furthering the case, but she was a little grumpy with Missy, who'd pinched her suspect. If only she'd run into Fiona. Now she was left with Patrick and his scary wife. Although it was probably just as well.

Missy was worse with alpha females than she was. Would roll over and let them attack. Not that Claire could see the alpha anywhere, let alone Patrick. She'd done a circuit of the dusty town and was back at the filled-in pool, feeling maudlin.

Was there anything more depressing than a drained swimming pool? she thought, whipping off her hat and wiping her brow. No more splashing about in there, no more fun and frivolity. She wondered if fun and frivolity were ever on Clay Dartmoor's agenda, or was he too ambitious for such folly? Had he always been terrifying to his children and a handbrake to his wife? A figure to be gossiped over by the neighbours and bemoaned by fossil enthusiasts and loathed enough that the book club had not one but now multiple potential suspects.

Once again she was reminded of the evil Mr Ratchett in Murder on the Orient Express. So feared, so loathed and yet tolerated for so long. Until someone snapped.

"Sad, isn't it?" came a voice to her right, and she turned with surprise to see Patrick Dartmoor standing there—like a gift from the Gods—hands shoved into his moleskin trousers, Akubra hat on his head.

He'd said almost the exact same thing the first time they'd spoken, at the Miner's Memorial in Broken Hill. She glanced around quickly, worriedly looking for Posey, but he appeared to be on his own. And, as it turns out, he'd been looking for her too.

"It's Claire, isn't it? Listen, I wanted to find you and thank you—all of you—for looking out for my dad."

She nodded, then asked gently, "No word yet?"

He shook his head, waved the phone in his hand. "Wi-Fi really is lousy, but he should've passed through a few towns by now, a few cell towers. He could've been in touch if he wanted to."

"You think something's happened to him?"

He looked at her surprised. "No, I think he's playing silly buggers." She couldn't help frowning at that, and he rubbed at his golden beard. "Sorry, but you don't know my dad. This is classic Clay Dartmoor. He's not calling in because he doesn't think he has to. Dad doesn't answer to anybody, least of all his kids. It's the way he's always been but... Listen, that's not what I wanted to speak to you about."

He glanced around and back, his tone heavy. "I'd never say this publicly—and don't bloody quote me because if you do I'll deny everything. But you seem like good people and you shouldn't be wasting your holiday worrying about my old man. He's okay. I know exactly where he is."

Now she was gasping. "You do?"

He nodded. Shrugged. Looked towards the horizon. "He's back in Broken Hill. Has hooked up with some... woman. Probably laughing at our messages as he hides away in a sleazy hotel."

Claire frowned. "You know this for a fact?"

Now he shook his head. "I know this because it's what he does. He turns to women when he's feeling lousy."

"But your mum's gone now, so why the secrecy—"

"Yeah, you're missing the point." He sounded annoyed, irritable as he glanced back to the Indian Pacific. She gleamed in the bright sunlight, twinkling, almost as if she was winking at them. Like a temptress. "Look, you know why we're on this trip? Not for the riveting stopovers, I can tell you that." His eyes danced across the dusty town now. "Dad was making his grand announcement—who would be the Chosen One, hand-picked by the Great Clayton Dartmoor to take over his precious bloody farm."

Then he laughed a joyless laugh, held his palms up and said, "Wow, big surprise, he handed it to Flynn." His tone was pure sarcasm. "That was always a given; he didn't need to turn it into a bloody circus. Thing is, when he told us that first night, after dinner, we didn't play our parts, tearing into each other like he expected. We were cool, and he couldn't handle it, so he did what he's always done when he feels small—runs into the arms of some bird who'll make him feel big again."

Claire dropped her head to one side. "That might have been his intention," she said gently, "but my friend really did see something that morning, Patrick. She's positive someone fell off the train, and we're pretty sure it was your dad. At least, she saw his green-and-white checked shirt."

"He probably chucked it off to keep us guessing."

Claire must have looked sceptical again because he kicked at the dirt, sending dust flying. "I'm telling you, you don't know him." He looked past her, clocking his family who were walking in their direction, a hazy blur from this distance. He shook his head. "None of them really know him either. I was the baby, see, the one stuck inside with Mum while they were out working the land. I was the one who consoled her every time Dad slunk in from some tart or another. Not them." He stepped closer. "I'm the one who saw how it wrecked her. Brought on her cancer. And do you think that stopped him? Not a chance."

He kicked the dirt again. "I couldn't believe it when I saw him with that bimbo in the pub in Perth. Mum was dying then. He couldn't stand it. Not the dying part but the fact she was getting all the attention. That's why he turned to the other woman. He's a child, Claire. A narcissist. It's what he does."

"I'm so sorry," she said, wondering why he was telling her all this.

He exhaled heavily and gave her an apologetic look, like he'd just wondered the same thing himself. He whipped off his hat, wiped the sweat from his own brow now, then yanked it back on and said, "Better get back. Posey'll be worried."

He went to go, then stopped and turned back. "Please, just... just let it go. Fact is my dad's a nasty character and we don't need any more confirmation of that. He's alive. Happier than ever I'd suggest because he's back where he wants to be—the centre of attention. Don't let him win.

Go back to your holiday and stop wasting your time worrying about him. He's not worth it."

Then he shoved his hands into his pockets and strode off towards his group while Claire stood looking after him, thinking how bizarre that exchange was. And how revealing. She wasn't sure exactly what Patrick was trying to achieve by telling her all that. Sympathy? Understanding? Or was he simply trying to get the book club off his scent?

Well, it hadn't worked. Right now Patrick smelled suspiciously like a son with a vendetta and had zoomed to the top of Claire's suspect list.

She watched for a little longer as he reached his pack, and they all turned and stared at her before continuing on towards the train. She noticed that Posey was missing, but the others were all there—his two siblings and his uncle. And she noticed again how identical they were, and it wasn't just the similar garb, the golden-red hair and the soft brown freckles. Despite a range of heights—Fiona the shortest, Flynn towering over everybody—they all walked in the same swift manner, shoulders back, heads up, eyes ahead, like they were on a red carpet, knowing they were being watched and giving nothing away. But they did give something away. There was something about them... Something was different... No, *someone*.

And that's when Claire clocked it.

One of them was not wearing an Akubra.

~

Tag wasn't a suspect! *Surely* he wasn't a suspect, Perry thought irritably as he made his way across the dusty terrain. What was Lynette on about? Silly girl, being taken in by the smarmy heir's lies. Still, he'd have to ask Tag now. No getting away from it, or the man. He'd just spotted the fossil collector all alone out on the furthest edges of the town, an intense expression on his face, staring down at the parched earth.

"Another toe?" Perry called out, joking as he approached.

Tag looked up, startled, and then smiled. "No such luck. Just lots of calcified shells. Back from when it was all—"

"Underwater. Yes, I know."

Tag winced. "Sorry. I must stop—what do they call it?—*mansplaining*. Especially when I'm mansplaining palaeontology to both a man and an actual palaeontologist. That's also what I'd call patronising."

Perry waved a hand in the air. "Don't worry, I'm enjoying your enthusiasm. So what do you do when you're not fossil hunting?"

"Me? Oh, I'm a science teacher. Or I try to be. I educate bored teenagers at a private college just outside of Fremantle. That's the beach suburb, just west of—" He threw a hand to his mouth. "Oops, I did it again."

Now Perry laughed. "It must be an occupational hazard, being a teacher and all."

"Hmm, yes, let's use that as my excuse." Tag chuckled as he bent down to study another old shell. "Amazing to think that this was once a shallow seabed—"

A loud wailing siren suddenly filled the air, and they both looked around. It was the first of two fire sirens that would be their call to re-board.

"Saved from another patronising lecture by the bell," Tag said, although he didn't stop his search, reaching out and grasping a small rock now, dusting it off, studying it up close.

Perry watched him for a moment, glad of the bell too. Glad he could avoid asking him difficult questions. He turned away, saying, "Well, good luck with your search."

"Same to you and your fellow sleuths," Tag called back, and Perry stopped. Turned around. Tag winked. "You're not the most discreet group on the train. I know you're looking into the Case of the Missing Wheat Baron."

Now Perry was wincing. "Everybody knows?"

"Oh, I doubt it. Most of our fellow passengers are too dazzled by the free food and booze. But I've seen you, whispering amongst yourselves. So you might as well get on with it and ask me."

"Ask you what?"

Tag dropped his head to one side. "Must I mansplain? You clearly want to ask something about the missing baron."

Perry smiled. "You did confess to being the last to see Clay Dartmoor alive."

"No, I don't think I confessed to that at all. We simply had a drink together. It was perfectly innocent. Just idle chit-chat. So you really think he's come to harm? Is that what all the whispering is about?"

"No one's heard from him since before Broken Hill. And I'm sorry, Tag, but I've heard you in full flight, I know you're passionate about fossils, so I'm struggling to believe you got Clay Dartmoor all alone and didn't broach your favourite subject."

He smiled. "You've read me like a book. Okay, sure, we might have had a little tête-à-tête about the merits of letting me dig at Dartmoor Downs."

"Tête-à-tête or mano a mano?"

There was a sudden flash of anger in Tag's eyes. "I was simply pointing out that Clay has *no right* to stop me from digging up Dartmoor Downs because he doesn't actually own it."

"He doesn't?"

He shook his head emphatically. "His clan stole it from the Indigenous Australians two hundred years ago, not so much as a handful of beads to thank them for it, and yet they act like they own the country. Absurd. In fact, no one owns the country. We are all custodians of this land."

Perry checked his watch and cleared his throat. "As riveting and as important as this discussion is, Tag, can we get back to the tiny bit of country around the Platinum lounge. What happened?"

"I simply pointed all this out to Mr Dartmoor and asked him when I could turn up with my trowel." He smiled now. "He said it would happen over his dead body"—he held up a finger—"do not take that literally. Then I might have called him a selfish, anti-science imperialist, or something equally ill-mannered, before I finished my drink and left the bar, Clay still alive and breathing. A tad offended, perhaps.

But certainly alive."

"Where's your Akubra?" Perry asked, throwing him.

Tag moved the hand to his head. Smoothed his silvery hair down. "Not really my style, or yours, by the look of it." He nodded at Perry's Fedora. "My lovely old *Boater*, however, is back on the train. Forgot to bring it with me. Why? Is headwear important to all this?" Then he squinted across at Perry's short-brimmed hat and said, "That's not much use in the desert. Although I suppose you spend more time in the bowels of museums these days than out fossicking. That's just for us amateurs, hey?"

"Do you really believe you'll find more specimens at Dartmoor Downs?" asked Perry. "Not the *whole* skeleton, surely?"

"Can't see why not."

"I can. Chances are predators disturbed the carcass before it was buried. Or there could've been some geological mishap, dissolution, erosion…"

"Such *negativity*." Tag tsked before grinning. "Or it might all still be there, just waiting for someone like me to finally take notice."

Now Perry was grinning. "Aren't you in luck then? With Clay missing and Flynn now in charge, you might get your chance."

Tag sighed and said, "If that's your way of saying I'm a suspect, well, bully to you. I may be into dead things, Perry, but I'm no killer." Then he smiled. "Besides, if I *was* going to throw Papa from the train, I would have got Papa to sign something first, saying I could dig to my heart's content. Now I have to start over, trying to persuade Papa's bratty boy to let me. And I suspect he's a homophobe like his father, so I don't like my chances."

"You think they're blocking you because you're gay?"

"Well… one mustn't be neurotic. But you and I both know the type. They're testosterone-fuelled philanderers, and *that's* where you need to be looking."

Perry stared at him, bemused. He was talking in riddles, but he didn't get a chance to call him on it because the siren began to wail again. "That's our last warning," he told Tag. "We'd better get back. I'm not sure we'd find it much fun to be marooned here."

"Oh, I think you'd be fun marooned anywhere," said Tag, winking and making Perry feel deeply uncomfortable. It's the reason he'd been avoiding the man.

*There was something about Tag...*

As they trod back, Perry asked, "So where should I be looking then? For Clay's killer."

"*Alleged* killer. You don't know he's dead yet. Do you?"

"Trust me. We have an uncanny sixth sense about this stuff."

"Oh yes? Did your sixth sense pick up that he had a visitor, old Clay, in his cabin early that first morning?"

Perry stopped walking. "He what?"

Tag plunged a hand to his lips, dramatically. "Ooh, did I not mention that?" He laughed, then continued on so Perry had to scramble to catch up.

"Who was it?" Perry demanded as Tag clapped his hands with delight.

"I should become an honorary member of your gang. I can see I've surprised you."

"Just tell me," said Perry, sick of all the nonsense. "You saw him with someone else?"

"Not saw, *heard*. Someone knocked on Clay's cabin door very early, as I said. I thought at first it might've been the conductor—you know, to wake us for Broken Hill. But I checked my watch and it was too early for that. So I turned over and went back to sleep. I was having the most delicious dream. I—"

"Did they go inside?" Perry cut him off.

"I assume so, but I can't really say."

"And what time was this?"

"Around four thirty."

Perry's heart skipped a beat. "Any idea who it was?"

He shook his head. "Sorry. I fell straight back to sleep. But I can tell you one thing. It was a woman's voice, and she was flirty." Then he held a hand to his lips and said,

"Oops, that was two things. See? I'm more than pulling my weight in the group already."

Then he smiled wickedly as Perry gulped, wide-eyed beside him.

# CHAPTER 18
## Rattling Onwards

Jacinta was chewing her lower lip nervously, looking this way and that, when she finally spotted Perry splitting away from Tag and rushing towards her carriage door.

"Finally!" the attendant said as he scrambled up the portable stairs where Alicia and Missy were also waiting. "Nearly sent out the search party."

She said it lightly, jokingly, as she ticked his name off her list, but Alicia felt for the woman. Clay Dartmoor's disappearance must be causing great consternation amongst the crew, and she suspected Walker was equally relieved to have Tag safely back in Platinum.

Perry barely acknowledged Jacinta as he turned to his friends, a glint in his eyes. He was clearly bursting with news, just as both Ronnie and Claire had been on their return, but Alicia gave him the same subtle head shake she'd given them. Now was not the time. Jacinta had promised to talk to them once the train was underway, and they didn't want a crowd for it. Things could get awkward.

Taking the hint and not looking happy about it, Perry returned to his cabin while the two women stood aside until Jacinta had secured the carriage again and the train had cranked back to life and was clacking down the track.

"Okay, let's make this quick," Jacinta said, glancing up and down the corridor. "The second someone comes along, I'm dust. The JM's sworn us to secrecy. It's important our passengers maintain their privacy."

"What if they haven't earned it?" asked Alicia. Jacinta frowned as though she didn't quite understand, so she added, "We know something terrible happened between you and Mr Dartmoor. Something very inappropriate."

Jacinta's shoulders stiffened. "How do you know that?"

Missy stepped forward and had the good grace to look sheepish. "It's my fault. I shouldn't've been snooping. And I wasn't, really. I mean I was just walking down the corridor, and I just happened to overhear you and Fiona talking—"

"Fiona? What did you hear?" Jacinta had a hand to her lips. She was clearly worried.

Alicia reached out and gave her arm a quick squeeze. "It's okay, Jacinta. It's nothing to be ashamed of. It wasn't your fault. Clay has form. He tries his luck with all the girls."

"Hang on, what?"

"Clay tried to crack onto Agnetha too," said Missy. "Claire saw him trying to give her his room key, the poor thing. It's just so sleazy and so *wrong*. You guys are just trying to do your jobs. You shouldn't be harassed at work. He's nasty, that Clay, and we're sorry he's gone missing and everything, but he shouldn't've tried with Agnetha, and he shouldn't have tried with you…"

Her voice trailed away as Jacinta looked like she was struggling to smother a smile. Missy swapped a look with Alicia and said, "It didn't upset you?"

"It didn't *happen*," said Jacinta, then she dropped her hand and shook her head. "You guys think…? Urgh! No… no, you've got it all wrong."

Missy's blush was now beetroot red. "Oh God, I'm so *sorry*. My mistake. I overheard Fiona apologising for a man, and I thought she meant—"

"What?" Jacinta was trying to process this and then began shaking her head, smiling again. "No… no, that was for something else. Ancient history."

Now they both looked confused. Alicia said, "You know the Dartmoor family from before?"

Jacinta's smile vanished. "I know Fi. From Agricultural College. The others not so much." She glanced at her watch. "I've got a staff meeting."

"I am truly sorry," gushed Missy again as Jacinta turned away. "It's just that Clay's been trying his luck and you are just his type—"

Jacinta turned back. "His *type*?" She did laugh then. It ended in a scoff. "I can assure you, ladies, I am most certainly *not* Clay Dartmoor's type." Then, spotting Alicia's confusion, she gave her shoulder a squeeze, just as Alicia had squeezed hers. "It's okay, Alicia," she said gently. "It's nothing to be ashamed of. It wasn't your fault."

Then she strode away, her laughter echoing behind her.

~

Posey Dartmoor idly flipped through the latest copy of *UK Elle* magazine, her feet tucked up underneath her, pretending to be deeply engrossed in a fashion spread as her husband pulled his leather R.M. Williams riding boots off and sent them flying.

Patrick then reached for a water bottle and took a few gulps.

"Bloody hot out there," he told her, and she glanced up innocently, smiled and kept flipping. He said, "So what did you get up to while I was doing all the hard yakka?"

She looked up again, thinking of her quest. How she'd failed again. She shrugged and glanced down at the page. "Nothing much." Then, as casually as she could muster, she asked, "So, you tell her? Like I told you?"

He nodded. "Not sure she bought it though."

"Why wouldn't she?"

He shrugged.

Posey smiled. "She has the hots for you. She'll believe anything you say. They all do. All the pretty girls who wished they'd married as well as I did."

She was flattering him, and he bought *that*. As he always did.

He grinned back. "Yeah, well, she can't have me. I'm all yours, babe. Besides, she's already married. I saw a ring. Bloody big one. She's not doing half bad herself."

Posey glanced down at her own enormous diamond. "So? Being married never stopped anyone. Certainly didn't stop your father."

His smile vanished. "I'm not my father, Posey."

Posey dumped the magazine and crept into his lap. Smothered his neck with kisses. "Of course you're not, honeybun." She sat back. "I'd never be with you if you were, you know that. And I hope you made that clear to her. What a slimeball Clay can be, I mean. Hope she realises he's not worth the effort."

"I hope she's not a bloody reporter."

"Oh, she's not a *reporter*! Or if she is, it's for *InStyle* magazine, and the PR won't hurt us there. No, you did the right thing, babes. You need to distance yourself from all of this. Get it all on record, and you need that lot to butt out."

He scowled like he didn't believe her. But then what did it matter, she thought? As long as they stayed united. That's all she cared about. Then she glanced down at her six-carat oval diamond and felt herself shiver...

~

The train rattled on, gathering speed as it made its way across the Nullarbor, the clickety-clack of the tracks getting faster and faster, the view swishing by, almost a blur.

And that's how the book club's brains were now feeling, sped up and blurry. Missy's in particular.

"That was so weird," she told the others after they'd regrouped in Ronnie's cabin, squished in even more with Lynette present. "Jacinta is most definitely Clay's type! She's a little older, sure, her hair's a tad darker, but other than that she's a cookie cutter version of Agnetha. And I know I heard what Fiona said. I don't think I got that wrong."

"What did she say again?" Claire asked.

Missy's eyes scrunched tight behind her zebra-print spectacles. "I'm sure she said something like, 'I begged him to leave you alone. I never knew he'd do that.'"

"She could be talking about one of her brothers," suggested Claire. "Maybe Flynn or Patrick did something abhorrent? Or her Uncle Phil?"

"Or maybe they hassled her one too many times for fresh towels this morning," said Ronnie. "I'm not sure this is even relevant."

"No, it's for something that happened years ago, back when they were at college together, I think. But you're right. Of course you're right. I'm just reading into it. Getting carried away like I always do."

Lynette was more intrigued by the notion that Fiona and Jacinta were old friends. "They seem such different *types*. I mean, one's a wheat baron's daughter, the other's basically making her bed."

"College does not guarantee a lifetime of wealth and privilege, Lynny," said Ronnie. "And perhaps Jacinta was there on a paid scholarship, or maybe she swapped careers, preferred hospitality."

"Anyway," said Alicia, "Jacinta fobbed us off, so hopefully we can get more out of Fiona at book club, which is in one hour, by the way." They all glanced at their watches. "So let's move on. Perry, you looked the most excited when you returned. What's the goss?"

He went to speak, but Claire flung her hand in the air and said, "I just need to quickly tell you something I discovered. Something Patrick told me."

Perry deflated but gallantly waved her on, and so she described her cryptic conversation with Patrick by the derelict swimming pool, and the club listened on, intrigued, aghast and in Missy's case teary-eyed.

"Oh, he sounds like the worst father ever," she said of Clay. "Poor Patrick. Knowing about the affairs, having to console his mum, and keeping it all to himself. That's too much for a little kid. It's *awful*."

"Yes, yes," said Claire, "but what do we think about Patrick's theory that Clay faked his disappearance and is holed up with some woman in Broken Hill?"

"I think it's a good theory to bandy about if you're a guilty man," said Alicia.

Claire exhaled. "Me too. But I thought I'd better mention

it. I mean, I believe what he says about his dad being a narcissist and running to the first woman he can find when he feels small or threatened. Clay did proposition Agnetha straight after the tense family meeting that first night, so that all fits. And he *might've* intended to catch up with some old flame in Broken Hill, but it doesn't change the fact that he's still missing. And it does seem rather odd that Patrick went out of his way to find me and spin me that sob story, begged me to stop investigating. But there's something else that muddies things a tad—"

"Nooo," whined Perry, bursting with his own news.

"I'm nearly done," she told him, pointing at the hat Ronnie had pilfered, which was now stored above her closet. "I think I know who left that."

She described how she saw the Dartmoors walking together in Cook and how one of them was missing his Akubra. "It was Flynn. He was hatless, and I think that's surprising. He's a farmer. Would be in the habit of wearing one outdoors."

Lynette frowned at that.

So did Perry. He said, "Okay, well, what I've just learned muddies things even further."

He then began to outline what Tag had told him, starting with the fact that he'd had "words" with Clay over drinks that fateful evening and finishing with the news that he was not the last person to see Clay alive. That honour goes to a woman. A flirty woman.

"*Flirty!*" he repeated in case they'd missed it.

That got their eyes boggling, and he grinned ghoulishly. "Forget the hat, I wonder if the culprit is a woman and, more exciting than that, a *lover* because I can't see any other reason a flirty woman would knock on a known sleaze's door in the wee hours of the morning."

~

Phillip Dartmoor was sitting in his own cabin just a few doors down, also thinking of Clay and his past conquests.

But he was recalling the misery his brother had wrought. How he'd broken Daisy's heart over and over, and not just her.

Scowling he stared down at the yellow notepad in his lap, at the names he'd scribbled, wondering if they could help. He crossed his legs. Groaned. Uncrossed them again. He was feeling guilty, useless, too, like he'd always been. A useless, baby brother.

That nosey book club woman had read him all wrong. She thought he was stronger... Better... Braver. If only she knew.

Sighing, he plucked a small photo from the back of the pad. A snapshot of him and Daisy at the old homestead. Was glad Ronnie hadn't found it when she'd barged in earlier. She'd have made more of a fuss even though the shot looked perfectly innocent. They weren't even touching. Just standing side by side, smiling coldly, staring at something to the right of the camera.

Probably Clay, he thought now. Who else could douse the warmth from a smile?

Ronnie was right about one thing though. Phillip did love Daisy... more, perhaps, than he should. So why did he never stick up for her? Or any of them? Why did he just stand by benignly when Clay picked at them and put them down and, worse, pitted them against each other? Why did he never stand up to the bully that was Clay?

No wonder Clay called him *Baby*...

And he wasn't the only one. Clay had nicknames for all of them. Daisy was Ditzy. Flynn was Dumbarse. Patrick was Sooky Paddy. And Fiona... Well, thankfully, he never did quite voice what he thought of his daughter. Didn't need to. It was in the curl of his top lip and the disdain in his glance. If Daisy didn't measure up, Fiona had no chance.

His mind returned to Daisy, and he winced now, remembering one Queen's birthday long weekend he'd stopped over at Dartmoor Downs and how she'd been running late getting back from the hairdressers in town. How she'd finally burst in, flushed and excited. Her pretty golden curls had been lopped off and straightened into a mod bob she called a pixie haircut. "Like Twiggy!" she'd announced, beaming.

She looked beautiful to Phillip, but Clay had erupted. Out of nowhere. Demanded she go into the bedroom and "fix it! Fix it now!" Like she'd dyed it pink and shaved it off.

Daisy had burst into tears and rushed out, and Phillip had just sat there like a useless lump, staring into the fire. No, worse than that, *smiling* into the fire, like they'd been discussing the weather.

Today they'd call it coercive control. Back then it was "just Clay".

He couldn't believe they'd all stuck it out for so long, especially Daisy. Wasn't at all surprised when she announced she had cancer. Because she'd been living with an insidious cancer for years, her sense of self corroded by a man who only knew how to love one person...

He shifted in his seat. Glanced out the window and scowled again. Hoped to God Clay was rotting out there somewhere, being picked at by stray animals. Didn't feel a jot of sympathy for the bloke. But he was worried. Real worried. And he was damned if he was going to let Clay keep eating away at the rest of them.

Not while there was now so much to smile about.

He tucked the photo away and turned back to the list he'd scribbled, circling the word *Gardener*...

# CHAPTER 19
## Surprise Revelations

The book club decided to compile a list of all the "flirty women" they could think of who would knock on Clay's door at such an indiscreet hour.

So far, the page was empty. It couldn't be any of the family, and they'd decided against Posey. She was brunette for a start and holidaying with her husband. Surely he'd notice if she'd slipped away that morning?

"It could've been anyone," said Missy. "I read that there are approximately two-hundred-and-forty passengers on this train and about forty staffers. Must be a lot of flirty blondes in the mix. Agnetha can't be the only one he tried his luck with."

"What *about* Agnetha?" said Perry, leaning forward as they all began to frown. "I'm not saying she was there to take up his offer, but maybe she was still steaming from his attempt and flirted her way in only to give him a piece of her mind. And, I don't know, things got ugly?"

Claire's jaw dropped. "You simply cannot believe that lovely young barwoman killed him."

He leaned back. Shook his head. "Not really. We can't even say that this early-morning visitor is the killer, can we? Flirty sounds friendly, not deadly. And it's like Ronnie said. It could've been about something entirely innocent. He could've booked an early wake-up or called for fresh towels…"

"How many towels do guests need?" asked Missy, confused, and they laughed at that.

But Ronnie wasn't laughing. She was staring hard at Perry. "We can't even be certain there *was* a visitor. I'm sorry,

I know you're rather fond of him, but Tag could very well be throwing you a line to protect himself."

Perry looked ready to dispute that, but Alicia had her pen up. "Okay, it's duly noted. Let's move on. Ronnie, did you manage to talk to the Gleesons?"

The older woman whipped her spectacles off and nodded. "Even managed to see a few happysnaps of their daughters, and I'm relieved to say, if we're sticking with the blonde motif, I don't believe there's a motive there at all. The Gleeson girls take after their father and have none of the 'Agnetha' about them."

She was being diplomatic, but Alicia understood and scratched them from her suspect list, then said, "Okay, so where does this leave us? We know Clay had a visitor about twenty minutes before he was thrown from the train. A flirty woman, but that's all we know. So we need to find out more." She glanced at Perry. "You need to talk to Tag again, see if he really is lying, or if not, what else he remembers. An accent? Any particular words, perhaps?"

Perry nodded, and she returned to her notes. "We know there was a lot of friction on the train that night and not just between Tag and Clay. We need to get the family to reveal more about that final meeting. See just how tense it got, and who was the tensest of all."

"We can check that with Fiona at book club," said Missy. "And Lynette, maybe you can pry some more out of Flynn at dinner tonight."

"How am I going to do that?" Lynette shot back. "Every mealtime he's huddled with his pack. They don't share tables, remember?"

"Ah, but they won't have a choice tonight. Not at Rawlinna, right?" Missy grinned, but they just stared at her blankly, so she reached for the Indian Pacific on-board magazine in Ronnie's magazine holder and flipped to a full-page picture of the guests dining around communal outdoor tables. "Did *nobody* read the itinerary before we left? It's an outback sheep station, peeps, and we all sit at these lovely, long tables under the stars. Sounds *divine*. But even better, it means they can't get away from us this time. They'll have to share, whether they want to or not."

That had them smiling, and Ronnie suggested they all split up and try to grab seats beside their respective suspects.

"Great idea," said Alicia, closing her journal and tapping her watch, "but right now we need to focus on just one."

By the time the book club got to the Explorer Lounge, the place was packed. There was a musician tucked into one corner, bellowing out a classic Aussie song, and half the room was chanting along—something about women glowing and men plundering.

"Blimey," said Missy, glancing around. "I should've thought to come earlier and save some seats. Didn't realise there was entertainment this arvo."

"*No*," gasped Perry, slapping a hand to his heart. "You didn't read the itinerary. Shocking!"

She stuck her tongue out at him while the others glanced around, surprised. The change in the bar was astonishing. From subdued clusters of two that first evening, the guests watching each other cautiously, now they were acting like one big gang, sharing stories across tables and singing and swaying in unison with the Men at Work cover.

"So what do we do?" asked Claire just as Fiona Dartmoor appeared from the adjoining doorway.

She took one look at the din and said, "Bugger this for a joke. Come on."

She led them into the dining car where Marvin was seated alone at a table, going through what looked like a staff roster. He glanced up as Fiona approached.

"Hey mate," she said like they were old buddies. "We're trying to run a book club, reckon we can hang here? It's not like you need to prep for dinner or anything right? Aren't we eating off train tonight?"

He glanced around and nodded heartily. "Of course you can. Help yourselves. As long as you don't mind me. I've got paperwork to get on with."

"No worries," she replied and then turned back to the

wide-eyed group. "Happy?"

The book club nodded, impressed by how proactive she was. That kind of confidence only came with wealth and power, thought Alicia, as they began to settle in across two tables.

But first she had a job for Lynette.

Using her sisterly code again, Alicia gave her a pointed look, then nodded back out and towards the bar. Lynette scowled, like she'd really rather not, but Alicia's look was now so spiky she knew better and followed her out.

As they stepped through the adjoining carriage doors, Alicia explained, "Agnetha's back at the bar. You should have a quiet word with her, girl to girl. Pretend Clay sleazed onto you too and see what she says."

"You seriously think Agnetha did this?"

"Not really, but it may be our only chance to check."

"Why can't you do it?"

Alicia scoffed, waving a hand between the two of them. "It'd be more convincing coming from you. Go on. Git!"

Lynette rolled her eyes as they continued through. After ordering a selection of tea from Agnetha, Alicia took the tray, then gave Lynette another subtle look before leaving her to it.

Lynette inhaled deeply, plastered a smile to her lips and turned towards the young bar woman.

~

When Alicia returned to the main group, no one seemed to notice that Lynette was missing. They were already in full swing, chatting about countesses and scarlet kimonos and whether a rattling train would really mask the noise of someone being stabbed twelve times in their bed, and it was clear which book they had chosen to focus on.

Good, thought Alicia, because we can use this.

"So what about the grander themes in *Murder on the Orient Express*, like vigilante justice and revenge?" she asked, keeping her voice light, her tone breezy as she distributed the cups. "Do we think it's ever okay to take justice into your own hands? Even if someone has done you wrong?"

Fiona smudged her lips downwards like she was giving it some thought while Missy fluttered her chipped nails in the air and said, "Oh we *always* talk about that when we do this one. I want to explore the other recurring motifs, like class and identity."

Alicia tried to give Missy one of her pointed looks—a look Lynette would comprehend—but the fool wasn't taking the hint as she rabbited on about the strict class structure in Christie's novels, how the servants are usually lesser characters, irrelevant, often overlooked.

"But in this book, they're front and centre. I mean, Princess Dragomiroff's German maid, Hildegarde what's-her-name, she's powerful don't you think? Just as pivotal to the plot as the chauffeur, the valet..."

Alicia smiled at her stiffly, her wide eyes imploring: *Shut up, shut up, shut up! I'm trying to get Fiona's take on the idea of revenge!* She wanted to know whether Fiona agreed that if someone does you wrong—say, disinherits you—you'd have every right to push them from a moving vehicle.

But now that she thought about it, now that she watched Fiona engage, Alicia couldn't quite wrap her head around that. Something didn't sit right. Fiona seemed too laid-back, too pragmatic for such hysteria. As she gulped her tea and nodded along, her face freckled, her laugh a genuine chortle, Fiona seemed like a regular country girl. Not a vengeful murderer.

But then... could you really tell anything about a person from a breezy book chat?

"Let's take a quick break," said Ronnie, struggling to her feet. "I need to use the facilities."

She made Perry scoot along so she could get out, then she added, "Don't say another word about the book until I get back. I don't want to miss a thing."

As she passed Alicia, Ronnie gave her a very gentle brush across the back, and that brush spoke volumes. This was *Alicia's* chance; Ronnie was handing it to her. Forget tricky words. Time for straight talking.

So she refilled their cups and said, "Any news on your dad yet, Fiona?"

Fiona shook her head, looking almost worried for the first time. "Hope he's okay."

"*Of course* you do," Alicia replied. "None of us really believe you wish him ill like you suggested when we first met, here in this carriage."

The others stared at Alicia aghast, worried she'd over-stepped, but Fiona just shrugged nonchalantly and said, "Yeah, well, my dad has a very special gift for pushing people's buttons, including mine. But it's all good now."

Alicia nodded, then prodded, "And you're cool with him giving Dartmoor Downs to your brother?"

That evoked a frown from Fiona. "News travels fast round these parts."

Alicia shrugged, also trying for nonchalance as Fiona shook her head and said, "Nah, mate, I'm not cranky about that. Flynn's worked bloody hard for Dad. While I was off partying at college, he had his head down, bum up, doing the hard yakka. So proud of my big brother. Top bloke."

That surprised Alicia, and she didn't know what to say, but then Missy surprised her even more by spotting the opening and saying, "Speaking of college, our lovely attendant Jacinta told us she knew you back then. Said you two were old buddies."

Fiona's eyes widened, and she looked up from her cup. "Old buddies?" She made a *pft* sound. "We were more than that. Jac and I had a massive crush on each other once."

That brought a whole new expression to Alicia's face.

~

Back at the bar, Lynette was struggling to work out how to broach the subject of Clay with Agnetha and do it discreetly. There was a steady stream of patrons, ordering all manner of drinks, including some very complicated-sounding cocktails that were keeping the bartender very busy.

That's when Lynette had an idea. "You don't need a hand back there, do you?"

Agnetha looked up from a shiny cocktail shaker. "You in the biz?"

She nodded. "I make a mean margarita, and my RSA is up to scratch."

Lynette was referring to her Responsible Service of Alcohol certificate, and Agnetha laughed.

"So sweet of you, but it's not allowed. I'll be fine."

Damn it, thought Lynette, glancing around. She couldn't just loiter here, looking like a spare wheel. Luckily, there was a small stand with used books nearby, and she grabbed one, plopping on a bar stool and pretending to read while she waited for her chance.

It came after about ten minutes. A middle-aged man had just ordered a wine, and he'd not only dropped a few dollars into Agnetha's tip jar, he'd added a flirty wink while he did it. It was another perfect segue, and Lynette closed her book and leaned in, conspiratorially whispering, "Looks like you get hit on as much as I do."

Agnetha laughed. "All just part of the job, right?"

"Sure," said Lynette, "but it can be seriously annoying. Especially when they're old and crusty."

Agnetha laughed again and reached for a cloth. "I'm not so fussed about the old ones; they're usually pretty harmless and they leave the best tips." She wiped the bench. "Doesn't really bother me. Bothers my partner though."

"I bet. It can't be easy knowing your girlfriend's alone on a train with rich guys having a crack."

"Oh, I'm not alone," said Agnetha just as two men approached the bar. They ordered beers and Agnetha nodded. As she flipped the lids off the bottles and began to pour them into chilled glasses, she told Lynette, "I'm really lucky. My partner also works here, on the Indian Pacific."

# CHAPTER 20
## Books, Looks and Musical Chairs

When Ronnie returned from the restroom, the book club looked like stunned mullets (as did Lynette when she'd passed the bar just now), and the elderly woman was delighted. Progress at last!

Before she could enquire further, however, Fiona said, "But enough about me, let's get this show back on the road, hey? Which actor do you reckon makes the best Poirot? Peter Ustinov? Kenneth Branagh? Or David Suchet?"

And so they had little choice but to return to the book—or the movies, rather, which is often where Christie discussions ended up. And before they knew it, the sun had dropped from the distant horizon, an inky darkness blotting out the view.

Marvin had long gone and the train was slowing down, like it was coming towards their next stop. As if to confirm it, Hana's voice suddenly crackled overhead: "Good evening folks, we're now approaching Rawlinna Station where we will be stopping for an outback dining experience." She proceeded to fill them in on the "former railway station, now the largest sheep station in Australia". That was an understatement. Rawlinna boasted something like sixty thousand sheep across more than a million hectares. That made Dartmoor Downs seem like a suburban block.

They all gasped and awed at the statistics, and then Alicia gasped again as she peered out of the window. She wondered how they could possibly be dining out there, quite literally in the middle of nowhere—when she caught sight of twinkling lights ahead.

And soon they were pulling into what looked like an

outback wonderland. Alicia spied an old railway station, lit up with roaring firepits and two rows of timber tables, flickering hurricane lamps on top. And above it all, a million twinkling stars.

"Okay folks, time to call this book club to order," said Ronnie as they gathered their things. "Special thanks to Fiona for joining us."

Fiona thanked them in turn, then they all made their way back to their carriage, a skip in their steps.

As they passed the bar, Alicia saw that Agnetha was still busily cleaning up, but Lynette had vanished. She hoped that didn't signal disappointment, but when she got to her cabin, her sister was bursting with news.

"You won't believe it. Agnetha's partner's also on this train, and guess who it is?"

Alicia took a moment and said, "It's not Jacinta, is it?"

That wiped the glee from Lynette's face. "What? Our attendant? No, where'd you get that idea from? No, no, Agnetha's shagging Arlo! You know? Arlo who works in the Platinum carriage." Then she reached for a black leather biker jacket and said, "Oh, and Agnetha says it's colder than you expect. Temps drop right down after dark."

Alicia grabbed her cashmere wrap and raised her eyebrows. "So Agnetha goes out with Arlo. Why are we excited?"

"Because it's just changed everything. We could be looking in completely the wrong direction. Maybe Arlo is the key."

"Sweet Arlo? Really?"

Lynette scoffed. "Sweet my foot." She dabbed some organic perfume balm behind her ears, then handed it to her sister. "Think about it—Arlo has been at the centre of this from the moment Clay went missing. He's the person who told everyone that Clay got off safely in Broken Hill. He's the one who pretended to tick his name off. Makes you wonder, right?"

Alicia nodded slowly. Yes, oddly it did. She sniffed the

balm—mmmm, smelled just like a tropical beach—then gave her wrists a dab, wondering if Arlo wasn't quite as sweet as he appeared.

~

While the passengers congregated in the corridor, awaiting disembarkation, Ronnie gave Perry the nod and pulled him back into her cabin. She was done with waiting.

"Easy tiger," he said as she secured the door behind them. "You know you're not my type, right?"

She shook her ivory-grey bob impatiently. "What happened during book club while I was at the loo? Because I know something happened. You all looked gobsmacked."

"We *were* gobsmacked. You mightn't be my type, Ronnie, but you could very well be Fiona's."

As confusion caused chaos with her wrinkled brow, he explained, "According to Ms Dartmoor, she and Jacinta were more than just college buddies, they were *lovers*."

Now Ronnie had the stunned mullet expression. "No!"

"No, I'm exaggerating. They were just friends, she claims it was very innocent, but they had a crush on each other. She was very clear on that. Says things might've heated up until someone put a stop to it."

"Clay," Ronnie said, and it was not a question. It was in keeping with the kind of character they were uncovering. "So what happened? Did she say?"

"Yes! Told us all about it. Well, some of it. Said she brought Jacinta back to hers one semester break, right? To hang out at the farm, ride a few horses, all very *Little House on the Prairie*. But then Daddy Dearest must've given some vibes or something because she says Jacinta backed right off and that was that."

"Vibes?"

"Yeah, she didn't go into it. Just said, 'You know how protective dads can get?' She made light of it, like it was no biggie, but…"

"But you wonder whether Fiona was holding a grudge against her dad for it. All these years later? Sounds a little unlikely."

He held up a finger. "Except Fiona's grudge wasn't years old—it was fresh. She told us she bumped into Jacinta on this train—*hadn't seen her since college*—and they got talking. *That's* when Jacinta explained everything." His eyebrows nudged up and down excitedly. "Makes you wonder. About *both* of them, right? Did Jacinta lash out when she ran into Clay? Furious with him for ruining her chance with his wealthy daughter? Did Fiona? I mean, imagine how angry you'd be, finding out after all these years that your dad might've sabotaged your first chance of love."

"And Fiona told you all of this? Apropos of nothing?"

"Well, Missy asked the right question, surprisingly. But yeah, Fiona just blurted it out." He smiled giddily. "Shocked the shirts off us too. You should duck to the loo more often, Ronnie, she opened right up."

Perry was joking, but he made a good point. Ronnie was the elder in the group, the same generation as Fiona's father, so it was understandable that the young woman would feel less comfortable discussing it in her presence. *Not* that she had any reason to, of course.

"Rightio, so where does this leave us?" Ronnie asked.

Perry pointed out the window, to the stream of passengers now sweeping past on the dirt platform below and jumped up. "It leaves *me* wanting to get out there and nab a seat next to Fiona, bond with her over the hardships of coming out. I might be able to gauge just how angry she was with Daddy Dearest that night and whether it was *Fiona* that Tag heard knock at his door early that morning, putting on a fake voice, ready to wreak revenge."

Then he stopped at the door. "Problem is, I need to speak to Tag about that too. See if he knows more."

"Stick to Fiona," said Ronnie, grabbing a shawl. "I still wonder whether Tag has an ulterior motive. I just don't trust the fellow, and I'm sorry Perry, but I don't trust you to see through him. Leave him to one of us."

He rolled his eyes. "Fine. I'll go back to plan A or should I say plan LGBTQIA."

Perry had left his run too late. By the time he and Ronnie joined the al fresco dinner crowd, most had settled into the wooden bench seats along the tables, including Fiona who was already surrounded by fellow guests, as were her family. The rest of book club were also seated, at the other end of the dusty platform, on the second long table, and Missy gave him a disappointed wave as he caught her eye.

She had saved him and Ronnie some spots, but this was not how it was supposed to go. They were supposed to be splitting up! He cursed Ronnie for causing their tardiness as they made their way across.

The dinner that evening was more rustic than their previous meals but equally delicious. It starred platters of barbecued lamb and vegetables and was followed by a mouth-watering chocolate mousse. But Perry figured they'd probably enjoy Vegemite sandwiches in this star-spangled desert setting.

Across the shimmering lamps, Perry spotted Tag about six people down and tried to grab his eye, but he was deep in conversation with a woman on his left.

"This was on my bucket list," murmured an elderly man to Perry's right.

"Oh yes?" he said, watching as he dribbled some thick gravy onto his lamb.

"Have wanted to visit Rawlinna for years, finally managed to find the time. How about you lot? Family group or...?" His tone was doubtful as his eyes swept across Missy and Claire, who were seated opposite and looked nothing alike.

"Book club," said Perry.

"Ah, now *that* makes more sense." The man sounded almost relieved, like he'd been trying to work it out for days. "You're certainly a motley crew."

"That's one term for us," Perry replied drolly.

He wasn't really in the mood for small talk, was still grumpy he wasn't getting any investigation time. They were due in Perth in less than twenty hours and were more muddled than ever!

"And mates with the Dartmoors I see," the man continued. Perry glanced up as he said it, and he explained, "Just that I saw you with Fiona earlier this arvo. She in your club is she?"

Perry half shrugged as he reached for a pepper grinder. "Oh, she's just a special guest. We only just met her on this trip. You know the Dartmoors?"

The man took the grinder Perry was offering and said, "Everybody knows the Dartmoors, mate, at least they do in WA." He ground some pepper onto his lamb, then reached a hand to shake Perry's. "David Jules is the name. Used to knock about with one of their cousins many moons ago. He had some stories I can tell you!" Then he chuckled again and turned away, not telling Perry anything as he called out to a man further down the table, "Hey, Johnno! How'd you go in Cook? Spot any of the ghosts you were hoping for?"

As they launched into a hearty discussion of the haunting outpost, Perry darted a quick look at Missy and gave her an excitable wink.

Missy wasn't sure why Perry's eye was twitching, but she was feeling twitchy too. This was not how this dinner was supposed to unfold! She had tried her hardest to nab seats next to the Dartmoors but somehow found herself herded to the opposite table, along with all the book club. She had a hunch Marvin was deliberately keeping the two groups apart, and she didn't really blame him, the poor sausage!

Several of the staff were looking stressed tonight and not just Marvin. Earlier she'd caught sight of Hana, the Journey Manager, and she was speaking into what looked like a satellite phone, a hand at her brow like she could not believe what she was hearing.

What had they discovered, Missy wondered. And how could she possibly find out?

"You look worried," came a chirpy voice beside her. "I hope it's not catchy?"

Missy glanced around to find three passengers to her left all staring at her, smiling. When they'd taken their seats earlier, they'd politely nodded hello but proceeded to converse amongst themselves, like old friends, and so she'd left them to it. But as Missy began to chat to them now, assuring them she was fine and asking them about themselves, she realised she was quite mistaken. In fact, they had only just met.

"We're all in the solo cabins," one of them declared. "Bonded by the loo, of all places."

They laughed at that and then introduced themselves properly as "Sara the pilot, Paul the flight attendant and Brenda the lawyer".

"Three professionals, one mission," said Brenda. "We're here to enjoy ourselves!"

Missy had laughed along at that and was soon swept up in their chatter. All three had been in Sydney for leisure when they jumped aboard, they told her.

"Squeezing a holiday in before we get back to the grindstone," Paul explained. "I've just been promoted to purser, Brenda here has made partner at Gardner Legal, and as for Sara…"

They all turned to look at the pilot, who gave them a quick salute and said, "I'm now officially a captain. Flying that plane right through the glass ceiling, baby!"

They cheered at that, and Missy cheered along, glancing across to Lynette, hoping to bring her in on this. *Her* career was soaring too, but she seemed lost in her thoughts, slowly chewing her food, frowning. Missy wondered about that. Why *wasn't* Lynette boasting more about her successes, like these three? Why did she seem so down? So *despondent?*

That's when Missy noticed that Ronnie was missing from the chair beside Lynette. As the three new pals continued yabbering, this time about hilarious office Christmas parties, Missy looked around and soon spotted Ronnie, striding across the platform, past the lively musician to where several of the staffers had congregated, Hana amongst them.

Missy continued watching as Hana broke away from the

group and began to speak to Ronnie. There was much shaking of heads and scratching of brows.

Whatever they had discovered, it was clear, even from this distance, that it was not good news for the Dartmoor family. Or at least for Clay.

Alicia was also checking out the staffers, but it was Arlo she was looking for, and he was nowhere to be seen. Good. She suspected he was using this opportunity to prepare the Platinum cabin beds while the passengers were preoccupied dining—setting them up, dropping chocolates on the pillows, switching on the low lighting. And that meant she could grab him alone.

Alicia had some fresh questions to ask Arlo. Well, actually, Lynette did, but Alicia felt like her sister had done a lot of the heavy lifting so far and decided to do it herself. Besides, Lynny was too busy enjoying the meal, trying to discern the precise ingredients used to marinate the lamb—was there a touch of lemon myrtle in there or was that lemon zest?

Alicia couldn't care less. She cared more for mystery, and right now there was one man at the centre of it. So she hid her wrap below the table, jumped up and made a show of being chilly—crossing her arms and rubbing her hands up and down her forearms—then mumbled something about getting a jumper and slipped away.

Head down, hands in her pockets, Alicia strode swiftly down the platform, back towards her carriage, then continued on towards Platinum. That's when someone called out to her.

*Of course* they did. Breaking into Platinum was like trying to access the Green Room at the Oscars!

"Everything okay?"

She turned to see an unfamiliar attendant trailing her down the platform. Alicia did her cold dance again and said, "Just grabbing an extra layer."

"That's fine, ma'am," he called back. "I just need your name and cabin number!"

Alicia quickly told him, then reached for the nearest doorway and flung herself aboard, hoping he wouldn't follow. And he didn't.

Exhaling, she looked around, realising she was between the Platinum lounge bar and its accommodation carriage. Another sigh of relief as she swept the adjoining door open and made her way through. Once inside, the first thing she noticed was a whooshing sound coming from an open doorway. She tiptoed closer and saw Walker with his back to the corridor, vacuuming, so she quickly stepped past and onwards. The doors of the next two cabins were closed, but the final one was open, and she could see Arlo in there, plumping a pillow. Bingo.

Leaning across the doorway, Alicia said, "Hey Arlo, can I have a word?"

The young worker looked up, surprised, half smiled, half frowned, his eyes darting out to the corridor as though checking for his boss. Or perhaps he was looking for backup.

Alicia said, "I know you're busy. I just want to ask you some questions."

He held up the pillow like it was a metal shield. "I'm truly sorry, but we're not allowed to talk to anybody—"

"Yeah, but I'm not just anybody, am I? I'm the one who saw Clay Dartmoor fall from the train, so I think I have a right to demand some answers."

He dropped the shield. "I... I don't know what I can tell you though. I mean... I don't really know anything. I did hear that the car companies came back with bad news. Mr Dartmoor didn't hire anything in Broken Hill. I think that's what Hana said."

"Yeah, see I'm not here to ask about that. I want to ask about your girlfriend."

Then she stepped inside and closed the door behind her.

Arlo looked doubly surprised now, and she wasn't sure if it was the door closing or the mention of Agnetha. Alicia didn't really want to be stuck in here with a potential killer, but she couldn't risk Walker finding her and turfing her out again.

"Everything good?" he asked.

She nodded. "But it wasn't so good the other night when Clay Dartmoor hit on Agnetha while she was working the bar. He pushed his room key on her; she was pretty pissed off."

Arlo frowned like he wasn't following, then there was a flicker of anger or disgust or something, so she added, "Were you pissed off too?"

"What?" He reached a hand to his face. Began picking at his skin. "How do you mean?"

"I mean, were you angry with Clay Dartmoor? Did you and Agnetha go and confront him about it, very early that next morning before the rest of the staff were up? Did something happen?"

She raised one hand, applied her gentlest tone. Hoped to God she hadn't made a fatal error, closing that cabin door. "I'm sure you didn't mean any harm, Arlo. You were just trying to protect your girl's honour. I don't think anyone would blame you."

Arlo had dropped onto the bed he'd just made, his eyes staring down at his lap. He didn't seem to notice that she'd just accused him of manslaughter at best. In fact, he seemed oddly relieved. When he turned back to look at her, he was almost smiling.

"Mr Dartmoor hit on Agnetha? Wow. What a freakin' sleaze." Then he shook his head and looked out of the window. "Now I don't feel so guilty that I stuffed up the roll call. I hope he *is* lost out there. The dirtbag."

~

It took until coffee and tea were being served for Perry to get his dinner companion's full attention again. As David Jules handed over the milk jug, Perry said, "So tell me about the Dartmoor cousins. Are you all still close?"

He shook his head. "Nah, my family moved away after high school, and of course I was never mates with Clay and Phil. They were an exclusive mob that lot, older and, like I said, a bit intimidating. Clay especially. The scariest of the Three Bears."

"Three bears?" said Perry.

"Yeah, that's what we called 'em. Clay was Big Bear of course, and some buddy I can't remember, he was Middle Bear, and then there was Baby Bear." He nodded his head towards the first table where the Dartmoors were seated, to the man who was slouched over, silently sipping from his cup, looking more like a teddy bear than a grizzly.

"*Phillip?*" That caught Perry by surprise. "Phillip and Clay were close as kids?"

It surprised Perry only because he had a brother too, and they had not wanted a bar of each other before the age of twenty. Were like chalk and cheese before then. And for some reason Perry assumed the same of Phillip and Clay, who seemed less chalk and cheese and more feather and flint, Clay being the flint of course.

"Oh, they were thick back then," the man was saying. "I'm surprised they're still mates *now*, was shocked to see them together on this train to be honest. Just glad it didn't wreck their relationship."

"What do you mean? What didn't wreck their relationship?"

"Hm?" The man shrugged. "You know, the way their old man divided them like that—giving Clay the Downs and turfing Phil out. Of course none of us were surprised about *that*. Clay always came out on top. That's why we called him Big Bear—and not just 'cause he was taller and scarier. But also 'cause he got all the best grades, the trophies in sport, the girl they were fighting over, and Dartmoor Downs, of course. The jewel in the crown."

But Perry didn't hear that last bit. He was stuck on *the girl they were fighting over.*

His mind darted back to the cutely freckled, sponge-cake-baking wife.

# CHAPTER 21
## Uncomfortable Conversations

The book club were feeling antsy. Dinner was over, the passengers were all back aboard, and the train was on its final leg, nonstop through the night and on to the westerly city of Perth, where they were due to arrive the following afternoon.

This had some of them panicked because they were still no closer to working out whodunnit, let alone how and why. They were now standing in a huddle at one end of the carriage, whispering between themselves. With the beds made up, it was impossible to fit into Ronnie's cabin, so it meant they had to congregate in the corridor and keep their voices low, one eye out for passing revellers. Or, more specifically, the Dartmoors, whose rooms were nearby.

"Hana put on a good act, but she's obviously very worried," Ronnie told them of her post-dinner chat with the Journey Manager.

She confirmed what Arlo had told Alicia—that all calls to hire car companies had come back negative. As did checks with the local hotels, Ronnie added.

"Patrick must have told Hana his suspicions, but there's no sign of the man and his supposed lover." Ronnie tsked, showing them what she thought of that theory. "The train drivers from the first leg—the leg in question—do not recall the door alarm sounding, so she's not sure what to make of that, but she's gone into emergency mode, nonetheless. The police have been alerted, and search parties are making their way to the area of track before Broken Hill where Alicia saw him fall off." Her eyes darted between the sisters. "Hana says the authorities are going to need to talk to you two. Wants you to stay behind when we get to Perth."

Alicia nodded, glanced at her watch and said, "Okay, so that leaves us sixteen hours."

Then she proceeded to describe her chat with the young attendant Arlo. "I don't think he did it," she told them. "He seemed genuinely surprised to hear that Clay hit on Agnetha, like it was news to him. Was angry, too, but more at himself for wasting time worrying about the guy."

"Agnetha probably didn't tell him to spare his feelings," said Claire. "It's not something you'd rub in your boyfriend's face is it? And it probably happens often. I really can't see how something so trivial would lead to murder."

Alicia chewed on her lower lip. "True. I'm just getting desperate."

"I might have an angle," said Perry, now filling them in on his dinner companion's gossip. "I'm boomeranging back to Phillip Dartmoor as our prime suspect because I know what it's like with brothers. They can be fiercely competitive; hold on to stuff forever. And from what my new mate David Jules tells me, Phil had a lot to let go of. Big Bear got the family farm, he got all the accolades at school and... wait for it... he got *the girl they were both fighting over*, whom I can only assume is Daisy."

He glanced at Ronnie, who had visibly drooped.

"Another lie then," she said. "That man insisted he was never interested in Clay's wife like that. Was quite adamant about it last time we spoke."

"Yeah, but Phillip's hardly going to confess his love for his brother's deceased wife to a nosey old biddy is he?" said Lynette.

Ronnie raised an arched eyebrow. "Thanks a lot, Lynny. I'll take that as a compliment, shall I?"

Lynette smiled to show she was joking, while the others agreed Phillip was the best candidate. He had plenty of motive, all of it laced with a lifetime of resentment and envy. And he confessed to being in his brother's carriage that morning.

"I've been thinking about why Phillip might've hung around for an hour or more," Alicia told them now. "I saw the body fall just before five, right? And he was ticked off the carriage at Broken Hill around six thirty. Maybe he spent that time cleaning Clay's cabin. Maybe that's where Clay was killed, and the place was a shambles or a bloodbath or something, and Phillip had to set it straight. It's a possibility, right?"

"An icky one," said Missy, nose scrunched up. "So why was *Flynn's* hat left in Clay's cabin then? And where does this leave his flirty visitor? The woman Tag heard. How does all that fit in?"

"Red herrings?" suggested Alicia. "We haven't really confirmed it's Flynn's Akubra, and for all we know the flirty woman was visiting a different cabin entirely. Tag never actually saw her. He just heard her."

They all exhaled heavily at that, and Claire said, "Bring on Perth!"

Perry was the only one looking lively. "Come on, folks. This isn't over yet. We need to get our butts back out there."

Ronnie groaned. "This butt is exhausted. I'm escorting it to bed."

Claire concurred. "Sorry, Perry. I'm tapping out too. Let's tackle it again in the morning."

"And if we hit the sack now, we could make some progress on our books," added Missy. "Take our minds off it."

Like anything—even the world's greatest mystery writers—could distract them tonight.

As they disbanded and made their way down the corridor to their respective cabins, Perry pulled the Finlays aside. "I'm sneaking into the bar for a bit, see what I can see."

"I admire your energy," said Alicia. "What do you expect to find?"

"Don't know, but I can't rest while there's a murderer running loose."

"Cripes," said Alicia. The very thought made her want to duck for her room.

Not Lynette though. "I'll come with you," she said.

"I agree. We need to hunt down the killer while we can."

Alicia waved them off worriedly, then wondered if it was the killer they were hunting or their new love interests, and she felt another prickle of trepidation because both Tag and Flynn had not officially been scrapped from the suspect list, so they could very well be one and the same.

~

Ronnie felt as old and dusty as the shadowy desert beyond the track, and she sighed wearily as she sat on her single bed, reaching for the chocolate on her pillow, thinking of her darling husband, long gone now of course. Bert would have loved this journey. Every little bit.

And she envied Alicia, starting out on her own journey with Liam Jackson, everything ahead of them, everything sparkling with hope and promise. As she nibbled away, her mind drifted then to the Dartmoors, to Clay and Daisy. Their bank balance certainly sparkled, but had there ever been hope and promise? There must have been once. Why else would Daisy choose Clay when Phillip seemed the kinder, sweeter choice? Was she bedazzled by all that sparkle?

She shook her head. If so, she was a silly, silly girl.

Ronnie knew more than most the lengths that people would go to get their share of a pie that wasn't always worth devouring. She had watched her own family destroy themselves over property and possessions, just as the Dartmoors appeared to be doing. It wasn't worth it, she wanted to tell them. Not really. One day, hundreds of years from now, someone like Tag was going to be picking through their remains, and who owned what simply wouldn't matter.

Of course, it was easy for her to say that. She was a very wealthy woman, thanks to her Bert. But it wasn't his money that made her happy. It was his love. His support. Their adventures together.

Sighing again, she popped the wrapper in the bin and

stepped into the small bathroom, glancing at the compact facilities. She really wanted to take a shower but wasn't sure she had the energy to tackle it all again as she had done that morning. Perhaps she should do as Iris suggested and grab her bath bag and towel and wander on down to the communal bathrooms?

And that's when Ronnie remembered Clay's cabin and gasped at her wide-eyed reflection.

*Oh, how stupid she'd been!*

There *was* a monogrammed hanky in his room after all. They just hadn't realised it at the time. And now it made sense why that person was lurking…

Yes, there could only be one reason.

One person…

She dashed out of the bathroom, feeling as energetic as a new bride.

~

If Perry and Lynette were really in search of Tag and Flynn, they were in for some disappointment. The bar was packed with revellers, but neither man was present, although they did spot Fiona wedged in a corner seat, scrolling through her phone, an empty beer by her side. She looked different tonight. Softer. She had replaced the checked cowboy shirt with a cuddly green jumper and had a slick of lipstick on, her lovely golden-red curls freed from their usual ponytail, draping her shoulders like a decorative curtain.

The fact that Fiona was here in the bar, away from her pack, was also unusual, and the two book club members swapped a surprised smile.

Then Lynette said, "You try your luck with her. I've got another plan."

As she turned back, Perry carefully made his way across.

"You're not with your usual crew," he said when Fiona looked up.

"My sibs? Nah, we just had some bad news from the train manager, so they're hiding out in their rooms."

"We heard," said Perry. "I'm so sorry. It's not sounding good."

She nodded. Shrugged. "Anyway, Jac's offered to help me drown my sorrows in a bit. But I could do with some company now if you wanna pull up a pew?"

"I do," said Perry. "Let me grab some drinks first."

While he fetched himself a gin and tonic and a fresh beer for Fiona, Lynette made her way back to Ronnie's compartment. She was just reaching her door when Ronnie came bursting out, catching them both by surprise.

"Where are you off to in such a hurry?" Lynette asked.

Ronnie replied, "I need to see a woman about a bag. You?"

Lynette glanced past Ronnie and into her cabin. "I need to see a man about a hat."

~

Perry suspected that Fiona was not as relaxed about her dad's disappearance as she made out, and after a few sips of their drinks, he pressed her on it.

She shrugged. "Just because my dad is... prickly... doesn't mean I don't love him."

"Of course," he said, thinking, and just because you love him doesn't mean you didn't kill him. Love and hate danced awfully close at times. "Did he ever accept your..." How to say this tactfully?

"Gayety?" she said, half smiling. "Who knows? We never discussed it."

"Ah, the old 'Don't ask. Don't tell'."

She raised her beer in the air. "Got it in one." Her tone was as bitter as her brew.

"Do you think your dad's vibe..." Again, how to put this... "Um, well, broke up what you might've had with Jacinta. Back at Ag College?"

She looked at him like he was thick. "Course it did. She *said* it did. And it was more than a vibe, mate. I was just being discreet. Dad always stressed that. Never give anything away—to the community, the press, whoever. They'll all twist it. Use it for their own means. 'Head up, kids, eyes front and centre!'" She'd deepened her voice to mimic her dad, but he sounded more like a drill sergeant. "'What they don't know for sure, they can't use against you!'" She tsked. "Like the whole world was out to get us."

"Nice way to grow up," said Perry, and she shrugged like she was used to it. "So what happened with Jacinta?" he prodded, quickly adding, "I'm not the press, Fiona. Not interested in using or twisting anything."

Which wasn't strictly true, but she bought it. Nodded. Said, "Oh, Dad was quite brutal apparently." She shook her head and looked out at the gliding darkness. "I'm so embarrassed. Never says a word to me, right? But somehow thinks it's cool to pull my friend aside and give her an earful."

She shook her head and gulped back more of the beer. Perry thought perhaps she was finished, but then she exhaled heavily and continued. "It was the morning we returned to college. I'll never forget it. We'd just packed up. Mum was about to do the long drive to the train station. Dad took Jac aside and was shaking her hand for ages. Smiling the whole time. I thought he was thanking her for helping out, feeding the chooks and dogs and stuff, or maybe thanking her for putting up with me." She scoffed at herself, her tangled red curls falling across her eyes. "Turns out he was doing quite the opposite."

Perry winced. "It was ugly?"

"You could say that, but only on his part. He called her a freak. Can you believe it? Told her it was *unnatural*, like being gay was so much worse than being a miserable, cheating…" She caught herself, smudged her glossy lips together. Took a loud breath. "Anyway, he told Jac to stay away from me. 'Tell no one about Fiona, or I'll destroy you.'"

"*I'll destroy you?*" Perry repeated. "That's a tad *Dynasty* isn't it?"

She nodded, her eyes fiery. "Exact words, Jac says.

No wonder she went cold on me the second we got back on the train to college. I blamed myself, thought I'd done something wrong. Then I blamed her. Hated her for years. When all along, it was him. And I never understood why."

"Until you got on *this* train and ran into Jacinta again."

She sneered. "I gave up everything for the farm, for Dad, for his precious bloody reputation. I kept my head up and gave them nothing to use or twist. I did that for *him*. And what do I get in return?" Her lips smudged downwards again. "Not so much as a back paddock." She was talking about the inheritance.

"I thought you were happy for Flynn."

Her eyes shot up. There was another flash of anger. "I was. I *am*. It's just... I dunno. I'm just disappointed." She offered a small smile. Then her voice turned wistful, her eyes watery. "Sure, it was young love, might not have lasted a month, Jac and me, but that was none of his business. That was for us to find out. He had no bloody *right*."

Perry reached for her hand, but she pulled it away and produced a tissue from her jumper sleeve. A bedraggled one, like these weren't the first tears she'd spilt over this. And he was reminded of the characters from his Christie novel *The Mystery of the Blue Train*, of the wealthy father who wants his daughter's partner out of the way. Rightly or wrongly, it was none of his bloody business either, and yet it soon turned bloody.

Was that what happened here?

He glanced around and back. Said very softly, very gently, "How did that make you feel, Fiona? Towards your father?"

She tucked the tissue away and glared at him. "How do you think it made me feel, mate? I wanted to hunt the turd down and run this train over him."

## CHAPTER 22
### Revealing Conversations

Ronnie knocked on the door of cabin three and waited. There was a murmur from within, and then Posey Dartmoor pulled the heavy door open, one pencilled eyebrow arched high. She was dressed in what Ronnie could only assume was loungewear, a ribbed, three-piece outfit in silvery grey with a tank top, drawstring pants and long, flowing cardigan, all of which hugged her curves like clingwrap.

"I'm dreadfully sorry to be such a nuisance," said Ronnie, channelling her best Miss Marple. "I'd ask my friends, but no one appears to be in their rooms, and this nail really is very annoying. I'm not one for manicures, you see, although I know they're all the rage with you lovely young people. Oh, and look at *your* nails! So perfect. I do find young people care so much more about their nails than my generation ever—"

"What can I help you with?" the woman said, cutting through, her tone more bored than anything.

"Who is it, babes?" came Patrick's voice behind her, and Posey waved one of those manicured hands back at him.

"Just one of the passengers," she called back, then said to Ronnie, "What do you need?"

"Nail file, please. That'll do it. Just need to get rid of this pesky bit."

"Oh. Right. Sorry, didn't bring one."

"Yeah, you did, honey," came Patrick's voice again. "There's one in your bath bag."

Posey offered a polite smile. "Sorry," she said again. "Can't help you."

She went to close the door, and Ronnie quickly said,

"That's a pity dear. I guess I could head to Clay's cabin and see if I can find one there. I noticed a lovely purple-striped bath bag in there just yesterday." She'd lowered her voice for this, kept her tone casual, but Posey's smile stiffened considerably as Ronnie hoped it would. It had been a bit of a guess, really, but who else would have such a lairy bath bag and wear Black Opium? Certainly not Daisy, by all accounts!

Ronnie lowered her voice even further. "I don't want to cause any trouble. Make an excuse and come to cabin eight."

Then she walked away while Posey's smile turned rigor mortis.

~

While Ronnie was freaking out the woman in cabin three, Lynette was surprising the man next door. When he opened his door, she held up the Akubra and said, "Hello again, Flynn. This yours by any chance?"

Flynn was still dressed in the jeans and chambray shirt she'd seen him in at dinner, but the shirt was untucked and the top buttons undone. His hair was tufted up like he'd been running his hands through it, and his eyes seemed a little glassy.

Had he been crying, she wondered?

Despite the rumple, he still smelled terrific. Like money, and lots of it.

He glanced from her to the hat and back, confused, then he grabbed it and said, "Yeah, thanks. Where'd you find it?"

"In your dad's compartment," she told him, watching his reaction.

He frowned with confusion, followed fast by suspicion. "What were you doing in—"

"It's a long story," she said, cutting him off. "The question is, why were *you* in there the morning he disappeared?"

Now Flynn just looked annoyed. "He's my dad, Lynette. I had every right to be in there. But I wasn't." She cocked her head to one side, her hair falling across her shoulder, looking sceptical so he added, "I never went into Dad's room. Couldn't even tell you which one it is. Why? What's going on?"

"And yet you left your hat in there," she said, ignoring his question.

"No, I didn't. Can't have."

"So where'd you leave it?"

"Can't remember."

She rolled her big green eyes at him, and for one worrying moment she thought he was going to slam the door on her.

But then he dropped the hat on his head, leaned against the doorframe and smiled. "So you *really* do think I did this. I'm still your number one mystery man."

That caught her by surprise. She offered a coy smile of her own, flicked the hair from her shoulder. "You're still on the list, sure."

"*List?*" He laughed. "So I've got competition, hey?" He stood back and opened his door wide. "Why don't you come in, Lynette, and tell me more about this *list*. Hmm? Maybe I can help knock it into shape for you."

The man's tone was playful, flirty, and she felt her legs turn to jelly. She shrugged as nonchalantly as she could, and he opened the door wider to reveal a bottle of clear spirits by the bed, a half-filled glass beside it. "Too many busybodies in the bar," he told her. "But I really don't like to drink alone."

Then he stepped back from the door and she hesitated for all of two seconds, knowing Alicia would kill her as she said, "Sure, don't see why not."

And in she went.

~

Was that Lynette's voice Alicia could hear out in the corridor? She considered getting up, checking for herself, but was now so engrossed in her Agatha Christie novel she wasn't sure she wanted to. She'd done exactly as Missy suggested and changed into her cotton PJs, tucked herself into the snug bunk bed and got reading, and before she knew it, she was back in St Mary Mead, in Miss Marple's parlour, clicking away at her knitting, her brain clicking away with her.

"There's something so anonymous about a train," Miss Marple says to young Lucy in the book. "If he'd killed her in the place where she'd lived, or was staying, somebody might have noticed him come or go. Or if he'd driven her out in the country somewhere—"

Alicia stopped reading and thought, *But this train isn't anonymous. Or at least, the Dartmoors aren't. Half the passengers seemed to recognise the wealthy family, and it wasn't just that. There were people on the lookout that night, people who might have noticed the killer and not even realised it!*

She threw the bedcovers off. Sat up.

What was she doing, lying here, cosily reading a book? This was her last chance to ask them. Her last chance to find out! That's when she, too, found her second wind.

~

Ronnie had barely been back in her room five minutes when there was a soft knock on her door. She smiled and opened it.

"Hello again, thank you so much for joining me," she said as Posey glared back at her before storming past and into the cabin. She got to the window, turned and folded her arms over her ample cleavage.

"I'm not sure what game you're playing," Posey grumbled, "but my family is going through some heavy shit right now, and I don't appreciate these bizarre insinuations."

"Then allow me to explain. Have a seat."

"No, thanks. I'll remain standing."

Ronnie shrugged. Dropped down onto the bed. "I would like to know if you own a purple bath bag and if it's the same bath bag we found in Clay Dartmoor's cabin after he vanished."

Posey's body tensed and she tightened her arms further. "Don't know what you're talking about."

"There's no use denying it, Posey," Ronnie told her. "We saw you. Perry and I. Second night on the train, just outside Clay's room. You were trying to retrieve it. Hide the fact that you were in there."

Now the younger woman looked worried. Really worried. Her arms dropped, and she pulled her cardigan tightly around her body. "But it's not what you think."

Ronnie said, "I think you used your bath bag as a prop very early that first morning on the train, pretending you were heading to the shared bathrooms when, in fact, you were paying your father-in-law a visit. All so your husband would not suspect a thing."

Iris mentioned the communal bathrooms to Ronnie over their first meal, and she realised now that it would make a very good ruse, a perfectly reasonable excuse for wandering the train at all hours.

Posey blinked. "Oh." Blinked again. "Then it is what you think. But there's an innocent explanation."

"Good," said Ronnie, tapping the mattress beside her. "Let's hear it, dear."

Posey hesitated for a moment, then slumped onto the bed. Cleared her throat, appeared to be sorting out her thoughts. Eventually she said, "Okay, yes, I did go to Clay's room early that morning. He's always up before the crack of dawn. I knew he'd be awake. I didn't want to miss my chance because I also knew he was getting off, and it might be my last. But like I said, it was perfectly innocent." She glanced up at Ronnie and suddenly glowered. "Don't give me that look. It *was*!"

Ronnie didn't realise she'd been frowning, so she rearranged her face and said, "I'm not here to judge, Posey. I just want the truth."

"The truth is I'm not Clay's type. Not one bit. Didn't mean we didn't enjoy a harmless flirt occasionally, but that's all it was, and that's all I was doing that morning. Trying to make Clay see reason."

"About Dartmoor Downs? The inheritance?"

"Duh!" Like Ronnie was thick. "He was being ridiculous.

Grossly unfair. Handing it all to Flynn while leaving his own grandkids in the lurch. Patrick and I are the only ones who bothered to provide him with heirs—an heir and two spares! Flynn's a childless bloody bachelor, but he gets the lot. How is *that* fair? He'll probably lose everything in his next divorce, God help us. I was simply trying to explain that, to make Clay see sense."

"And how did that go down?"

She turned away. "Not well as it happens." She glanced back. "He was still grumpy from the night before. Sulking that we didn't all cheer like a pack of loons when he handed Flynn the deeds, like that was something to celebrate. Probably still drunk, too, knowing Clay. Clearly hadn't got much sleep, was still in the same clothes he wore at dinner, bed barely slept in. Anyway, I could tell I wasn't getting through, so I cut my losses and left. That's all there is to it."

Now Ronnie did let her face mirror her doubt. "You were the last one to see Clay alive, Posey. How do I know you didn't hit him over the head? Like you said, he might still have been drunk. It wouldn't have been hard."

She scoffed. Scoffed again. "You really think I killed my father-in-law? And then... what? Dragged him all by my lonesome through the train and somehow managed to chuck him out. I'm half his size! And I'm not even sure how you'd go about doing that, but I can assure you I didn't. I might have been anxious, but I'm not desperate. And I'm certainly not stupid. That would've been a bloody stupid thing to do." Her eyes narrowed. "Besides, who says I was the last to see him alive?"

Ronnie shot her a sharp look. "You weren't?"

Posey shrugged and folded her arms over herself again. Looked a little smug as she said, "No, as it happens. Somebody else came to the door while I was in there."

*Another one?* thought Ronnie, the wrinkles draining from her face entirely.

# CHAPTER 23
## Scary Conversations

Missy was determined to follow the brief. She would finish her Agatha Christie short stories if it killed her! But first she needed a soothing peppermint tea. Her energy was too high, her nerves a little frazzled by what had been going down.

"Fancy a cuppa if I go get one?" she asked Claire, who did seem to be lost in her book, snuggled into the lower bunk.

"I'm fine," Claire replied, then her eyes danced across Missy's oversized hot-pink polka-dot pyjamas.

Missy grinned. "Let's hope no one busts me out in the corridor."

Not that she really cared. Missy giggled nervously at lots of things, but being caught in her jammies was not one of them. And just as well because it was like musical doors out here!

First she spotted Lynette, stepping furtively into Flynn's cabin—goodness! Alicia would have a coronary!—then she spotted Alicia stepping out of her cabin and heading towards the lounge. She would've mentioned Lynette's rendezvous, except Alicia looked flustered enough as it was and gasped something about the night managers as she rushed past, so Missy let it drop.

She had almost finished making her tea when she heard the carriage door to the solo cabins on the other side of the tearoom swish open, followed by a burst of familiar laughter.

It was the three new besties Missy had met at dinner. The pilot, the flight attendant and the lawyer. They'd discarded their warm jackets and were clearly heading to the lounge, still in a party mood by the sound of it.

And again she envied them. *Had* the book club been taking this trip too seriously? Was Lynette right after all? Should they have skipped the mystery and focused on the fun?

"Hey Missy!" one of them sang, spotting her as she peeked out.

"Hey!" she called back, blushing, not because she'd been caught in her PJs but because she could not recall the woman's name. And they'd just spent an entire meal together! Now *that* was embarrassing.

Missy did remember that she was the lawyer in the group. That's right. She worked for Gardner Legal—

She stopped, eyes boggling. *She worked for Gardner Legal!*

Now Missy recalled the scribbles Ronnie had spotted on a notepad in Phillip's cabin: Andrews, James, barber and *gardener…*

Dumping her cup, she stepped out of the tearoom and called the lawyer back.

~

By the time Alicia got to the Explorer Lounge, Perry was deep in conversation with Fiona and did not look like he wanted to be interrupted, so she gave him a sly wink and kept walking.

It was now well past eleven and the bar was still busy, the passengers making the most of the final night on board. Yet Alicia could find no one at the bar when she stepped up, so she called out, and that's when Agnetha popped her head around the corner.

"Oh, hey, another glass of sparkling wine?"

Alicia shook her head. "Are your night managers around? Everything's fine. I just need a quiet word."

Agnetha glanced about. Leaned across. Whispered, "So you heard about…?" She nodded towards Fiona.

Alicia nodded back. "Terrible news. How're all the staff coping?"

Agnetha leaned back. "We're devo'ed of course. Poor Arlo, especially. He's the one who thought he'd ticked him off safe and well."

"It's not his fault."

"I *know*. I keep telling him that." She dropped her head to one side. "I think it's finally clicked because he seemed cool last time we spoke."

Alicia smiled. *She* might've had something to do with that, setting him straight about what a lecher the missing man was. She leaned in now and said, "Listen, Agnetha, I'm going to give you some unsolicited relationship advice—take it or leave it. Always keep your partner in the loop. No matter how trivial. Not telling is always so much worse than the news you're trying to protect them from. Believe you me."

Alicia was thinking of Jackson and his close friendship with his police partner, Indira Singh. How she'd let her share of doubts creep in. How it almost broke them up.

Agnetha nodded slowly, not sure how to take that, as Alicia stepped back.

"Speaking of secrets," Alicia continued, "here's one you can keep." She pointed towards the Platinum carriage. "I know I'm not supposed to go that way, but I'm going anyway. You're welcome to stop me, or you can pretend you never saw me."

"Saw what?" said Agnetha, turning towards the back fridge.

Alicia smiled and continued on, through the empty dining carriage, the NO ENTRY doorway, and into the Platinum Club. There were several couples in there now when she strode through, all glancing up at her curiously, and she offered them a hearty smile and kept right on walking all the way to the accommodation carriage where, lo and behold, a staff member suddenly appeared to block her pathway.

Alicia couldn't help laughing.

"My God, Walker," she said. "You should work in a VIP club. You have Door Bitch down pat."

He cracked a lopsided smile at that but did not budge. "You know you can't be here."

"Yes, yes, apparently I'll turn into a pumpkin or something. At the risk of that, I just want a very quick word with your night managers." He raised an eyebrow, a worried eyebrow. She said, "Nothing's happened, don't panic. I just need to ask about the other night."

"No can do. They're official witnesses and are not to speak to anyone until they've reported to the police."

"Does that mean they saw something? The killer perhaps?"

He folded his arms and said nothing.

She laughed again. "You are the consummate professional, Walker. Hana should give you a pay rise." Then she turned to leave when something occurred to her, an unchecked fact. And she wasn't a fan of those.

"Hey Walker," she said, "I just have one quick question for you, and I promise it won't hurt." She stepped closer. "Why *did* I see you coming out of Clay's cabin the morning he went missing? And don't tell me you were cleaning, because I know Arlo had already done that."

~

After Flynn had shut his heavy cabin door, Lynette felt awkward. She wrapped her tanned arms around herself and glanced about. The space was tight during the day, but with the bed out it seemed even tighter—and shockingly intimate. The mattress was the only place to sit, so she lingered by the window, watching as he ducked into the bathroom and retrieved a second glass. Rinsed it, then poured her a drink.

Handing it to her, he said, "So, Alan Taggart didn't work out as a suspect?"

Lynette shrugged. "We're looking into him."

"I'm glad to hear it. Take a seat." He motioned the bed. "Who else you got on your suspect list?"

She hesitated a moment longer, then sat on the very edge of the mattress, crossing her long legs, pulling her cotton dress down to cover her knees. She took a quick sip of the drink. It was straight gin, dry and good. Very good. She tasted pink peppercorn, cranberries and cinnamon, a touch of rosemary perhaps. Glancing at the label on the bottle, she saw that it was by the Dartmoor Distilling Co. Patrick's brew. Flynn caught her glance and raised an eyebrow. He was referencing the brewer, not the brew.

"Yep," she said, "we have been wondering about both Patrick and Fiona."

"Really? So Paddy and Fi make the list. Which one you reckon did it? Or are they in it together?"

"This is not a game, Flynn. Your dad's missing."

Now he looked annoyed. "Yeah, and I'm supposed to be cut up about it, but you'll forgive me if I'm not."

There was defiance in his thin blue eyes. He was staring hard at her, daring her to be shocked, but she kept her own gaze steady. He rubbed the scar on his chin and said, "You have no idea what it was like growing up a Dartmoor. You see us for five seconds on a train and think you have it all sussed."

She leaned forward. "You know what I saw? I saw a bunch of kids who are terrified of their father, which I find really sad. Heartbreaking, in fact. And I saw an eldest son who wants to make a difference in the world and his dad doesn't seem to give a crap. Does that about sum it up?"

That caught Flynn by surprise, and he looked impressed, before the annoyance returned.

"I wouldn't say we were *terrified* of him." He scoffed, but a lot of that was pride, so she let it drop. "You're right about one thing though. Dad doesn't give a crap—about me, my plans, any of us. So why should we care about him?"

She didn't answer as he drained his glass and poured himself another shot. He tried to splash some into her glass, but she pulled it away, so he dropped the bottle back to the floor. "Look, I didn't wish my dad dead, but we were all pretty testy after that meeting we had, the one the whole train seems to know about. The one where I was handed the keys to Camelot..."

He was talking about Dartmoor Downs and his tone was bitter, surprisingly so. If Lynette had been handed thirty thousand hectares, she might've been more appreciative.

"Dartmoor Downs is a curse," Flynn told her, echoing

Jock Gleeson and reading her mind again.

It was uncanny, the way he did that. Perhaps Alicia was wrong and her soulmate *was* living on the other side of the country after all.

"It killed my marriage," Flynn was saying. "Killed Mum too. They were never happy out there. Like birds in a gilded cage. And not just them. Dartmoor has ruined family after family, split up brothers for four generations. I saw how it emasculated Uncle Phil. He puts on a good show, but he's a miserable shadow of a man. Pathetic, you ask me. Anyway, I was putting a stop to that. I told Dad, thanks, but no thanks. Not without Fi and Paddy."

*Now* she was surprised. "Really? You said that?"

"Why not? This isn't the 1800s anymore. I told him we should own it together, work it together, do it our way. That way the land thrives, the business thrives, and so does the family."

She smiled. "Impressive. How did he respond?"

"Exactly like I thought he would." He pulled the hat off and rubbed a hand through his clipped golden curls. "It's like I'd told him I was turning it into an ashram. No, worse than that. Like I'd spat in his face. He was angry. Real angry. And not just angry... disappointed. Yeah, that's it. He just wanted me to kiss his feet and leave it at that. Wasn't expecting me to have some conditions of my own. Certainly wasn't expecting us kids to have our own ideas, our own plans. We were a united front, and he didn't know what to make of that. He'd done such a good job of dividing us all for years. He said, 'That's not the way we do things in this family' and I told him they are now. 'Things are changing, Dad.' That threw him for six. Couldn't stand it. He wanted chaos. So he's creating it now."

Her eyes narrowed. "What are you saying?"

He rubbed a hand across his scar again. "I'm saying if anything happened to Dad, *he* made it happen."

She was still confused. "Are you saying he... *jumped*?"

"No! God no. It's just..." Flynn blew out a puff of air. "I have no idea what happened to him, Lynette, but I know my dad and he's a poor loser, and he lost that night. He knows I won. He knows he can't change it. Sure, he can refuse and insist I work it alone, but he's not gonna live forever, is he? What's to stop me implementing my changes after he's gone?"

Lynette didn't respond, but she could think of a more pertinent question, like what's to stop Clay bequeathing it all to a dog shelter the second he gets off the train, just as he had joked to Tag? Clay still owned Dartmoor Downs when he vanished. Nothing had been signed over yet, as far as she knew.

Was *that* why Clay was thrown from the train? Not to cause chaos but to put an end to four generations of it?

Flynn watched her closely as she thought this through, and it looked like he was trying to read her mind again, his narrow eyes darting across her face, voice animated.

"Lynette, it's the only thing that makes sense. Us working it together, I mean. Dartmoor Downs has become a beast. It's all very well for Dad to say he managed just fine on his own, but when he got it, it was half the size, hadn't diversified into different markets. It's a massive operation now; too big an operation to manage alone. And I haven't got a wife and three strapping kids to help me. Sure, Dad's assembled a good team, plenty of casuals during seeding and harvest, but…" He caught himself. Laughed. "Listen to me, poor little Landed Gentry."

She laughed along. Liked his self-awareness. "Yeah, First World problems, right?"

"But it didn't *need* to be. A problem I mean. That's why I encouraged Fi to book this trip. She wanted it to be a kind of memorial, for Mum, you know? She brought along some old photos of her, gave us each one. Wanted us to make a fuss and all that."

Ah, thought Lynette. So *that's* why Clay had a picture of Daisy in his cabin. He wasn't pining after his departed wife after all. Not sentimental in the slightest.

Flynn clearly wasn't either because he confessed, "I was more interested in getting the whole business of Dartmoor

Downs squared away. Thought it'd be easier if we told Dad our plans, together, on a family holiday." He snorted. "Look how that turned out. Maybe I'm not fit to run this family. Just like he said."

"That's not true and you know it."

He smiled. His eyes turned sheepish. He edged closer on the bed. "I feel like you get me, Lynette. You understand."

She rolled her eyes at him, like he was being corny, but he edged closer again. "No, you see it. Clearly. You see *me*. I can't remember the last time a woman actually saw me."

Lynette felt a small tug at her heartstrings, felt her legs turn to jelly again.

He offered another sheepish look, then he dropped his head to the side and said, "Why are you really here?"

"I told you why. We're a busybody bunch of Miss Marples."

"No, you. Why are *you* here? Now?" He indicated the cabin and then the bed. Placed his glass on the floor and reached a hand up to stroke her face as he added, "And there is *nothing* Miss Marple about you, babe."

That caused Lynette's heart to flutter as his eyes drifted down her body and his smile turned wolfish. She felt tempted—God, she was tempted!—but she couldn't stop thinking of Alicia and how disappointed she'd be. And not just Alicia. She was thinking of Clay now, and Daisy.

Had Clay been this charming back when he was Big Bear?

Lynette smiled coyly and leaned back. "Good try, Flynn. But that's not happening. Not tonight."

He dropped his hand but held on to the smile. "What's the harm?"

"No harm, but it's not why I'm here."

His smile tightened. "So why are you here then?"

"I told you! I came to ask about the hat."

He blew out a fresh puff of air. "Yeah, right."

He gave her another wolfish grin and scooped up his hat, dropping it onto her head. Then he took a loose strand of her hair and began to twirl it.

"We connected that first night, at the bar. You and me.

Let's not pretend that didn't happen."

Lynette whisked the hat off and dropped it on the bed. She scoffed. "You are a very attractive man, Flynn Dartmoor, and you know that better than anyone. But I'm honestly not looking for—"

"Bullshit!" he said suddenly, catching her by surprise. His voice softened a note as he added, "You've been stalking me from the start. Like a sick puppy." His hand reached up again, this time taking her behind the neck. "Don't act like you don't want this. We both know you do."

He went to pull her closer and she pulled back, angry now. But he didn't let go.

"*Flynn*," she said, her tone tense as she attempted to get up, but he held her tight. She glared at him. "What the hell do you think you're doing?"

He was still smiling, acting coy. "What? Scared your book club will find out? Is this against the rules?"

"It's not happening. Now *back off*."

She pushed one hand hard against his chest, but for a brief moment it felt like he would not let go. His smile had turned into an ugly smirk, almost a grimace, and she felt a sudden, rising panic.

"My God, Flynn," she gasped, "you are just like your father!"

That did it.

Flynn's smirk vanished and he burst like a balloon, dropping his hand and falling back away from her, to the side of the bed. She grabbed the opportunity and leapt to her feet, rushing to the door, surprised how wobbly her legs were. When she reached it, she wrenched it open, and only when she was in the safety of the corridor did she dare to turn back and glower at him.

But Flynn was not looking at her. He was flopped over, his bushy eyebrows wedged together, staring at his chest, shocked and bewildered.

Like he'd just been stabbed through the heart in his bed.

When Lynette got safely back into her cabin, she looked

around frantically for Alicia, but she was not there. She grappled for the door lock and applied it quickly, then she turned around, slid shakily to the floor and burst into tears.

~

Posey was putting on a good show, her eyes wet with what Ronnie could only assume were crocodile tears.

"You *have* to believe me," she was saying. "I'm not lying. It's true!"

They'd gone through it now, several times, and Ronnie kept trying to catch her out, but she was adamant. Someone else had come to Clay's door very early the morning her father-in-law had disappeared.

"I wasn't the last to see him alive. I wasn't," Posey persisted.

"So who was it?"

"I don't know! I didn't hear them, but someone was there. And luckily Clay was smart enough to realise how it'd look, so he shoved me in the bathroom before he opened the door."

"You didn't catch a glimpse? Hear a voice? Man? Woman?"

She shook her head firmly, her glossy black hair shimmering as she did so. "I told you. I was in the bathroom." Ronnie still looked sceptical, so she added, "Look, okay, I had the door open a smidge, and I *think* it was a man, although I don't know why I'd think that because I never heard their voice, but I did hear Clay say something like 'Oh hello there!' and then 'No, no, no!' and then I heard him say something about talking in the corridor. And next thing I know the door went thud and he was gone."

"So where did he go?"

"I don't know! I wasn't hanging around to find out. After I heard the door shut, I waited a few minutes and peeked out, but everything was quiet. I waited a bit more, then thought, bugger this for a joke and pissed off back to my room, fast as I could."

"And you didn't see Clay again? Or anyone on your way back to your cabin?"

She shook her head. Released a long exhale, and Ronnie felt relieved for her too. Because if Posey was telling the truth, that mystery visitor *had* to have been Clay's killer. And luckily for her, they had walked *away* from the Gold carriage, towards the front of the train. After all, that's where the exit door key was stolen from. If they had walked the opposite way, Posey might very well have collided with them on her way back to her Gold cabin. And God knows where that would have left her.

Probably on the side of the tracks with Clay.

"Why didn't you say anything earlier?" Ronnie demanded. "This is crucial information. That might have been his killer."

"Hey, I didn't know he was going to vanish that morning, did I?" Posey was back to scoffing. "And like I'm really going to admit to being in my father-in-law's room by myself when it was all perfectly innocent. I saw how *you* reacted. Imagine what my dim, darling husband would think!" She grabbed Ronnie's arm. "You *can't* tell him. He can't know! He won't understand; it'll only complicate things, when I was there for all the right reasons. Really I was! I was just looking out for our kids."

Ronnie wasn't interested in her excuses. "It's not up to me now, dear. The police are officially involved."

She was aghast. "What? Oh God. You have to help me. Can you sneak back in, get my bath bag for me? I've tried several times now, missed Cook trying to retrieve it, but I can't seem to open the blasted door. Can you help?"

"Not even if I wanted to, dear." Which she didn't. "Hana has the cabin locked down tight. No one's allowed in on police orders."

Posey gasped again, her eyes wild. "Oh bugger! Patrick is never going to understand. What if he doesn't believe me?"

"I'm not sure *I* believe you, Posey. I'd like to think you didn't do this but—"

"I didn't! Someone else was there. And don't think for a

second it was Patrick. 'Cause it wasn't! He was still asleep when I got back to our room—fast asleep. He doesn't know about any of this. I'm his alibi, and that's all there is to it."

Not quite, thought Ronnie. They only had Posey's word for the fact that Patrick was asleep in their cabin, that he wasn't Clay's second mystery visitor, chasing down his wife. Perhaps Patrick had caught them together and lashed out, killing his own father, and she was now covering up for him like the good wife.

There were several "good wives" in this tale, thought Ronnie, but she wasn't convinced this one was the real deal.

"*Please*," Posey persisted. "You *have* to tell the police I wasn't involved, because I wasn't. There was someone else at the door..."

"You're going to need to do better than that, dear. Who was it? Think back!"

"I can't! I didn't see him! He didn't speak!"

"So how do you know it was a man?"

Posey shrugged, looked annoyed. "I don't know. I'm telling you, he wasn't making much sense, Clay I mean. That's why I thought he might still be drunk. He was talking in riddles or fairy tales really..."

"Fairy tales?"

"Yeah." She sniffed, her eyebrows narrowing. "That's right. He said something about Cinderella or Rapunzel..."

An icy trickle slid down Ronnie's spine as she recalled something Perry had said earlier, something he'd heard at dinner. "It wasn't Goldilocks, was it?"

Posey blinked. "Yes! That's it!" She raised a small fist like she'd just won a trivia contest. "Yeah, I did hear the word Goldilocks." She dropped her head quizzically. "So I guess it could've been a woman. It's odd though, right?"

"Not as odd as you think," said Ronnie, her mind whizzing back to the three bears, or one bear in particular. And to an old colour photo of a woman with long, golden curls...

# CHAPTER 24
## Baby in the Corner

Baby Bear was in the Explorer Lounge, sitting in the exact same seat that Ronnie had found him in the day before. It was now their final morning on the train. The day was dawning swiftly through the window beside him, the harsh flat desert now giving way to lush rolling hills, vibrant valleys and farmland, but Phillip clearly wasn't watching, his brow knotted, his jaw tense and moving, like he was chewing on something when the only thing in front of him was a cup of coffee.

She ordered an English Breakfast tea from the bartender, then strode across and took the seat beside Phil, not bothering to ask this time. He looked up and did not seem surprised to see her either. He had deep, dark shadows under his eyes, clearly hadn't slept a wink.

"You've spoken to Hana," she said, and he nodded. "And you finally believe us? That he went overboard."

He dropped his chin into his neck. Rubbed a hand across his forehead. Exhaled heavily. "I think I always believed it... Just didn't want to face it. It's like a nightmare. My poor brother."

"Big Bear, you mean?"

He looked up, his expression confused. "What?"

Ronnie took a sip of her tea and sat back. "There was a man at dinner last night," she told him. "A man you went to school with, years ago, by the name of David Jules?"

He stared at her blankly. "Don't remember any David Jules. What of him?"

"He had some interesting things to tell us about you and your brother."

He grimaced. "Everybody's got an interesting story about the Dartmoors. Take it with a grain of salt."

"Ah, but this David fellow speaks with some authority. He went to school with one of your cousins. Few years younger I believe. Any case, he remembers you well. Remembers your brother too. Told Perry how everyone called you Bear. He was Big Bear and you were Little Bear."

"Baby Bear, yeah, so?" Phillip still looked confused. Not a skerrick of alarm in his voice. "That was a lifetime ago. What's this got to do with anything?"

She took another sip of her tea. "How much did you love Daisy?"

The change in tack turned his confusion to irritation. "I told you, everybody loved Daisy. Including me."

"What about Clay?"

"What about him?"

"Did he love her. Like he should."

Now there was a spark of anger. "Clay didn't love anyone like he should. She was no exception."

"He treated her badly?" Ronnie already knew the answer to this and he shrugged, a kind of acquiescence. She said, "That must've infuriated you. I mean, why would he fight so hard for her, then treat her so poorly?"

The confusion was back. Then the irritation. He grabbed his cup and took a good gulp. Said, "Honestly, Ronnie, now you're the one talking tricky. I'm not in the mood this morning—"

"Then let me cut to the chase. You tell us all that you and Clay were close, but you're human, Phillip. No one would blame you if you harboured resentment towards your brother. He got everything, didn't he? He got Dartmoor Downs and he got Daisy, a woman you confess to loving. A woman you said died too young, that Clay did not deserve."

"He *didn't* deserve her, not for one second," he replied, his tone surly, "but I don't know how many times I need to spell this out for you: I loved Daisy in a *brotherly* way. That's all."

"That's not what this fellow told Perry. He said you and Clay fought over her when you were young, and Clay beat you there too."

The confusion was back, so too the anger. "Well, that's a blatant lie. And what the hell would *this fellow* know anyway? Don't even know who you're talking about." He clunked his cup back down. "I don't need to listen to this rubbish!"

He barked out that last part and began to stand, so she held up a hand and said, "I'm sorry, Phillip. I know this is invasive, but please hear me out. I wouldn't be intruding on your grief if I didn't need to, but I just learned something. Something important."

He hovered, staring hard at her like he didn't believe her, so she quickly added, "Somebody visited your brother in his cabin very early the morning he vanished."

In fact, Clay had two visitors, but she had decided not to out Posey. Not because she wanted to protect the woman—the truth was coming out whether Posey liked it or not—but because it wasn't important right now, would only confuse matters.

Phillip's brow had furrowed, his jaw had tensed, but he'd also settled back into his chair, so she continued. "Don't ask me how I know this, but someone was heard knocking on Clay's door less than two hours before we got to Broken Hill. I'm sorry, but I do have to ask, was that you?"

His furrow deepened. "There was a man? At Clay's door? Who told you this? What did they see?"

Now he sounded worried, and she tried to keep her tone light as more passengers began filling the lounge on their way to breakfast. "I can't say if it was a man or a woman, but the name Goldilocks was mentioned, so I can't help wondering—"

"Hang on, *Goldilocks?*"

Now he looked utterly muddled. Which was making her feel a little muddled too. "Yes," she said. "And we know Goldilocks was Daisy, so—"

"Whoa! Just a sec." He had one finger up. "Why would you think Goldilocks is Daisy?"

She tsked. "Because we're not idiots, Phillip. We know you were part of the Three Bears at high school. That's what your old friend said. That you and your brother fought over a girl, and Clay ended up with her, so I can only assume that girl was dubbed Goldilocks. What else would she be called? I do know my fairy tales. Have I got that wrong?"

He slowly shook his head. "No... we did call her Goldilocks... we did fight over her... but..." Then he sat forward. "But Daisy wasn't Goldilocks."

Now Ronnie looked flummoxed. "She wasn't?"

"How could she be? Daisy was still in Kindergarten when we were at high school. She's nine years younger than Clay. I know he's a pig, but... Why would you think...?"

"But I saw the photo!" Ronnie cried now, feeling very much like an idiot. "In Clay's cabin. Daisy had lovely golden curls, just like Goldilocks. And the kids do too."

"*Clay* has golden curls," he shot back. "Or he used to before he lost most of it. That's where they got them. Daisy was a brunette. Her hair was straight. She curled it and dyed it for Clay." His eyes turned dark then. He shook it away as he sat forward. "So... are you saying *Goldilocks* was at Clay's door that morning?"

"I don't know if she was there as such..." Ronnie frowned, totally muddled now. "But let's back up a bit. If Daisy's not Goldilocks, who is?"

He frowned. Scoffed. Shook his head. "What do you mean, *who is?* You've been hanging with Goldilocks this *entire* trip."

~

Goldilocks's long curls had thinned considerably and turned a soft, warm shade of grey, and she was clearly brushing them out when Ronnie knocked on her cabin door, because they hung long and loose down past her chest, and she was wielding a hairbrush.

Ronnie must have been staring at her hair because Iris laughed and said, "Yes, I'm a little long in the tooth for all this." She swept the curls back. "My locks have always been my pride and joy. My folly, too, if you ask the girls at the CWA. But I can't seem to find the will to cut it. Like I'm Samson and I'll lose all my powers."

She chuckled at that, and Ronnie smiled along. Yes, if the stories were to be believed, Iris certainly had power back in her youth. Did she still? That was the question.

"Actually," said Ronnie, "I heard you once looked more like Goldilocks."

That froze the smile on Iris's lips. She was surprised and then... What was it? Worried? Fearful? She quickly blinked it away. "Well, I wasn't always a dumpy old lady," she said. "The young ones forget that, don't they? Think us old biddies were always old biddies, forget we once had blood pumping through our veins. Still do. Some of the time." She winked. "I bet you had the lads lined up in your day."

Ronnie smiled. Shrugged. "That was a long time ago."

Iris chuckled and waved her brush in the air. "And you can't dwell on the past now, can you?"

"Ah, but you see, I have a terrible feeling someone did," said Ronnie. "Someone on this train."

Iris flinched. Her arched cheeks paled. The worried look was back. "Is there something I can help you with?"

"Yes," said Ronnie, "there is. When you're finished up here, do you think we could have a word? My book club and I? Just get yourself to the diner and you'll find us from there." Then she smiled benignly and added, "Perhaps you could bring Jock along so we can get things *just right.*"

Ronnie didn't stick around to see the look of horror that was now etched clear across Iris's face. Like Goldilocks had just been woken by a hungry bear.

The Explorer Lounge was a teeming, boisterous space when the book club walked in, but this time they didn't hang around or beg to use the dining room. Marvin was waiting for them and ushered them through the Queen Adelaide Restaurant and into the Platinum Club where Walker met them at the entrance. This time he welcomed them in.

"Follow me," he said. "There's a private lounge you can use."

"And the Gleesons?" asked Ronnie.

"I'll make sure they get there," said Marvin, giving them a cheerful salute.

And so they continued on, past the curious stares of the Platinum passengers having breakfast and through the accommodation carriage, past Clay's cabin, which had a makeshift DO NOT ENTER sign posted to the door.

Eventually they got to what Walker called the Chairman's Carriage, a private lounge that was even fancier than the one the Platinum class was using.

"This is for groups who want to book an entire carriage to themselves," Walker explained. "We've had all kinds of celebrities use it. But it's free now, so help yourself."

"Thank you so much," said Alicia.

Walker smiled in his lovely lopsided way. "Mr Dartmoor wasn't our favourite passenger, but he didn't deserve to be thrown from this train. And the Indian Pacific doesn't deserve it either. So if you think this will help, I won't stand in your way."

Then he bowed and left them to it, Alicia beaming after him.

Walker had done a complete U-turn since they'd spoken last night. He and his team had now become fellow sleuths, helping them solve the mystery of the missing man. And it started with two hats. Two mislaid hats, in fact. It turns out Clay had accidentally left his old beat-up Akubra in the Platinum bar after drinking with Tag that first night, and the night manager had found it many hours later. Not knowing who owned it, she had popped it behind the bar for Walker to chase up the next morning, which he'd tried to do, failing in his endeavour to find its owner (never assuming for a minute that it belonged to the richest man on the train).

Meanwhile, earlier that evening, Clay had reserved this very carriage—the Chairman's Lounge—for his family meeting, and that's where Flynn had left his new, tan-coloured Akubra. It was Walker who had picked that one up and, assuming incorrectly that it belonged to Clay, had dropped it into Clay's cabin the next day.

*That's* why Alicia spotted him coming out of Platinum's cabin number two. It turns out that hat was very much a red herring, and Flynn hadn't been in his dad's room at all. He was telling the truth to Lynette. (*Not* that Lynny knew that when she strode willingly into his compartment late last night!)

Alicia flashed her sister a frown, but Lynette could barely meet her eyes this morning, kicking herself enough for both of them it seemed.

Ronnie caught the look as she took a seat and said, "Yes, I heard about what happened, Lynette. Honestly, dear, I never would have handed over that hat if I knew Flynn was going to assault you."

Lynette's eyes flashed. "He didn't assault me! I mean… not really… I got away. And anyway, I could've screamed at any time and you would have heard me."

"You know, that's what keeps bugging me," said Missy, settling in between Ronnie and Alicia even though there were plenty of spare seats. "Why did Clay not cry out, get help that morning?"

It was a good question, one they still needed an answer to. And perhaps they would finally get it, they decided, as they watched the Gleesons enter the room.

Iris had not wasted any time grabbing her husband and getting herself to the diner where Walker met them and escorted them to the private carriage. The attendant had refused to answer questions, and that had them intrigued. Or at least that's how Jock appeared.

"What's all this about, hey?" he said, his tone still jolly. "Feels very cloak and dagger."

"And what a lovely space," said Iris, glancing around lightly, as though trying to keep things equally as light.

But it was too late for that.

"Take a seat," Ronnie told them. "We hope this won't take long."

Jock glanced across to his wife, who just shrugged back and sat on the opposite side to Ronnie. "What's this all about?" he asked again, his tone a little less jocular as he dropped down heavily beside Iris.

Ronnie said, "It's about Clay Dartmoor. You must know by now he's missing."

He shifted in his seat. Glanced at Iris again, but she was looking out of the window as though the view was more scintillating.

He said, "Yeah, it's all anyone can talk about out there. Waste of breath, you ask me." His eyes darted across the group. "Is that... is that what you lot have been doing this whole time? Trying to work out whodunnit? Hmm?"

His eyebrows nudged up and down and he was being jolly again, but Ronnie did not crack a smile. "It's what we do a lot of the time, Jock. Work out whodunnit. Not because we're nosy"—although they were, unapologetically so—"but because Alicia here saw the man get pushed from the train just before five the morning he vanished."

Now both Gleesons stared across to Alicia, eyes wide.

"So it's true? You *saw* that?" asked Iris.

Alicia held up a hand. "I saw him fall. I never saw who pushed him."

Iris made a good show of hiding the heavy breath she was exhaling.

Ronnie said, "You know, Patrick's wife admits that she visited Clay very early the morning he disappeared?"

"Posey? Really?" said Iris. "That's suspicious."

"Oh yes, we thought so too. She tells us she popped a bathrobe on and grabbed her bath bag and slipped down to Platinum. Says she took her bath things so that if she got busted she could pretend she was trying to find the communal bathrooms."

Iris edged her lips downwards. "Clever ruse, I guess."

Ronnie nodded. "I know you used the communal bathrooms too, Iris. I wonder... did you use them early that first morning on the train?"

Iris looked stunned then almost amused. "Yes, I did now

you ask. I wanted to get a head-start on the solo passengers. But it wasn't a *ruse*, Ronnie. How silly! I really did go there."

Then she turned to Jock. "I did." Like he was the one who needed convincing.

When he said nothing, she glanced back at Ronnie. "You can believe what you want, but I never went down to Clay's room because it's pretty bloody clear what you're implying, and I take offence. Although I suppose I should be flattered." Her tone was snippy. "Like I said, young'uns forget we have blood in our veins, but the truth is I really am too old and too boring to be sneaking into strange men's cabins at all hours."

"But *was* he a stranger?" asked Perry suddenly. "Really?"

He was seated in a corner couch, and she looked across at him. Shrugged.

Perry shrugged back. "It's funny you were both so determined to give us that impression. When we first met, you told us you knew the Dartmoors—it was the first thing you said. And yet you were very casual about it, called them 'distant neighbours'. Several times. Never explained that in fact you were all the best of buddies once, went all the way back to high school."

"Before that, if you must know," Iris snapped, sweeping the grey hair from her eyes. "We all met at our tiny primary school in the local village. Just thirty-seven kids at that school. Of course we were buddies; everyone was."

Jock glowered suddenly. "This is all very confusing. Why are you grilling my wife? What is this about?"

Ronnie smiled and adjusted her silver spectacles. "It's about a fairy tale, actually. *Goldilocks and the Three Bears*. Or at least, that's where it began, with a very silly story— one my Murder Mystery Book Club would never read. After all, there isn't a murder in it, at least, not recent versions."

In fact, an early 1831 rendition of the fairy tale was extremely grisly. It featured three bachelor bears and, instead of Goldilocks, a silver-haired old lady, not unlike Iris now. In that telling, the bears are utterly unforgiving, attempting to burn, then drown the interloper and finally managing to impale her on a church steeple.

But they weren't here to discuss that story, although it was the springboard that finally set the book club on the right trail. Ronnie looked directly at Iris. "You were more than school buddies with Clay Dartmoor. You were his Goldilocks, he was your Big Bear. And we now know that Clay's brother, Phillip, was Little Bear, or Baby Bear, as Clay liked to call him. And both men were in love with you."

Phillip probably still was, thought Perry to himself from his corner, recalling again how Phil had looked at Iris that day at the Miners' Memorial, how he'd touched her hair so gently, so achingly.

Iris smudged her lips downward. She was acting blasé, like none of it mattered. "So they called me Goldilocks, big whoop. And sure, I dated Clay for a bit, but I never ended up with him, nor with Phil. One was too much of a bighead, the other too much of a wuss."

Perry raised a hand, glad of the segue. "Yes, that's true, Iris. Neither of them was quite right, but they didn't need to be because that's not the whole story, is it? You see, it's Goldilocks and the *Three* Bears. I dismissed Middle Bear when I was told about him last night—just fixated on Big Bear and Baby Bear—which was foolish. Because, of course, Middle Bear is an equally important part of the story. That's why they call it the Goldilocks Principle. One is too harsh, one too weak, and one is *just right*."

His eyes swept to the man beside her. "And that was you, wasn't it, Jock? You were Middle Bear."

# CHAPTER 25
## Who's Been Sleeping in My Bed?

The smile Jock was now offering the book club was more sheepish than bearlike. He shrugged his bulky shoulders, like it was no biggie, then he took his wife's hand and said, "Well, as my darling Iris says, that was a long time ago."

"Surely not so long that Clay would forget you," said Perry, eyes boring into the man. "And yet that's how he behaved on this train, or at least that's the impression we got. Never even glanced in your direction as far as we could tell. Which is odd because you were once part of his inner circle. And not just you, Iris as well. He snubbed you both." Perry's attention turned to Iris, who looked surly. "We wonder, did he do that because he was still hurt, Iris, that you chose Middle Bear? That you decided Jock was *just right*, or at least he was for a while."

Iris blinked back at him, jaw twitching, then gave her husband's hand a shake. "He still is just right!" she snapped. "You are, my love, and you always will be."

Jock nodded, but his smile now just seemed sad. He turned to Perry. "Clay ignored us 'cause he's a sore loser. Yeah, I got Goldilocks; he didn't. So what of it? It's all in the past. Childhood nonsense. We grew up, moved on."

"Moved on or fell out?" asked Alicia now. "With Clay I mean?"

He flinched. Shrugged. "So we didn't stay friends. That's not a crime. Like Iris says, Clay was a bighead then. Always too competitive. I used to find it amusing. Soon realised it was pathetic. He might have more land, old Clay, doesn't make him a better person. I could've had as much land if I wanted. More if I'd put some grunt into it."

"Jock…," his wife began, but he shook her off.

"I'm just saying. Our farm could be ten times the size if I had my priorities screwed up like he did. My family's property wasn't much smaller than Dartmoor Downs when we first met. But Clay couldn't have that, could he? So competitive. So much to prove. After he took over, he started expanding, big time. Bullying neighbours into selling. Desperate to be King of the Crop. But he didn't get our land did he, love? Couldn't bully us into selling."

Iris smiled sadly, then looked away.

"Except you must have been worried that he would one day," said Ronnie. "You're not in good health are you, Jock?" She offered a sad smile of her own as she glanced down at his enormous barrel chest. Ronnie was a trained nurse. She knew the tell-tale signs of high blood pressure, diabetes, heart disease…

He shrugged. "Like I told you, I'm my biggest customer. Too many tasty scones."

"His heart is dicky," said Iris. "What of it?"

She was sounding irritable again, and Ronnie glanced at her.

"I think your husband was very concerned about his dicky heart, convinced he'd die before you, and worried— very worried—that you'd sell your property on to Clay when he did."

"Well, that's just rubbish," she said. "Because I promised him I wouldn't." She turned to her husband for backup, but he had a cloaked look in his eyes. "I *wouldn't*," she said more forcefully. "I've always told you that."

He didn't respond, and fear suddenly skittered across her face. "Jocky? Darling?"

That brought him to his senses. He blinked and grabbed hold of her hand again. Feigned a wide smile. "Course, my love. I know that."

"Ah, but do you?" said Ronnie. "Really? I mean can you be truly sure your wife and daughters won't want to move on after you're gone? Won't be tempted to sell to someone like Clay who *really* wanted your land." He didn't answer then, and she smudged her lips downwards. "Anyway, that's by the by. We don't think that's why Clay vanished. Nothing to do with your farm."

Now both Iris and Jock visibly exhaled. And Iris had had enough. She got to her feet. She turned to face them. "I don't know what's happening here," she said, shoulders rigid. "But I know an attack when I see one, and I've had a gutful. Come on, Jock. Let's go and have some breakfast. If we've still got our appetites left."

But he didn't stand up. He had a sad, defeated look in his eyes.

"Jock?" she said, stepping towards him. "Please, let's go."

Her tone had turned desperate, imploring, and the book club understood why. Iris didn't want the truth to come out, but it seems that Jock did.

He shook his head firmly, tapped the lounge beside him, and said, "Sit down, Iris."

Iris hesitated, just briefly, eyes darting from Jock to the door, but then she rolled them and returned to her seat with a huff, openly glaring at the group now.

"Let's go back," suggested Ronnie, who'd been chosen to run the show. She'd been the one to figure it out, so it was hers to bring home. "Back to the fairy tale, because that's where it all began. We know that all three bears fought over you, Iris, and that you ended up with Middle Bear, Jock."

"This again!" she said, slamming one palm against her thigh. "So? I ended up marrying Jock. I chose Jock in the end, and I never once regretted that decision." Her eyes were on Ronnie, but she was talking to her husband, that much was clear. "Jock knows this. He has been a good and faithful husband, and I have been a good and faithful wife."

The book club nodded. Ronnie said, "We believe you."

Iris released another heavy rush of air. "Good." Glanced at her husband and frowned.

The book club were watching him too. He was staring at his enormous belly. Expression rigid. Shoulders hunched.

Ronnie said, "The problem is, it's not us that need to believe you, Iris. It's Jock. And he doesn't believe you, do you, Jock? Or at least he didn't believe you on the morning that Clay vanished. When he saw you leave your cabin, bath bag in hand."

"What?" said Iris, grabbing Jock's hand. Giving it a shake. "I told you I was going to the bathroom... I told you—"

He looked up, eyes beseeching. "But how could I be *sure?* I mean... you walked in that direction."

"*What?*" she said again, trying to understand. Then she scowled. "I got a bit lost... disoriented, that's all. I turned back. I did! Ask the night watchman woman. She saw me. She pointed me to the solo carriage. Walked me down, in fact. I promise! I never went to see Clay!"

Ronnie already knew this to be true. Walker had confirmed it with the night managers, but Jock was now shaking his head. "But... I wasn't sure... I just needed to check—"

"Oh my God!" Iris dropped his hand and flung hers to her heart. "What did you do?"

He shook his head. Dropped it into his belly again.

Ronnie glanced across her group. They all had a spark in their eyes, but they knew they were on shaky ground. They had to tread carefully. She cleared her throat and said gently, "You were the one who knocked at Clay's door that morning, weren't you, Jock? Posey was in Clay's cabin then. She didn't hear your voice, but she did hear Clay say something about Goldilocks."

Iris slapped her thigh again. "There you go! That must've been Phil! Tell them, Jock. That was Phillip! Baby Bear! You were never there. *Tell them!*"

She was screeching now, imploring again, but Jock's eyes had turned watery. He seemed choked up.

Eventually he swallowed hard and cleared his throat. He said, "I just needed to check if you were in there. I wanted to see for myself."

Iris grasped her throat. "What?"

His eyes looked up and straight to her. "There was someone in there! I could hear a woman. I... I thought it was you... I demanded to see, but he wouldn't let me in, Iris!

Wouldn't tell me who it was. So... I... I couldn't be sure. Then he slammed the door and pulled me down the corridor. Told me to calm down, but how could I calm down when I thought you were in there?"

"But I wasn't!"

"I know that *now*. But then... then... I... I..."

"What?" she gasped. "Then you *what?*"

"I was so upset, my darling. So hurt. We were near the exit door. Clay and me. I... I saw the key in the little red box. I thought, I need to get off this train. I didn't want to live anymore, not if you were in there... I just needed to get off. I smashed the box. I grabbed the keys. I wanted to open the door."

"No," moaned Iris, shaking her head madly. "No, no, no!"

He nodded, tears streaming down his ruddy cheeks. "I just wanted it to end. *I* was going to leap off, don't you see? That's what I was going to do! But then I looked back and he was smirking. *Smirking,* like he always does, and that's when I realised—he was playing me, just like he played me all those years. And worse! He'd done it deliberately! He wanted me to jump."

"*What?*" she demanded, her face contorted with anger and confusion. "Why would he want that?"

"Because he wanted *you!*" he roared, taking them all by surprise now. His head was up, tears were gushing down his cheeks. "Don't you get it? *You* were the one thing Clay never had. He had the money and the land, the two strapping sons to work it." His eyes darted towards the book club. "You know he sent me sympathy cards when my girls were born? *Sympathy cards!* Who *does* that?"

Iris gasped, looking horrified, like she hadn't known, and he turned back to her.

"I didn't tell you because I didn't want to hurt your feelings and because I didn't care. Don't you see? I never cared about any of Clay's bullshit because none of it mattered. I had my Goldilocks. And he didn't. He *didn't!*"

He sniffed, his eyes shifting to the exit door in this

carriage. He sighed heavily.

"I stood by the door for ages, just clutching the keys. It was clear what I was going to do... but he didn't try to stop me. Like I said, he just smirked. And that's when I realised, if I opened that door, if I jumped, he'd win. Not only would he get the land—*because don't tell me you wouldn't sell to Clay if the price was right!*" His tone had turned snarly. He quickly softened again. "But it wasn't the land, Iris. It was *you*. I could see in his eyes. If I jumped, he would win. We'd be broken apart. It's what he wanted!"

Iris was aghast. Hand slapped across her mouth, head shaking, begging him to stop.

He continued, gaze to Ronnie now. "It happened so quickly, before I could think it through. One minute he was smirking at me, the next he was flying off. I know I must have opened the door. I know I must have grabbed him, pushed him, closed it again... I was just so *angry* with him for that smirk. He'd been smirking at me since we were five! I'd had a gutful!"

He shook his head. Sniffed. Wiped his eyes. Then he looked out at the lush farmland that was now sweeping past the window. "We weren't going that fast, rounding a bend. There was scrub along the track, bushes everywhere. He would've landed in one. I'm sure he landed in one... I thought maybe... maybe..."

"Maybe what?" Iris cried, horrified. "Maybe he'd be *okay*?"

He shrugged. Sniffed again. "I never meant for it to happen. If only he'd just told me you weren't in there—"

"*I* told you I wasn't in there!" she screamed, hands flying about. "You came back! You saw me in our cabin!"

"Yes, but by then it was too late... It was done. I'm so *sorry*."

He buckled over his enormous belly again, shoulders shuddering as he wept, and Iris stared down at him, eyes plump with her own tears. And for a moment, just a moment, her expression softened.

"Oh Jocky," she whispered.

And he looked up like he'd been thrown a life raft. His nose was dribbling snot, his eyelashes clogged with tears. He grabbed her hand. "I'm so sorry," he said. "I didn't mean for any of it to happen. I… I just knew that if I jumped he would finally have you. Which is all he really wanted. I couldn't let him win. I couldn't let him have you. Don't you see?"

And that's when Iris did see, very clearly now, and she was suddenly breathtakingly furious. "*Have me?*" she said, shaking his hand away and scrambling to her feet.

When she turned to look at him, her eyes were black balls of fury. "You bloody fool!" she snapped. "He would never *have* me! What do you think I am? A piece of land up for grabs? The winnings in a poker game? And *so what* if he ended up with our farm? Who cares? It's soil and grain! But *I'm* not for sale, and I never bloody was! How many times did I have to tell you that? I never wanted Clay."

She thrust a hand to her face and wiped her own tears away. Took a deep breath and said, "Maybe I imagined life with him on occasion…"

He looked up then, horrified, and she smudged her lips downwards.

"Of course I did!" she spat at him. "Who wouldn't? That year I dated him at high school, I got a taste of the good life. All that money. *Three* giant homesteads. Lovely antiques, like that beautiful grandfather clock I fell in love with. Not like our dreary old junk. But it wasn't just that. Imagine never having to stress about bills again. No begging the bloody bank for an overdraft. I gave up a lot when I chose you, Jock Gleeson, but I thought it was worth it. Clay was a bully and a bighead. Full of hot air and self-loathing. And I knew he'd make a terrible husband, which he did. The number of times poor Daisy came sobbing on my doorstep, so browbeaten, so diminished. I told her to leave him, so many times, but she never did."

She shook her head as he looked away. "Give us some credit, Jock," she almost whispered. "I knew it was all smoke and mirrors. I never loved Clay. Not like I once loved you."

That brought Jock's face whipping around again because she'd used the past tense. It was like she had roared it, and he stared at her pleadingly, eyes red and raw, shoulders quivering like jelly.

"Yes, *loved*," she hissed now. "The whole reason—the *only* reason—I rejected Clay and married you was because I knew that none of his money would make up for the fact that *he* was the brutal one, the nasty one, the violent bear. But now…" She gasped. Held her palms out towards him. "It turns out you're just as brutal and nasty and violent as Clay."

"No!" he cried, head shaking over and over.

She nodded. "But worse, Jock, worse, because you're also irredeemably stupid! And how can I possibly love a man who could be so brutal and violent and stupid?"

Then she steadied herself, swept a hand through her once golden curls, and strode out of the carriage while he watched through tearstained eyes as his fairy tale shattered around him.

Before collapsing into himself like a beat-up old teddy bear.

# CHAPTER 26
## Reality Bites

The city of Perth was fast creeping up on them, the valley turning to fields to paddocks and backyards. The group were all together in the lounge, enjoying a final glass of Bollinger. Yes, the French stuff this time (Marvin had insisted upon it), along with a basket of those giant cookies Alicia had been drooling over in the Platinum Club earlier (this was Walker's doing).

But it wasn't a celebration.

Clay's body had just been located, concealed in bushy scrub alongside the track, east of Broken Hill, just as Jock had told them, his bones broken, his brain smashed in by the fall. It was a gruesome find, a terrible end for anyone to endure, and it did not fill the book club with any sense of jubilation.

"Silly us for thinking we'd actually read our murder mysteries on this trip," said Missy, smiling sadly as she chomped into a cookie.

"Silly us for thinking we'd actually celebrate Alicia's engagement," added Lynette, not smiling in any way, shape or form.

"Well, we have been rather busy," said Claire. "No need to beat ourselves up. Do we know where they are now, the Gleesons?"

Alicia nodded. "Iris is in her room, refusing to talk to anybody, and Jock is being held in a separate cabin somewhere, officially under house arrest, according to Walker. My new best friend." She smiled properly now. "He's a sweetheart under all that bluster. Tells me they've got two attendants on the door, but I don't reckon Jock'll do a runner. He seemed desperate to confess, don't you think? That was the easiest 'grand reveal' I can recall."

"And the saddest," said Perry, who'd grown to like the man. "The Gleesons were such a lovely couple."

"*Were*," stressed Ronnie. "Until his fear and neurosis ruined that. Iris was right. Her husband was so stupid. She chose him and yet he never quite believed it."

"But once doubts creep in…," said Alicia, thinking of Jackson and his detective partner again.

"Stirred on by Clay!" said Claire, now tsking. "How cruel of him not to tell Jock that it was *Posey* in his compartment that morning, not Iris. He must have known that would send Jock wild. I don't think for a moment he did it to protect Posey's reputation; he did it to hurt Middle Bear because Middle Bear got Goldilocks. He played on Jock's fears."

"Are you suggesting Clay deserved it?" asked Perry. "Like the evil Mr Ratchett?"

"Not as such," said Claire. "But I do think he brought this upon himself. I mean, I know you shouldn't victim blame, but my goodness, what a nasty piece of work Clay was. And what a dangerous game he was playing. Making everyone dance to his tune. And it sounds like Jock was about to do just that—throw himself from the train—when he realised that was exactly what Clay wanted. So he changed the tune entirely. I'm not saying he should have, but I'm not going to weep over Clay either. He clearly didn't care about anyone or anything but himself and his farm, certainly didn't care about his wife and kids. But he came up against a man who cared so much for his wife he was prepared to die for her." She sighed wistfully. "A true crime of passion."

"Ooh, I think that's too generous, possum," said Missy now. "I think it was more about ego. Jock said it himself, didn't he? He couldn't let Clay win. It was like they were still at school, squabbling over Goldilocks, like two dogs peeing on a post as my dad would say. Jock couldn't stand the idea that Big Bear got her in the end, or he thought he did.

It's *so* pathetic."

It was another classic insight from young Missy, and they all agreed.

"What about the third dog?" said Perry. "Anyone speak to Baby Bear?"

Ronnie held up a hand. "I had a quick word with Phillip earlier. The Dartmoors are all lying low in their rooms too. All distraught, of course, and absolutely shocked with the revelation that Jock was involved. I don't think the kids had a clue they'd all been so close once, and Phillip insists he had so little to do with the Gleesons after high school, after they married, that he didn't realise things were still raw between Jock and Clay. Not until he pulled Jock aside in Broken Hill and asked about his health and the farm, kindly suggested they could help him out, and then got an earful."

"Ah, that was the altercation we witnessed," said Perry.

Ronnie nodded, eyes turning to Alicia. "Phillip sends his apologies by the way. Says they should have taken your concerns seriously. From the start."

"Fools," she replied.

But Ronnie believed there was an ulterior motive there too. "I think the Dartmoors all secretly suspected each other. After that tense meeting with Clay the first night, I think they feared one of them might've lashed out. So they tried to quash it all and send us on a wild goose chase." She looked at Claire now. "Like we were ever going to believe Clay had snuck off with some floozie in Broken Hill."

"And that's why Phillip had that list of names you saw scribbled on his notepad, Ronnie," said Missy.

She was the one who'd worked out they were the names of Perth law firms. After running into the three Perth friends by the tearoom last night, Missy remembered that one of them was a lawyer, a lawyer who worked for a firm called Gardner Legal, and it had reminded her of the word *gardener* that Ronnie had seen written down in Phillip's room. In fact, all four firms specialised in criminal defence, according to Brenda.

"Yes," said Ronnie. "Phillip would never admit this to

me, but he clearly feared one of the kids had done it. I guess he wanted to hush things up until he could get them proper representation. He did tell me he regretted not being there more, for the kids and Daisy. Was quite emphatic about that."

"Uncle Phil steps up at last," said Alicia. "Sad, really. I wonder if it even occurred to Clay as he went flying through that exit door that the train was full of people who would be relieved to see him gone."

"You know, I was thinking," said Claire, tucking a strand of black hair into her velvet turban, looking like something from an Agatha Christie movie. "This is such a case of what-if. What if Posey hadn't visited Clay early that morning and overheard the word Goldilocks? We might never have caught Jock."

"What if Iris had just used her own en suite bathroom?" said Missy. "Then Jock never would have followed her out and ended up at Clay's cabin in the first place."

"What if the Dartmoors or the Gleesons hadn't chosen this particular week to travel on this particular train?" added Alicia.

"You could go back even further," said Ronnie. "What if the Dartmoor brothers hadn't befriended Jock and Iris back at school? Or Iris had chosen a different bear. Or someone else entirely? I mean, where does it end?"

"I know where it started," offered Perry. "What if the Dartmoors hadn't stolen the land from the indigenous people two hundred years ago? It's like that's where the curse first began."

On that they all agreed, several of them now shuddering.

"Here's a fresh question then," said Claire. "What happens now? To Dartmoor Downs, do we know?"

They all turned to look at Lynette, who'd been uncharacteristically quiet.

"How would I know?" she muttered. "Flynn can lose it in a poker match for all I care."

"Fair enough too," said Ronnie. "But Phillip confirmed what Flynn told you, Lyn. He did insist his fellow siblings co-own and co-manage it together. And Clay was furious. Phillip thinks it's because Clay never had that kind of love for him, that kind of generosity of spirit, and it left Clay looking like the mean one. And he didn't like that."

"Ooh, such a horrid man," said Missy. "And really, when you think about it, full of neuroses. Needing to be king all the time, to have his way."

"It's domestic abuse," said Ronnie. "He didn't beat anyone up, according to Phillip, but it was just as insidious. Classic coercive control. And he wielded it over all of them. Dangling Dartmoor Downs like a carrot, keeping them in their boxes, never letting anyone get too confident, until Flynn did. And Jock, that morning. So very sad, but I guess that's one silver lining. Now the kids are free to do as they please. Call time on the divisive Dartmoor patriarchy."

"Fiona will be relieved," said Missy. "To be able to stay and help run the property."

But Perry was shaking his head. "Personally, I think Fiona needs some time out in the big smoke. Needs to find her people. Maybe even bond with Jacinta again." Then he twiddled his earring and added, "Jacinta's *my* new bestie. I could've kissed our attendant last night when she came into the bar. I was just thinking Fiona had shoved her dad off the train and was feeling dreadful for her. I really didn't want Fi to be the culprit! But then Jac showed up and set me straight."

It turns out, the timing was all wrong. Yes, Jacinta had revealed all to Fiona while on this train, telling her the truth about her father and the threats he'd made. But she'd done that the morning *after* Clay had vanished, when Fiona burst in while she was cleaning her cabin. That's when they got chatting and the truth was finally revealed. Fiona was livid. But by then Clay was long gone.

"That's why Fiona was so angry when we first met her in the diner," Perry explained. "But she's not angry anymore. Just sad. About all the missed opportunity." Then he winked and added, "But she'll catch up. I'm hoping she'll join Jacinta and me in Perth. Jac's offered to take me bar-hopping.

Tag's tagging along."

"Of course he is," said Ronnie, also winking.

Perry didn't bother distancing himself from the fossil collector this time. Realised it was just nerves; he really liked the guy. "You're all welcome to join us, too, if you like."

Lynette held one hand up. "I'm in. I think I need to swap sides. Might have more luck."

"You don't need luck," said Ronnie, but she waved her off.

Reaching across the table, Lynette scooped up her champagne glass. "Enough of all this negativity, people. It's time to get back to Alicia's romance."

"Oh, I think we've missed that train, honey," said Alicia, laughing.

"No, no," said Lynette. "We still have to finish our toasts."

"Honestly, it's fine—" began Alicia.

But Lynette was not having it. She slammed her glass back down. "Yes!" she bellowed. "We are doing this, so *stop!*"

Alicia blinked at her, speechless as several people around them looked across.

"Sorry," Lynette said quickly, lowering her voice again. "But stop acting like your marriage is no big deal, Alicia. It is. To me. It's massive, okay?"

"Okay," said Alicia, wincing now.

Lynette frowned. "You don't get it, sis. You're leaving us. Max and me."

She was talking about their beloved Labrador, and Alicia sighed. "But Lynny, I'm not—"

"But you *are*, honey. We won't be together like we used to be. Who am I going to experiment on with my cooking and swap good books with? Poor Max will be the size of a house, and he's a really slow reader."

Missy giggled at that joke, but no one else was laughing. The air was tense. Alicia placed her glass down and grabbed her sister's shoulders. Gave them a gentle shake.

"Lynny. I'm not leaving you and Max. I'm just leaving our share house, but we'll see each other. Often."

"How often?"

"At least every fortnight at book club," offered Missy, now bringing scowls from the rest of them and a worried gasp from Lynette.

Alicia shook her sister again. "Whenever you want. You just need to call. You're not just my sister, Lynette, you're my best friend. You think *Jackson* can compete with that?" She made a *pft* sound. "Besides, he's even slower at reading than Max."

Lynette tried to smile at that but was still so raw with emotion. Eventually she said, "I know I can call you. I know that. It's just... you won't *be* there, and not just to swap books. What happens when I come home with an absolute flop of a guy, like I always do? Who's going to set me straight and make sure I'm safe? Look at what happened last night with Flynn. I'm the real fool here."

Suddenly Alicia was shaking her sister angrily. "Now *you* have to stop! You are not a fool, Lynette. Not even close." She dropped her hands and shook her head. "A fool would have stayed and let the rich guy butter her up. Would've been charmed by his sleazy antics. But you weren't, Lynny, not in the end. Your instincts kicked in. You saw him for who he is and you pushed him away, got the hell out of there. That's not foolish. That's smart."

"A smart woman would never have got into that situation in the first place," Lynette persisted, but Ronnie wasn't hearing it now.

"Poppycock!" she called across to her. "A woman is perfectly entitled to have a drink with a fellow without him taking liberties. I will have no victim shaming here! This is what's wrong with the world." Then she leaned forward and said, "But I can tell you what's wrong with you, dear, if you'd like to hear it."

Now Lynette was wincing, and Alicia turned and glowered at Ronnie. "*Seriously?*"

"Sorry, Alicia," Ronnie told her, "but I think this will help, and it needs to be said." Then she turned her attention back to Lynette, whose shoulders were now up around her ears, her head to the side like she was preparing for an avalanche. Ronnie said, "You need to stop living your life like it's a cosy mystery."

That caught them all by surprise.

"Huh?" managed Lynette.

Ronnie shrugged like it was a no-brainer. "You act like a young, dynamic woman, but the truth is you want everything to be nice and safe and work out neatly in the end, with your sister by your side, a cup of hot chocolate, a cute dog and a warm fire." She leaned forward. "*That's* why you've been choosing inappropriate men. You knew they wouldn't work out and you'd be free to go home to your cosy nook. And it's also why you took so long to leave that poorly paid waitressing job when everyone knows you're capable of so much more."

"Maybe that's also why you're not digging on your new job, Lynny?" whispered Missy now, worried she'd get it wrong again.

Ronnie smiled at her. "Exactly! You're terrified of anything intruding on the cosy little life you created with Alicia and that stinky mutt."

She was also joking, but no one was smiling along, least of all Lynette. Her eyes had narrowed, her jaw was set.

So Ronnie quickly added, "But don't you see? This is your chance! Just like the Dartmoor children, you're free to start living your life more fully, to close the cosy book and find something more suitable, more thrilling. More *you*. Alicia wasn't going to be there forever and nor should she! It's not her job to vet your boyfriends; that's up to you. And *only* you. And I promise you this, Lynette. When Mr Right— or *Ms Right*—comes along, not only will you recognise them, but you'll be free to invite them in because you won't be so worried they'll intrude on the lovely, cosy life you've created."

When she'd finished talking, Ronnie sat back and offered a smug, knowing smile, and the others all watched Lynette closely, waiting for an outburst, wondering how she'd take that.

Lynette had closed her eyes, and a small tear trickled down her cheek now. She reached a hand up and gently wiped it away. Then she flung her eyes open, arched one eyebrow high, and said, "Thanks a lot, Ronnie. I'll take that as a compliment, shall I?"

She was parroting Ronnie from an earlier conversation, and it broke the tension.

Ronnie chuckled and there was a collective exhale, followed by a nervous giggle from Missy. Then Alicia jumped up and flung her arms around her sister. Missy said, "*Aww!*" and suddenly did the same, and before long they were one big, cuddling mess.

Then Lynette flung them all off and said, "Okay, enough with the public displays of affection." She wiped away another tear and reached for her glass. "I'm taking Ronnie's advice and going with my gut from now on. And my gut tells me we're not far from Perth and we still have a lot of champers to consume. So come on, hens, let's do a final toast to Alicia."

This time Alicia sat back and allowed them all to gush about her and Jackson and what an adorable couple they were, then she told them it was her turn to do the toasting.

She pointed her flute at her sister. "Firstly, to Lynette. Ignore everything Ronnie just said; there is nothing wrong with a cosy life, just replace me with someone equally as fabulous! If that's at all possible. Okay?"

Lynette sniffed and nodded and then Alicia turned to the others. "I want to thank you all for this wonderful trip and for believing me when I saw something strange through a train window." She lowered her glass and added, "Well, for believing me *eventually*." She winked. "And I want to thank you all for being the kind of people I would never want to hurl from a train in the dead of night. Let's just hope it stays that way."

And finally, there were tears of laughter, genuine laughter, and then someone noticed their glasses were empty, and somebody else jumped up to fetch a fresh bottle, and somebody complained about a hangover, and someone else told them to "suck it up, buttercup, you only get married once", and before they knew it, the train was pulling in to Perth and the Murder Mystery Book Club had reached the end of another extraordinary mystery.

And all while barely opening a book.

*~ the end ~*

# ACKNOWLEDGEMENTS

There are so many people to thank for this book, starting with my sister Simone, who not only loved the idea of sending the club off on a murderous train journey—à la the Orient Express—she encouraged me to contact the Indian Pacific (yes, it's a *real* train) and make it happen. And so I did!

An even bigger THANKS then to the train's incredibly gracious and surprisingly enthusiastic PR team who were happy to play ball. Special mention to Giselle Whiteaker and Ella Chronowski of Journey Beyond (the people behind the Indian Pacific and its equally iconic sister train the Ghan). Giselle was so unfazed by my desire to plant a murder on her beloved locomotive she even allowed me to drag my photographer (aka hubby) along, and we have the stunning cover to show for that.

This really is a Bucket List adventure, and everyone on board went above and beyond, but there are some honourable mentions, starting with our real-life Guest Experience Manager, Dylan Tyers. Talk about unfazed! He not only escorted us on a tour of the train, bubbly in hand, breezily pointing out spots to stash a body should the plot require it, but he then answered my pesky follow-up questions months later without missing a beat. Thanks for your time and generosity, Dylan. Any errors, while inadvertent, are entirely my own.

Big thanks, too, to the bar manager Brett Rawlins, who suggested the best time to bump someone off—between midnight and six, in case you're wondering, and I really hope you're *not*—as well as our hospitality attendants Debbie Ahearn, Matthew Milne and many others who answered my weird and worrying questions without batting an eyelid, as well as Brittney Howe, the Journey Manager, for welcoming us so warmly.

A very special thank-you to Associate Professor Diego Garcia-Bellido of the SA Museum whose lecture mid-journey really was a highlight (champagne notwithstanding). That excursion inspired me to create the character of Tag and make palaeontology a pivotal part of the plot. Thanks also, Diego, for checking my copy without a hint of mansplaining. Once again, any errors are entirely my own.

Just like my book club, the hubby and I made instant friends along the way, and while my characters are entirely fictional (honest they are!), I *might* have misappropriated/mashed up some of your names, nationalities and jobs in the interest of plot. And for that I say sorry, thanks, and that'll teach you for letting a crime writer share your booth. Seriously, you should have done a Posey and told Dylan to move us along.

Special mentions: the hubby, Christian, for a cover image that could not be more perfect; my son Felix for gifting me the journal that helped make it so; my designer son Nimo for pulling it all together so beautifully; my mother, Dianne, a frequent flyer, for her tips and tricks aboard the train; my other sister, Michelle, for her knitting know-how; Elaine Rivers for being such a supportive early reader; Annie for her editing prowess; and to you, my loyal readers, for accompanying me on another fast-paced ride.

Speaking of rides, a final thank-you to the Indian Pacific. It really is an iconic way to cross this wide brown land, and I tried to make the journey as authentic as possible so you could enjoy it right alongside the book club. However, this is a work of fiction, folks. *Fiction.* That means some elements of the journey were tweaked in the interests of plot, pace and poetic license, including where the on-off list is stored, how the exit doors can really be opened, and almost everything about the crew, especially the drivers, who would *never* ignore an exit alarm, let alone a flying human (no matter how irksome he is). Once again, any and all errors are mine and mine alone.

Now, I wonder where I can set my next holiday—I mean *book club adventure…*

# ALSO BY C.A. LARMER

### Blind Men Don't Dial Zero
### (Sleuths of Last Resort 1)

POLICE say the case is open-and-shut: The heir to a massive
fortune slaughters his parents, confesses to the crimes, then
turns the gun on himself. His grandfather says, "Not so fast."
With the case now closed, Sir George assembles his own
crack team of detectives—five amateur sleuths with a nose
for mystery and a need to prove themselves—then pits them
against each other to solve it.

"This is a fantastic read! lots of twists and turns and a real
page turner! Quirky, interesting and complex characters fill
this interesting adventure! I loved the book!"
*Charlene @Amazon*

"Will have even the most seasoned sleuth baffled as these
amateurs tackle a wealthy family, loyal employees, and
unsavoury boyfriends. You will find this action-filled journey
unforgettable and hard to put down"
*Peggy Jo Wipf for Readers' Favorite*

### Killer Twist (Ghostwriter Mystery 1)

KILLER TWIST is the first stand-alone mystery in the
popular 'amateur sleuths' series featuring gutsy ghostwriter
Roxy Parker and her motley mates.

"Roxy is a compelling character and I couldn't help but adore
her. She's 30, hip, very inquisitive, and fiercely independent.
A great cozy."
*Rhonda @Amazon*

"A fun read … an easy style … Lots of local flavour."
*Parents' Little Black Book @ Amazon*

**calarmer.com**